DRAGON
RUN

PATRICK MATTHEWS

SCHOLASTIC PRESS

NEW YORK

Library of Congress Cataloging-in-Publication Data Available

ISBN 978-0-545-45068-3

10 9 8 7 6 5 4 3 2 1   13 14 15 16 17
Printed in the U.S.A.   23
First edition, March 2013

The text type was set in Apollo MT.
Book design by Phil Falco
Map design © 2013 by Mike Schley

FOR CONNOR AND NICHOLAS,
IN THE HOPE THAT ALL YOUR DRAGONS
ARE SMALLER THAN MINE

Castle T'lirian

Sadraki

Mountainway

North Road

Castle
Surflienne

Dockside

Pilgrommor
House

Riverway

The River
Flienne

The Water's
Blessing

The Uillian

Brighton

Stelton

CHAPTER 1
TESTING DAY

Al rubbed the palms of his hands on his trousers, then jammed them into his pockets.

It was Testing Day, the last morning of childhood. Today, he would learn his rank. Score a seven, and he'd start training to be one of the most powerful people in the county. A one, on the other hand, would make him an outcast, forbidden from owning property or even fathering children.

"Nervous?" Wisp asked. The taller boy had a canvas sack slung over one shoulder, and he shaded his eyes against the morning sun. Red and brown leaves rustled in the branches above their heads, and a fresh autumn chill danced on the breeze. They were standing under a tree at the edge of a field filled with people. The imposing stone edifice of Castle Surflienne loomed over them all, its gates closed and guarded.

Al shivered. "Yeah."

Wisp opened his sack and lifted out a carefully rolled black leather vest. He pulled it on over his white linen shirt. "Relax. Your folks are both fours. You'll be fine."

Al didn't answer. He wasn't just worried about himself. He was, after all, the son of Orion Pilgrommor. The worst he could expect was a rank three. Wisp's parents, however, were only rank two, and Al didn't know what he'd do if his friend ended up a rank one.

Wisp finished smoothing his vest out. "Not bad, huh?"

"Very sharp," Al said drily.

"That's not all." Wisp pulled a wide-brimmed black leather hat out of his bag. It was weathered and water-damaged, and had a red suede band tied around the base of its crown.

Al laughed. "You've got to be kidding. You're actually going to wear that?"

"Not me," Wisp said, holding it out. "My dad said to give it to you. 'The luck of the Evans,' he said."

Al took the hat. "What does that mean?"

"I have no idea." Wisp rolled up the empty canvas bag and reached up to balance it on a tree branch. "There," he said. "Should be safe there. I'll come back for it after the test."

The hat felt heavy in Al's hands. He looked back toward the castle, at all the families waiting to have their twelve-year-olds tested. While the other boys of his station were wearing brushed short coats and shiny boots, he had on his regular clothes, stained and worn from working in the fields. In those clothes, and with his tan skin and ear-length brown hair, Al looked the part of a poor farmhand's son. He held the hat out to his friend. "It goes better with your clothes," he said.

Wisp didn't take it. "Why aren't you dressed up? Your sister got all dolled up for her Testing Day, even had a big party."

"I think that's why my parents told me to just wear my work clothes," Al said. He turned the hat around, examining it. Feathers were marked in deep red on its band, running end to end around the whole hat, but too faint to see except up close. "She only scored a three."

Wisp stilled. "*Only* scored a three," he echoed.

"I'm sorry." Al turned to his friend. "I didn't mean it like that, Wisp. You know it doesn't matter to me, but it's different with my mom."

Wisp didn't answer.

"C'mon! You know how she is."

"Sure."

Al tried again to give him the hat back. "You wear it."

"No." Wisp pushed his long black hair out of his face. Thanks to years of hard farmwork, both the boys were lean and athletic, but Wisp was taller than Al, and thinner, with quick hands and sharp features. "It's yours now," Wisp said.

"Okay," Al said. "Thanks. I guess."

He didn't feel like arguing, not that he would have won anyway. Wisp was only a couple months older, but he always seemed to be in charge. Besides, Al had bigger things to worry about. This was Testing Day, and there just wasn't any easy way around what was coming. Even if things went well, he'd be losing friends. It had already started this past summer, when his parents had hired special tutors for him. Instead of working the farms with the other kids, he'd spent the past months trying to master what his dad called "the necessities": languages, heraldry, fencing, and numbers. It was all to prepare Al for his life after Testing Day, when he would be a rank four, or maybe higher, and on his way to great things.

Wisp poked Al in the ribs and pointed out Trillia arriving with her family. Her long red hair had been braided and piled on top of her head, and metal straight pins jutted from its edges. White powder covered her normally tan face, and she wore a purple formal gown that made her look roughly three times as large as normal.

Al stifled a laugh and waved to get her attention.

She stomped over to them, her face angry. "Don't say a word," she hissed. "Not one word."

"About what?" Wisp asked, his own face the picture of innocence. "Nice pins, by the way."

"Wisp Evanson," Trillia said, poking him in the chest with one white-gloved hand. "I swear I will pull these pins out of my hair and jam them up your skinny —"

"I think you missed a spot," Al interrupted.

"What?"

"Right there," Al said, pointing at her forehead. "I think I can see your natural skin color."

She turned her glare on him. "Don't think I won't beat you up. Right here. Right now. Right in front of everybody, Mister too-good-to-get-dressed-up."

Al raised his hands, laughing. "You win, you win!"

She sighed and brushed at the expanse of fabric around her waist. "Can you believe this? Nobody dresses like this. What were they thinking?"

"Actually," Wisp said, jerking his head toward Al, "he's the one who's out of place."

"Yeah," Trillia said. "Why is that? You're dressed for the fields."

"Just lucky, I guess." Al's dad employed Wisp's and Trillia's parents, as well as everyone else who worked the fields just south of the castle. Al had been surprised when his parents had told him to wear his work clothes today, but he hadn't argued. Nobody argued with Orion Pilgrommor, especially not his own son.

"Hey," Wisp said. "I think I hear the gates."

Trillia snorted. "Don't be ridiculous. You can't hear anything over the —"

The castle gates swung open, pushed by two large soldiers wearing metal armor. A tall man stood in the opening. His black hair was pulled back in a ponytail, and his tabard bore the purple and yellow flower of Lord Archovar. He raised a long brass horn to his lips and blew three short bursts. A hush rippled through the crowd, and the man dropped gracefully to one knee, bowing his head. On either side of him, the men at the gates echoed his gesture, as did the guards on the wall above.

The people in the field dropped to their knees as fast as they could, bowing their heads and closing their eyes. Al went to one knee, but kept his eyes open, staring at the dead leaves on the ground.

Glancing sideways, he noticed that Wisp also had his eyes open. The boys shared a look, then watched the dragon's shadow soar across the field and disappear behind the castle. Nobody moved or spoke. Even the babies seemed to know better than to cry. After a few more tense breaths, the man sounded his bugle again.

Trillia jumped to her feet, flashed Al and Wisp a smile, and ran for the castle. Other kids followed with less enthusiasm, flooding through the gates and past the man with the ponytail. Their families crowded around the gate, not allowed inside.

Al looked back to Wisp. His friend's face had grown pale.

"Well," Al said. "This is it."

Wisp nodded tightly.

Unable to come up with any words, Al raised the ridiculous hat with a flourish and put it on, pulling it down low over his brow.

Wisp laughed, and the two boys left the shelter of their tree. As they walked, Al felt his stomach knot. What if he didn't measure up? Rank three wasn't bad, but it wasn't good enough for his mother. And what about Wisp? Rank ones were rare, but they happened.

"I think I'm gonna be sick," Wisp said as they walked into the courtyard between the curtain wall and the keep.

"Me too," Al said. He'd always thought of Testing Day as a great festival, but now that it was his turn to be tested, he was scared. The other kids around them looked pinched and strained, their faces every bit as gray as Wisp's. Some chewed their fingernails. Others just stared at their feet. More than a few were crying.

Once the last of the kids had entered, the gates behind them clanged closed. The man with the ponytail pushed his way through the crowd and climbed the steps to the keep door. "Welcome to Testing Day," he announced in a clear tenor voice. He spread his arms. "Today is the day you find your place in the world."

He seemed to be expecting some sort of cheer, but none came. "Castle guards," he continued, "will come out of this door and lead each of you to your test. Once you get your mark, you will be taken out of the castle by the East Gate, where your families will be waiting." He took a breath. "Please form a line at the base of these steps."

No one moved. The sound of someone whimpering carried quietly over the courtyard.

"Oh, for luck's sake," Trillia said loudly.

She bounded up the stairs, pulling hairpins as she went. When she reached the platform, she shook her head, throwing braids and the last of the hairpins in every direction.

The man stepped back, raising one eyebrow.

"So here I am," Trillia said, putting her hands on her hips. "You gonna test me or what?"

As the man's mouth dropped open, the courtyard exploded with laughter and applause.

She straightened and spun around to face her audience. "That's more like it. Now, who's after me?"

A blond boy with a determined face and shiny black boots stepped up the stairs. Behind him, a line started to form. The man with the bugle nodded his head to Trillia and opened the keep door.

"Leave it to Trillia," Wisp said.

"Yeah." Al laughed. A steady stream of men were coming out to take kids into the keep. Al and Wisp watched in silence as Trillia and a handful of others disappeared. After the first group, the line slowed down. Al touched Wisp's arm and gestured toward the door.

Wisp shook his head. "You go."

"You'll do great," Al said awkwardly. He wasn't used to trying to reassure Wisp. "I know you will." He took a breath. "And even if you don't," he said, "we'll always be friends."

Wisp met his eyes, wearing an expression Al couldn't read. The taller boy gestured with his chin toward the door. "Go on, Al," he said. "I'll see you later."

Al joined the line, feeling self-conscious in his worn clothes and silly hat. The next guard to emerge was a disheveled man with a two-handed battle-ax strapped to his back. A girl at the front of the line moved to join him, but he waved her away and pointed to Al. Surprised, Al took a breath, squared his shoulders, and followed him into the keep.

Black-and-white marble tile covered the floor of the receiving room they entered, and intricate chandeliers hung from its vaulted ceiling, filling the room with light. The walls were lined with high-backed chairs, each with a colorful banner hanging behind it. The banners represented the current noble families, but they didn't mean much. The dragons and their Magisters appointed whomever they wanted, whenever they wanted. Nevertheless, it was an impressive display.

The man with the ax grabbed Al's arm. He smelled as if he hadn't bathed in weeks. "Come on, kid," he said. "I've got someone I want you to meet."

They walked across the room to where another guard waited, this one wearing a sword and a much cleaner uniform. He wore no insignia, though, no sign of allegiance to any lord. Even the axman, as shabby as he was, had Lord Gronar's emblem on his breast: a river running out of the mountains.

The swordsman's eyes went to Al's hat, and he raised his eyebrows.

The guard with the ax laughed. "Thought this one would get your attention."

"Shut up," the swordsman growled in UnderEarth.

Al's eyes widened. He'd been studying the language of the earthers all summer, but he hadn't thought anyone else in the county knew it.

"It's from the Third, isn't it?" the axman said, still speaking in the foreign language.

"That's done with. They're all dead and gone."

"Not you," the axman said.

"Look at his face, you idiot. He can understand us." The swordsman pointed to Al. "You can, can't you?"

"Yeah," Al said in the same language. "I didn't think anyone here spoke UnderEarth."

"They don't." He glared at the man with the ax, still speaking in UnderEarth. "Now both of you shut up and follow me." He looked at Al, his expression hard. "It's time for your test."

Al followed the men through corridors and up stairs, his mind spinning. The inside of the castle passed in a blur of thick carpet and gem-covered chandeliers.

Suddenly, he was in a well-appointed sleeping chamber, with a thin man in a leather apron guiding him to a chair. A table stood next to the chair, with an assortment of knives and needles glittering in the light from the window. A red cloth bag sat beneath the table, its top buckled closed.

Al sank into the chair. "Um," he said. "Where's Lord Gronar? I thought the testing was done by a dragon *and* a skincarver?"

The skincarver chuckled. "We haven't done that in more than ten years. Lord Gronar will be testing you through me." He pulled a chair over next to Al and sat in it.

Al was disappointed. Castle Surflienne belonged to Lord Gronar, with the human nobles there ruling in his name, but Lord Gronar seldom visited. Al had hoped to finally lay eyes on a dragon, see him for real. "The dragons don't test us themselves?" he asked. "Why?"

"Mainly because the dragons don't always trust each other." He stopped, suddenly pale. "But of course, that is not an issue between Lord Archovar and Lord Gronar." He took a breath. "Now please just give me a moment."

The skincarver pulled off his right glove, revealing a tattoo that swirled across his palm and up into his sleeve. Al leaned over for a closer look. He'd never seen a real porta before, the skincarving that allowed Potentia to enter the body and granted its wearer the ability to work magic. This one looked like layers of green vines twisted together, with thorns jutting out at odd angles, and long triangular leaves.

The man smiled politely. "This won't take a moment. You probably won't even notice. After I'm done, I'll give you your rank mark. Do you understand?"

"Yes," Al said.

"I have to tell you that it is illegal to mar or deface your rank mark. It is a crime that is dealt with very severely. Now, if I could have your hand for a moment?" The man held out his tattooed hand.

Al swallowed. This was it, he thought, the big moment, the instant that would make him a noble, would separate him from all his friends. He took a breath and placed his hand in the other man's tattooed palm. As the skincarver closed his eyes in concentration, Al let his breath out. He'd expected something more dramatic. Instead, he was just sitting in a room holding hands with a strange man. Other than a slight tingling in his palm, nothing seemed to be happening. He looked at the two guards standing in the doorway.

The axman smiled at him.

The swordsman chewed his bottom lip and stared at Al's hat.

The silence stretched on and on. The skincarver's tattooed palm felt surprisingly smooth in Al's hand. Al wondered how Wisp and Trillia were doing. He hoped he'd still be able to see them once he was a rank four, at least on holidays.

After several minutes, the guard with the ax spoke up. "Excuse me, master carver? We've got a lot of kids down there and only five carvers. We can't afford to take this much time."

The skincarver's eyes opened abruptly. He shook his head. "Of course." He smiled. "Of course, you are right. It's just that this was my first time."

Al didn't need to see the guard's puzzled expression to feel alarmed. His first time? That didn't make any sense. If there were only five carvers, this one must have already seen several kids today.

"Is something wrong?" Al asked. "Did I do something?"

The carver shook his head, but didn't meet Al's eyes. He slid his bag out from beneath the table. "No, nothing at all." He opened his bag and rummaged in it. "If you could turn around please, your mark will only take a second."

Al stood up and turned his chair so it faced away from the carver. Then he sat back down, bracing himself for the pain.

The carver reached around him and put one strong hand on his chest. "This is going to hurt, but please try not to move. That will help things go faster."

When the blade touched the base of Al's neck, he yipped. It was, quite inexplicably, red-hot. It didn't just cut, it also burned, and left a burning path behind it as it moved. He gritted his teeth, focused on not making any more embarrassing noises. He had known he'd be getting a rank mark, of course. Every adult had one in the same place, right where the neck met the spine. They were complicated swirling designs, each one unique, but featuring the bearer's rank in its center.

Most people kept their rank marks covered, but Al had seen a few. His dad's was a crenellated castle wall, with vines crawling up it, and the number four emblazoned in bright gold in the center. His mom's was more understated, a field of purple flowers, with the four a vibrant green.

Al had looked forward to seeing what his would be. He just hadn't realized how much it would hurt. By the time the carver was finished using his blade, tears were flowing down Al's cheeks. He wiped at his face, trying to stay still as the man switched to using his needles.

At last, the carver pushed back and smiled at him, ignoring the tear tracks. "See? That wasn't so bad." He picked a clean small knife up off the table. "Now I just have one more thing left to do."

Al thought he was going to faint. "You can't be serious. Another one?" The skincarving on his neck felt like it was on fire.

The man laughed and shook his head. "Oh no. Nothing like that. Just a small mark is all. It's customary. Please roll up your sleeve and hold out your arm."

Al rolled his sleeve up past his elbow and placed his arm on the table, with his palm flat on its polished wooden surface.

"It might help," the man said, "if you look away. Many people can't stand the sight of their own blood."

Al was happy to oblige. He focused on the two guards standing by the doorway while the carver cut a small mark on the outside of his forearm. The swordsman's face looked to be carved out of granite, his eyes facing straight ahead. The axman returned Al's gaze, his expression soft. Al closed his eyes, ready for more pain, but this time, the knife didn't burn. After making a single cut, the carver pressed hard against Al's flesh and wrapped bandages tightly around his arm.

He stood and pulled Al to his feet. "Thank you for coming. These men will see you to your next station."

"My next station?"

"Hurry now. I've taken far too much time with you and set everyone back, and now I have to deliver a message, which will only make things later. Please don't make it worse."

Al turned to the guards, trying to ignore the pain in his neck, but neither one would meet his eyes. They guided him quickly to another room, this one much smaller, and with no windows.

A short balding man sat at a table in its middle, leafing through a pile of papers. "Come in, come in."

Al approached, his guards close on his heels.

"Not you," the man said to the guards. "What are you doing? Go get another candidate."

The guards hesitated, looking at each other. "You go," the swordsman said. "I'll stay."

"It's only a hat."

"Maybe."

The axman nodded, his face grim. "Good luck," he said, then walked away.

The man at the table held a stylus poised over a blank piece of paper. "Name?"

Al's neck burned and the cut on his arm stung. The pain of the carving had left him exhausted. He leaned on the table. "Excuse me," he said. "Could you tell me my rank? Have I done well? Have I done poorly? What's going on?"

"Your rank? How am I supposed to know? That's what you're here to tell me. Guard, what is going on?"

The swordsman's voice was flat, completely devoid of any emotion or inflection. "Zero," he said. "He is rank zero."

CHAPTER 2
NAMES

Zero?

Al's knees felt weak and he almost dropped to the floor. No one was ever a zero. The ranks didn't go lower than one.

"No," he whispered. "It can't be. It's not possible. My parents —"

The swordsman put a hand on his shoulder. "Shut up, boy. You are what you are: a zero."

"But it can't be!" Al yelled. "My family, they —"

The guard's grip tightened painfully. "Shut up," he barked. "Shut up now!"

Al's mouth clicked shut.

"I'm sorry," the man at the table said. "But I'm sure it will all work out. Your family will understand. You'll be fine." He raised his stylus over a piece of parchment. "Name?"

Al looked down at him numbly. *Fine*, he thought. *Sure.* The best he could hope for was for his parents to support him. He'd never amount to anything, never marry, never have kids. He was nothing, a zero. The word echoed through his brain.

The man with the stylus repeated himself. "Name?"

Al opened his to mouth to answer, but before he could speak, the guard grabbed him with both hands and jerked him backward. He flailed his arms, trying to catch his balance, then was spun around to face his assailant.

"Think, boy!" the man hissed in UnderEarth. "You want a rank zero in your family?"

The man at the table jumped to his feet. "That is enough," he yelled. "Guard, release the boy this instant!"

"He was about to attack you," the swordsman said. "I could see his weight shift."

"What?" Al said. "No I wasn't."

"You will leave this room this instant," the man barked at the guard, "and consider yourself reported. This boy is harmless."

The guard ducked his head, released Al, and left, closing the door behind him.

The man at the table sat back down. "What did he say to you?"

Al returned to the table, thinking fast. The guard had used UnderEarth, knowing that the clerk wouldn't understand them. Why? "I'm not sure," he answered. "I don't even know what language that was."

The man nodded. "Sounded like UnderEarth. Though why he'd think you would understand is beyond me." He paused, clearly thinking things over, then lifted his stylus. "Let's get back to business. What's your name?"

Al took a breath before answering. "Al."

"Full name, please."

Al stared at his hands. The guard was right. If this man found out who his family was, they would be forever disgraced. His dad might even lose his position as Overseer, and his sister's wedding would definitely be called off. Nobody would marry someone who might have a zero for a child.

"Full name, please," the man repeated.

"Alman," Al lied. "Alman, uh, Chairson."

The man wrote the name, his stylus making scratching sounds as it moved across the page. "And your parents? Where do they live?"

"They died," Al said, trying to piece together some sort of history the man might believe, "in a fire."

"A fire?"

Al nodded. "Two years ago," he said. "Over in Dockside," he added impulsively. Dockside was a town just west of the castle, on the river Flienne. Al had never been there, didn't know anyone there. It seemed like the safest choice.

The man's stylus had stopped writing. He narrowed his eyes at Al. "A minute ago you were yelling about your parents, and now you're telling me they're dead?"

"My real parents are dead. I live with some dockworkers that took me in after the fire," Al said. "I told them my parents were nobles, that they'd be rich once I was ranked." He chewed his lip, hoping the man would buy it. Did they put people in prison for lying like this? He didn't know. "They're going to be angry that I lied."

The official peered at his face, then sighed and started writing. "Okay, I understand. And your birth parents were named Chairson, like you?"

"Yes." Al said. "Elouise and Robert." Those were the first names that came to mind, two of the tutors who had worked with him over the summer.

The man made a final mark on his page and stood up. "There. That wasn't so hard now, was it?"

Al smiled weakly.

"Normally, this is where I would say congratulations, but in this case," he said, gesturing to the door, "good luck to you."

Feeling numb, Al walked to the door, opened it, and left the room.

The swordsman was waiting for him. "Did you give him your real name?"

Al shook his head.

"Good. Then all we have to do is get you out of the castle. Follow me."

The guard turned and strode away, moving so fast that Al had to run to keep up. After several turns, the man entered a tight spiral stairway. Al sped after him, almost falling down the stairs in his hurry. Three flights later, the man stopped abruptly to take two oil lanterns out of a wooden case built into the wall. Handing one to Al, he lit the other and resumed leaping down the stairs.

Al followed, still not sure what was happening. Where was the guard taking him? And why?

After several more floors, the stairs ended in a small stone room with a single metal door. The guard put his back to that door and placed his lantern on the floor beside him. Al slowed, nervous. Other than the stairs, there was only one exit out of that room. There were no furnishings or decoration, save for a rope hanging from a hole in the ceiling.

The guard waited, the lamp casting his shadow large on the door behind him. "Come down here, boy. You've no time for cold feet."

Al stepped down the last few steps. "What's going on?"

"What's your connection to the Third?" the guard asked.

"I don't —" Al said. He put his lamp on the step behind him. "I don't know what you're talking about."

"Your hat. Where'd you get your hat?"

"A friend of my father's gave it to me."

"Unlikely." The man's sword whispered out of its scabbard and pointed at Al. "I've put my life at risk by bringing you here. Speak the truth."

Al stumbled backward and fell against the stairway. "It's true! He sent it to me for Testing Day, said it might bring me luck. 'The luck of the Evans,' he said."

The man's eyes narrowed, and a muscle in his jaw twitched. The tip of his sword lowered to the ground. "The luck of the Evans?"

"Yeah, whatever that is."

A sound somewhere between a laugh and a sob choked out of the man's throat. "The luck of the Evans," he repeated. He took a shuddering breath and sheathed his sword.

Al stood. He was pretty sure this was a guardroom, and the rope hanging from the ceiling was some sort of alarm. If he could reach it, he could get help. He inched toward it.

The guard shook his head. "Don't pull that," he said. "You're not in danger. Not from me, at any rate." He pulled off his left glove and tucked it in his belt. "Let me see that arm."

Al's eyes widened. A tattoo covered both sides of the man's hand, disappearing up his sleeve. It was faded blue and green, some kind of a bird with a long curling tail. The guard had a porta!

"You're a zero," the man said, unwrapping the bandages

19

from Al's arm. "You know what that means?" He dropped the bandages on the floor and turned Al's arm so the skin-carver's incision faced the lamplight, then pressed the skin next to the cut the carver had made. "See that?"

Al peered at the dark lump under his skin, a sick feeling growing in his stomach. "What is it?"

"Something to let them track you. As soon as we left him, the carver sent a messenger to fetch the Cullers. They'll be here soon. They'll come for you and your family."

Al had never heard of the Cullers, but he could guess their function. He'd spent his whole life on farms, knew all about culling a herd. "But I told them my parents were dead."

"Won't matter. The Cullers don't take any chances. Their job is to make sure there aren't any zeroes, and they don't care if they take a few ones, twos, or threes in the process."

"You mean they'll kill me?" Al whispered. He stared at the black bulge beneath his skin.

"Unless you stop them." The swordsman pulled his dagger from his belt and held it in his right hand. His left hand, the one that was covered with the tattoo, held Al's arm in a vice grip. "You ready?"

"I don't understand," Al said. "Why even put a rank mark on me, if they're just going to kill me?"

"Because they want you to go home to your family. The Cullers don't just kill zeroes. They eliminate bloodlines. You go home. Your family takes you in. Then the Cullers show up and you all die. Later, at the funeral, they start tracking down your extended family. Now . . ." The man tapped Al's arm with the knife. ". . . are you ready to get that thing out?"

Al gritted his teeth and nodded. Moving with quick efficient motions, the man carved a semicircle around the black bulge, then folded the flesh back with the blade of his knife. Bright red blood flowed out of Al's arm and dripped on the stone floor.

"Grab it," the man urged.

Breathing hard through his clenched teeth, Al dug the fingernails of his left hand into the gash and pulled out the black metal bead. "Got it," he grunted.

"Wait," the guard said without letting go of his arm. "Just give me a moment." He closed his eyes and took a deep slow breath. As he exhaled, the muscles in his face loosened. He inhaled again and blew the air out through pursed lips. Al watched, fascinated. With each breath, the man's face grew more relaxed and peaceful.

A tingling sensation raced up Al's arm and into his body. He gasped. It felt like ice water splashed through his veins, like he was freezing from the inside out. The tingling turned to a heat that grew hotter and hotter with each passing heartbeat. And then, just as suddenly as it had arrived, the sensation was gone.

The guard took a final deep breath and pulled his glove back on while Al looked at his arm in wonder. The wound was completely gone, along with the pain. His whole body felt invigorated, like he'd just woken up after a long night's sleep. Even his neck didn't hurt anymore, not even when he rubbed his new tattoo. "Wow," he breathed. "Thanks."

The man turned to the door. "You have to get out of here."

Al swallowed. "Where? Where can I go?"

"Anywhere you want, except for home." The guard pulled open the door. A narrow dark stone corridor was on the other side. "You're hunted now, kid. I've bought you some time by sneaking you out this way, but not much."

"But I've never been anywhere but my dad's lands," Al said. "I don't know where to go."

"Easiest thing is to go to the docks and hop a ship. Whatever you choose, get rid of that bead as quick as you can."

Al started to open his hand, but the guard grabbed it and closed it around the bead.

"Not here," he hissed. "As soon as that bead breaks contact with living tissue, the Cullers'll know not to follow it. Right now, you have a couple guys following you. Drop that bead, and you'll have a dozen or more searching the whole area."

Al clenched his fist around the bead. The metal felt cool and slippery. "What about you?"

"Don't worry about me." He pushed Al toward the open door. "That hall connects to the catacombs. Head west and you'll end up at an exit near Dockside."

Al looked at him helplessly. He had no idea which way west was.

"That way, kid." The guard took Al's hat off his head and handed it to him. "And hide this cursed thing, will you? It's a dead giveaway."

"Thank you," Al said, taking the hat and tying its chin strap through his belt. "You've saved my life, my family's lives —" He stopped. "I'll never be able to repay you."

The man pushed him through the doorway and handed him his unlit lantern. "If your dad knows an Evan, I'm the one who should be repaying you."

"*An* Evan?" Al said.

"Go," the man said. "Now." He closed the door.

Suddenly, Al was in a darkness so complete he couldn't even see himself. Dust swirled into his nose and mouth, kicked up by the breeze the door had made as it closed. He coughed and spat, then groped about to find the lever on the lamp that sent a spark into its wick. As he clicked it, the flame flickered, strengthened, and steadied, filling the narrow stone corridor with a steady yellow glow.

Al wiped his mouth with the back of his hand. Everything was happening so fast. He felt out of control, jittery, and uncertain. He focused on the gray stone blocks of the walls around him, wondering where Wisp and Trillia were. Among the three of them, Wisp had always been the leader. He was the strongest and fastest, the one to get them out of the trouble that Trillia inevitably dragged them into. Now Al was on his own, and he didn't know what to do.

No time, he thought. He didn't have time to stop and think. The Cullers were after him, and as long as he had the bead, they could find him.

He strode for the door at the far end of the hallway. It was polished oak and heavy, but swung open easily enough, revealing the backside of a tapestry. Shielding his lantern, Al backed through the thick fabric, until he was standing in the room beyond, a large low-ceilinged chamber.

Stone sarcophagi filled the dusty room like rows of school desks, and the walls were covered with large tapestries that showed armies and heroes Al didn't recognize. He shone his lantern around until he found a door in the general direction the guard had indicated was west. Beyond it were more narrow stone passages, more rooms filled with dead people. After a few minutes, he started jogging. It wasn't long before the jog turned into a run.

As he ran, Al couldn't help but think that the Cullers might already be on his trail. He sped up, moving as fast as he could without spilling the oil in the lamp. Its light danced crazily off the stone walls, highlighting the clouds of dust he kicked up with each step.

The catacombs were broad and deep, and Al lost track of how long he spent down there. By the time he found a narrow spiral stone stairway leading up, he was panting, and a stitch had started in his side. He climbed the steps as fast as he could, finally reaching a broad chamber that blazed with daylight.

Squinting in the sudden brilliance, he turned off his lantern. Tall grasses and open sky beckoned through a metal gate on the far side of the room. Placing his lantern on the floor, Al ran to the gate, unlatched it, and pulled. It resisted at first, then swung noisily on its hinges. Relief surged through him, and Al stepped into the tall grass.

He'd escaped.

CHAPTER 3

HIDING

Al pulled the gate closed behind him and turned away from the catacombs. To the west, down the hill that held Castle Surflienne, he could see the roofs of Dockside, a chaotic collection of stone and wood buildings stacked alongside the river Flienne. He had never been there. Too dangerous, his parents had said, and he'd believed them.

After hiding his hat in the tall grass, he took a moment to examine the bead the guard had pulled out of his arm. It didn't look magic, didn't smell or feel any different than a smooth pebble.

Clenching it in his hand, he half ran, half skidded down the steep slope. The buildings seemed to grow as he approached. Some three stories tall, others four, they towered over narrow alleys and filthy streets. Al slowed to a stop in the weeds, a few short paces from the jagged broken edge of a stone walkway. The stench of old fish hung over the place like a cloud, and the cobblestones in front of him were stained with splashes of fluid he couldn't identify.

The metal bead in his hand felt strangely warm, like an egg lifted fresh from beneath a chicken. Did that mean it was doing something? He had no way of knowing, but he did know he had to get rid of it, and soon.

His plan, the one that had come to him while he ran through the catacombs, was to put it on a boat. With any luck, that would lead the Cullers far away. Between that and the lie he'd told about living in Dockside, they'd never find his family.

Holding one hand over his nose to block the smell, he stepped onto the street. Though he couldn't see it behind all the buildings, he knew the river was straight ahead. All he had to do was reach it, find something to stick the bead in, and leave as quickly as possible.

Few people were on the streets, and those that were paid him no attention. Al strode purposefully, trying to look as though he belonged. When his street ended with no sign of the river, he tried the nearest alley, only to reach a dead end. He walked back and broke into a jog, following streets as fast as he could, always trying to make his way to the river. The paths twisted and turned with no apparent pattern, and were surrounded by buildings so tall that he couldn't see past them. With no landmarks or signs, he had no way of telling which way he faced, let alone which way to go.

He slowed to a walk, not sure what to do. Who designed a city like this? It made no sense. He leaned against a stone building. The bead in his hand felt positively hot now. It hadn't been that warm earlier. Did that mean the Cullers were getting closer?

A chicken cart rattled past, pulled by a man who gripped its two long poles. Al jumped up and ran alongside. "Wait," he called. "Please!"

The driver came to a stop, his eyes darting around the street. "What do you want?"

"Are you going to the river?"

"Yeah," the man said suspiciously. "I'm delivering these chickens to the docks. Why?"

"I need to get to the river. Can you help?"

"Get away from me, kid," the man said, pulling the cart forward.

"Please," Al shouted over the clucking and scratching of the chickens. "I'm lost! I just need to get to the river."

"Go away!" the man yelled, breaking into a run.

As Al pumped his legs to keep up, an idea came to him. The chickens were going to a boat! He reached into the wire enclosure and held his hand out flat, with the bead in his palm. As soon as his hand opened, a beak pecked down, taking the bead.

Al slowed and stopped, then sank to a heap on the side of the street. He'd done it. Now, he just had to stay out of sight until the bead and the Cullers left Dockside. Then he could go home and see his family, try to make a life for himself, maybe as a farmhand or scullery boy.

He put his face in his hands. *A zero*, he thought. He was a zero, a nothing, a nobody. A sob formed deep in his chest, and he gulped for breath, trying to force it back. It came anyway, a wracking shivery gasp that convulsed his whole body.

The ranks were the dragons' way of improving humanity, a measure of how well they matched up to the ideal the dragons had tried to create. Rank seven was the perfect person. Rank ones were the dredges, barely above animals.

I'm a zero.

Eyes closed, he rocked back and forth as the tears flowed down his face. He knew he had to leave, knew he was lost in a strange city, knew people were hunting for him, but now that he'd stopped for a moment, he couldn't get his mind away from it. How did a zero live? Where could he go? Did it even matter? Wasn't he *supposed* to die?

The sound of hooves clopping on stone brought Al's head up. He scrambled to his feet, rubbing the tear tracks off his cheeks. Two men approached on horseback. They wore pants dyed a deep green, and white silk shirts open at the throat. They reined their horses in front of Al and stared down at him without speaking.

Al's heart pounded in his chest. The horses' tails hung flat and their heads drooped. The smell of their sweat enveloped him. They'd been run hard, he thought, and recently.

Still the men didn't speak. Al tilted his head to look at them. Were these the men following him? Was this what the Cullers looked like? Scabbarded rapiers hung from their hips, and their eyes had dark shadows under them.

One man had taken off his riding gloves. He had green eyes and black hair, and held a black stone in his hand. He moved it back and forth, staring at it. "It's not him," he muttered.

The other man grimaced. "You sure? He fits the description."

"Stone points toward the river."

Al glanced around the street. There was nowhere he could run that these horses couldn't follow. His eyes settled on their gear. The saddle flaps had been stamped with the image of a sheaf of grain. If these were the Cullers, he thought, then that must be their symbol.

"Did you see a boy run by?" the man without the stone

asked. He had flat brown eyes, and his eyebrows were down and angry.

Al licked his lips. "No."

"You sure? We're looking for a boy, about your age."

Al shook his head, too scared to speak.

"We don't have time for this," the man with the stone said. "If he makes it to a boat, we'll be chasing him all winter." He gestured with his hand. "The stone points toward the river."

His companion waved him quiet. "Roll up your sleeves, boy. I want to see your arms."

Al rolled up his sleeves and held his hands out.

"Palms down."

"Sorry," Al said, turning his arms over.

The man leaned over to examine them. "No wound," he said. "Not even a scar. We should check his mark, just to be sure."

"He doesn't have the hat or the scars, and the stone says it's not him." The man with the stone nudged his horse into a walk. "Come on. We're wasting time."

After one more look at Al, the Culler shrugged and rode after his companion.

Al watched until they were out of sight, then ran in the opposite direction. He kept running until he managed to find his way out of Dockside.

After retrieving his hat from the grasses at the door to the catacombs, Al ran until he was well north of the castle, and then cut east across the horse pastures to the only place he thought the Cullers might not think to look for him: the swamps. Tucking himself just far enough behind the line of trees to not be seen, he started on the long walk home. This late in the year the bugs weren't a problem, but the deep mud sucked at his boots and he worried about snakes.

As he passed the castle, music and laughter drifted to him from the Testing Day festival. He sniffed reflexively, hoping to get a whiff of the spicy meat pies or the hot bubbling cider he remembered from previous years. Instead, the smell of stagnant swamp water surrounded him. He forced his feet to move faster. He had to stop thinking about things like festivals. They weren't for him anymore. They were for people of rank. *People who matter*, he thought glumly.

The sun had all but disappeared by the time he reached the southern edge of the swamp, and the night air was cold. He stopped at the edge of the trees to examine his father's fields. With the autumn harvest two weeks past, they were littered with broken stalks and deep wagon ruts. On most days, men would be working to clear those fields. Not on Testing Day, though. Everyone was either at the festival or home eating dinner.

Al hurried toward the hill that held his family home, feeling new energy surge into his legs with every step. His father would know what to do. It wouldn't matter to him what Al's rank was. All he had to do was make it home. He ran faster. Insects chirped and trilled around him. The full moon hung bright and clear in the sky.

He slowed as he drew closer. No smoke rose from his house's chimney. No light shone from its windows. That was unusual. His mom always made sure to keep a fire crackling on the front hearth, usually with some stone soup bubbling in it for any farmhands that were in need. Since they weren't at Testing Day, his mom should be sitting on the front porch next to their open door, rocking in her chair and waiting for him. Al looked around. Only two of the cottages at the base of the hill had smoke drifting from their chimneys, the Hermans' and the Sopfias'. The rest, including the Evansons', were still and dark.

Al's fist tightened on the brim of his hat. He'd never seen it so quiet, but then he'd never been here the night of the festival. That could explain it. He walked the gravel path past the houses of the people he'd grown up with. No lantern light flickered in the unshuttered windows. No laughter drifted on the air. He hunched his shoulders and hurried up the hill to his front door.

The door was locked. Al rattled the brass doorknob, trying to force it to turn, then looked in the front window. The sitting room was dark and silent. Al shook his head. This didn't make any sense. His parents never locked their doors, not even at night. It was something his father insisted on, a way of letting the farmers know that they were always welcome.

Al ran to the side of the house. Dropping his hat, he climbed the trellis to his bedroom window. It was locked as well. He cupped his hands around his eyes and peered through the dark glass. His bedroom was completely empty. There was no bed, no chair. Even the rug was gone. It looked as though it had never been lived in.

A hollow panic filled Al's stomach. He dropped to the ground, eyes wide. Had the Cullers already found his parents? Was this what happened when they caught up to you? Did they make everything seem like you had never existed? He pulled his knees to his chest and pictured the two men on horseback in Dockside. Was that why their horses had been so lathered? Had they first taken his family and then galloped to Dockside to catch him?

Al picked up his hat. He needed to get away from here. Whatever had happened to his family, it wasn't safe for him to stay any longer. Crouching low, he ran down the hill to the back of the Evansons' house, then leaned against it to catch his breath. The moon cast deep shadows around him.

Were they watching? Had they killed his family and then left someone behind in case he came back?

He examined the empty fields, studied the hillside leading to his house. If the Cullers were out there, Al certainly couldn't see them. He forced himself to calm down. The moon was bright enough that he would have been easy to spot climbing the trellis next to his house. That meant there wasn't anyone out there, no men on horseback waiting to scoop him up.

Even so.

Al took another look around, convinced he shouldn't be out in the open, then reached over to Wisp's window and pulled. Wisp's family wouldn't mind him hiding there for the night, not even if he was a zero. If he were really lucky, Wisp would be the one to find him there. He would know what to do. Wisp always seemed to know what to do.

Holding his hat in his hand, Al clambered through the opening and into the dark room, then closed and latched the window.

As it clicked, Al heard the soft sound of breathing behind him. He spun, squinting his eyes to see better.

A man sat in the darkness, a sword lying across his lap. His face and features were in shadow, with only the metal of the sword gleaming dully in the moonlight that shone through the window.

CHAPTER 4

FAMILY

"I-I'm sorry," Al stammered, staring at the slice of moon-light on the sword. Beneath the metal blade, the man's legs were covered by a black layer of hardened leather. "I have the wrong house. I thought this was empty." His words came out fast and jumbled, almost overlapping each other. "I just wanted a place to sleep. I didn't think anyone would —"

"Stop," the man interrupted. "Excuses won't help you against a Culler. Don't even try."

Al sucked in a startled breath. He recognized that voice. "Mr. Evanson?"

"Close the curtains, Al. We need to talk."

As Al pulled the heavy cloth across the windows, he heard Mr. Evanson move behind him, then the familiar sound of a lantern clicking to life. Yellow-orange light filled the room. Al turned back around.

Mr. Evanson stood in the doorway, adjusting the wick of a lantern that hung from a hook on the wall. It was a scene Al had watched countless times over the years, during sleepovers with Wisp. This time, though, things were different. The man adjusting the lantern wasn't a farmhand, but a soldier, and a soldier wearing armor unlike anything

Al had ever seen. Layers of dark leather covered Mr. Evanson's body, with blackened metal guards over his forearms and thighs, and the faded red outline of a feather on his chest. His long gray hair was pulled into a tight braid and tucked down the back of his armor. A sword hung in its scabbard on his left hip, and two long parrying daggers hung from his right hip.

Mr. Evanson smiled. "Not quite what you're used to, is it?"

Al shook his head. Wisp's father was a farmhand, and not a very good one at that. He was clumsy with the animals, had no instincts for the growing season or when to plant or fertilize. As much as he liked Wisp, Al had always wondered why his father had given the Evansons a house so close to theirs. It was a place of importance, typically reserved for the farmers themselves, not the hands, and certainly not a rank two hand.

Mr. Evanson crossed his arms. "How'd you get away?"

"A guard helped me. He recognized your hat and snuck me out of the castle, warned me about the . . ." Al trailed off. How could Mr. Evanson have known he'd be on the run? "You knew?" he asked. "You knew I was a zero?"

Mr. Evanson nodded.

"But how? Nobody knows before Testing Day. It's not possible."

"Remember the fortune-teller last year?"

"Yeah," Al said slowly. There were always crazies at the Testing Day festival. That was part of the fun. Some claimed to do magic, others to tell fortunes. No one took them seriously. With the use of Potentia strictly regulated by Lord Archovar, everyone knew they were fakes. They were fun

34

to watch, though, and last year, there had been a real flamboyant one, draped in bright robes and wearing a mask made out of feathers.

"Your father hired her to come test you. She has a powerful command of Earth Potentia and was sensing people through the ground. After the way your mother reacted to your sister's low rank, your father wanted to know ahead of time what your rank would be."

Al considered. The fortune-teller could have been barefoot under her robes, he supposed, and no one would have known. He tried to remember what his tutors had said about how Earth magic worked. "She had an Earth porta on her foot?"

"Yes."

"And she could tell I was a zero?"

"She couldn't be sure," Mr. Evanson said. "There's a reason no one gets tested until they're twelve. It could have been that you just hadn't developed yet."

Al's mouth tasted sour. He'd been a zero for a whole year, and no one had told him? He slid down the wall to sit on the cold stone floor.

"Your father didn't want to believe that you were a, uh —"

"A zero," Al interrupted harshly. "Go ahead. It's okay. That's what I am, right?" He banged the back of his head against the wall.

"When he told me what he'd learned, I warned him about the Cullers, that if you were a zero, they would kill your whole family." Mr. Evanson shook his head. "He didn't believe me at first. He thought the Cullers just hunted down people who'd changed their rank mark."

Al closed his eyes. "But you convinced him."

"Your father's a smart man, and well connected."

The image of Al's empty room floated behind his eyelids. "I get it," he said. "He had to choose between the family's safety and mine."

"Your father did everything he could think of to prepare you. He hired the best tutors, gave you as much training as he could. Your sword master is something of a legend, among those who know about such things."

"And he sent me to Testing Day with your hat," Al said, "to let your friends know to rescue me from the Cullers."

Mr. Evanson shook his head. "The hat was my idea. I hoped someone from the Third might be there, might lend a hand if you needed it. It was a long shot."

Al opened his eyes. "So my parents sent me to be tested" — he tried to keep the bitterness out of his voice — "knowing that if I was a zero, the Cullers would kill me."

"No," Mr. Evanson said. "The Cullers' job is to eliminate empty bloodlines. They wouldn't kill you there. They'd bring you to your family first, make sure they had everyone together. Then they'd kill all of you."

The hairs stood up on the back of Al's neck. He'd come so close to giving them his real last name. If that guard hadn't stopped him, Al's whole family would be in danger. He shook his head. "I don't understand. Dad's plan was that if I tested to be a zero, the Cullers would bring me back to my house, and find it empty? How would that help?"

Mr. Evanson chuckled. "There's a reason I'm dressed like this, a reason your father ordered everyone away tonight, a reason I'm sitting in the dark looking out the only window that has a clear view of your house."

Al's eyes widened. "You? You were supposed to save me from the Cullers?"

"Your confidence is overwhelming."

"But you . . . you're Wisp's *dad*. You're not a soldier!"

"I was, once upon a time."

"I still don't understand," Al said. "Why is my room empty?"

"If you did manage to get away, your family didn't want any way for you to be traced to them. Your dad hired someone to cleanse your house of any traces of your Life Potentia and paid to have the records altered. The boy everyone thought was their son is actually an orphan they were raising. They haven't seen him since he was tested."

An emptiness seeped into Al's gut, chilling him. He hadn't just lost his family. It was like he'd never had one. He drew his knees to his chest and wrapped his arms around them. "But you're going to take me to them, right? I mean, I get that I'm an orphan and all, but I still get to see them?"

Mr. Evanson shook his head. "No, Al. Your dad's work is too important. He can't sacrifice it, or the rest of his family. Not even for you."

The color drained from Al's face. "Too important?" His dad was an Overseer, in charge of managing and taxing twelve separate farms. Each farm employed about ten people year-round, working their fields and livestock, and more were hired during harvest season. Yes, it was a big job, but how could it be more important to him than his own son?

"I'm sorry," Mr. Evanson said gently. "You can sleep here tonight. Wisp and his mom are camping at the festival. I'll need you out tomorrow, though. The Cullers are on your trail. You have to get far away from here as quick as you can."

Al nodded, swallowing hard to try to keep from crying, his eyes fixed on the floor. By the time he looked up again, Mr. Evanson had left.

Now I really am a zero, he thought. *Even my family thinks so.*

CHAPTER 5
A NEW BEGINNING

Al woke before dawn, just as he had every morning since he was old enough to do chores. He yawned and sat up, disoriented. Someone had opened the window, and the crisp cool air of early autumn filled the room. He moved to the window and leaned on the sill, looking up at his house standing cold and silent on its hill. The events of the previous day came back to him in a dull rush, like a headache that wouldn't go away.

Al tried to push the sadness away. With any luck, the Cullers had followed their black bead down the river, chasing whatever barge happened to be carrying the chicken that had swallowed it. That should buy him enough time to put some distance between himself and the farm. But what then? No one would hire a rank zero. The thought felt like a giant rock hanging over his head. No matter where he went, no matter what he did, at some point, they'd find out he was a rank zero.

A ragged V of birds flew through the gray sky over his house. Al felt a lump in the base of his throat, but forced it down. That wasn't his house anymore. It was just a house, no different than any other. He clenched his fists. How could they have abandoned him like this? Parents didn't do that to their children. He didn't care what his dad's job was. It couldn't be that important.

Once again, Al forced himself to stop thinking about his parents. He needed to focus on what to do next, how to survive. *I wish Wisp were here*, he thought. Wisp would know what to do, where to go, how to hide out until the Cullers had given up.

"All done crying?"

Al looked over his shoulder. Mr. Evanson stood in the doorway, holding a large travel-worn leather bag. He was back to looking like the typical farmhand Al had grown up knowing. Al turned back to his house. "Probably not," he said.

Mr. Evanson smiled and dropped the bag on the bed. "Maybe this'll help."

"What is it?"

The bag was a four-foot-long leather cylinder with a wide strap running along its length. Mr. Evanson untied the flap over its top. "A care package your parents left for you. Food, money, and something else. Take a look." He tilted the bag toward Al and lifted a flap on its inside.

Al's eyes widened. A metal scabbard had been attached to the inside of the bag, and the pommel of a sword jutted out of it. He grabbed the leather-wrapped hilt and drew the blade out. It was designed for stabbing, and balanced almost the same in his hand as the practice sword he'd been using all summer. The blade was as wide as three fingers at its base, with a fine edge on one side and a sharp point at the end.

"Wow," Al breathed. The image of a feather had been etched into the metal of its pommel.

Mr. Evanson laughed. "Thought you might like that. Go ahead. Give it a swing."

Al moved through the five parries he had learned. Despite being heavier than his practice weapon, the blade actually seemed to move faster.

"That's not bad," Mr. Evanson said. "You've got a real solid stance. Can you move?"

"Yeah," Al said drily. "I'm real good at moving." He stepped back and then sideways, turning and moving as though parrying invisible attacks from different sides.

"It's called foundation, Al. It's the most important thing, and you've got it down perfect. You studied for three months under Master Ruipert, the best sword master money could buy. Don't discount that. You've had more training than most soldiers I've known."

Al lowered the blade. "I guess. Just don't ask me to attack anything. Parry, counter, parry, counter. That's all we did. For three months, that's all we did. Unless someone tries to attack me, I'm helpless."

Mr. Evanson laughed again and held up the bag for Al to slide the sword back. "That does sound pretty crazy." A strip of leather was attached to the scabbard. Mr. Evanson looped it around the hilt and tied it down, then tucked the flap over the hilt of the sword. Between the leather covering the metal scabbard and the flap over its hilt, the sword was completely covered.

Mr. Evanson reached deeper into the bag and pulled out a glass jar. "Ahh, that's the stuff." He cracked the wax seal with his thumb, and then dug out a double fingerful of sticky red jam.

"Hey," Al said. "That's mine!" He recognized the jar. Nothing was better than his mom's redberry jam. Spicy and sweet at the same time, it left a slow burn that ran all the way down his throat.

Mr. Evanson paused before putting the glop of jam in his mouth. "Call it my pay for watching this stuff."

"Aww."

"Get some biscuits," Mr. Evanson said as he chewed. "We'll share."

Al dug into the bag. It was filled with biscuits and strips of dried meat, but no more jars of jam. The bottom held a wool blanket, an oiled tarp, and two empty waterskins. He pulled out two biscuits and handed one to Mr. Evanson.

"Thanks."

"What am I supposed to do now?" Al asked. He broke off a piece of biscuit and dug out as much jam as he could manage.

"You've got to leave."

"Can't I just hide out? There's that cave by the river, and I know Wisp and Trillia would bring me food. I could just lay low for a while."

"Put your friends between you and the Cullers?" Mr. Evanson pointed at Al with his biscuit. "Would you really do that?"

"No." Al sighed. "I guess not." He chewed on his biscuit, barely tasting the jam. "But where should I go? I've never been anywhere."

"Don't know. Some place far away."

Al considered. The quickest way off the farms was north to the swamp, but he really didn't want to go back to slogging through mud. The next best would be due east, into the hills. Once there, he could follow them south to the rest of Lord Archovar's lands, or north to the mountains where the earthers lived. Of course, the Cullers would probably expect him to pick one of those two directions. "How long would it take me to cross the Thumb?" he asked.

Everyone called the hills the Fingers. On a map, they looked like a giant hand extending down from the mountains. Al lived west of the Thumb, between it and the river Flienne.

"It's going to be cold up there," Mr. Evanson said around the last mouthful of jam. "Why not go to Dockside and get a boat?"

"I told the guy at the castle that I lived in Dockside."

"Ah." Mr. Evanson licked his fingers clean. "It'll take you at least three days on foot. If you go straight across, you should bump into Brighton. You might have luck finding work there."

Al walked to the window and looked at his house again. He didn't know anything about Brighton, but at least it was a destination. Better that than just running randomly. "This really is happening, isn't it? I'm never going to see you again, or Wisp, or my family."

Mr. Evanson tied the bag closed and picked it up. "Never's a long time, Al. You need to focus on the now, and right now you have to get going. Stay to the field breaks, and try not to be seen. By anybody."

The field breaks were the spaces between the planted fields. No one wasted time tending them, so they grew wild. Some had trees. Others were filled with bushes or tall grasses. Al knew them well from the many hours he'd spent playing in them over the years. He slipped the leather bag's strap across his chest, and Mr. Evanson adjusted the buckles until it was snug. The strap ran across his body from his shoulder to his hip, holding the bag diagonally on his back. The bag stuck up over his shoulder, and the scabbard hidden in it felt hard against his spine, but it wasn't too uncomfortable.

Mr. Evanson helped Al out the window and patted him on the shoulder. "Go quickly, Al. These first few days are the most important. The Cullers will pick up your trail again, but it could take them months. If you get far enough away, you might be able to find the breathing room you need to hide yourself so deeply that they'll never find you."

Al bit his lip. Was that the best he could hope for? "Thanks." He took one last look at his house, then ran for the field break, staying bent over to keep his pack from hitting the backs of his legs. Halfway there, he glanced back and saw Wisp's father still standing at the window, his arms crossed over his chest and his face hidden by the shadows of the house.

At the edge of the field, Al pushed through to the far side and ran along it, heading east. In the early morning, no one would see him against the weeds, but he knew that as the sun rose, he'd be easy to spot. He chewed his lip, trying to come up with a better way to stay out of sight, but couldn't think of one. Instead, he tried to run faster.

The bag weighed him down, and it wasn't long before his back ached from running while bent over. When he reached the next field break, he straightened and switched to a fast walk, then tried taking the bag off and holding it in his hand while he ran. Once it became too heavy to carry, he slung it onto his back again. By switching between the three different techniques, he found he could keep moving.

The sun rose behind Al as he ran, urging him to move faster. Every time he stopped to catch his breath, he remembered the Cullers on horseback in Dockside. They could ride across these fields in a fraction of the time it was taking him. His only hope was to get to the hills without being seen, and then get as deep into them as he could.

At noon, Al stopped at a well to drink and fill his waterskins. The well stood at the edge of a pasture filled with cattle, and Al pulled up the bucket to refill the animals' trough. His back and legs hurt, but not any more than after a day working the fields. A cow lowed at him.

"Shh," he said with a laugh. "Don't tell anyone you saw me." He pulled some dried meat out of his pack and resumed running.

The fields near the hills were not as flat as he was used to, but rolled with the contours of the land. The swells and slopes made it easier for him to stay out of sight, but also made the running significantly more difficult.

By evening, the cultivated lands had given way to forest, and Al trudged between the trees, his pack on his back. The land continued to rise beneath his feet, and the trees here had already lost most of their leaves. Al continued until the sky overhead was red with the setting sun, then he collapsed against a tree, shivering.

The sweat he'd worked up during the day felt cold and clammy against his skin. He rummaged in the pack for his blanket and pulled it out. As the blanket unfurled, a small fabric pouch fell to the ground with a clink. Al wrapped the blanket around himself and laughed. Mr. Evanson had mentioned money before, but he'd forgotten all about it in his rush to get away. He untied the pouch and dumped its contents on the ground.

Coins of all denominations fell out: drakes, royals, crowns, clouds, even a collection of nuggets. It was more money than Al had ever seen in one place, but there was something else as well; a piece of parchment had been folded up and tucked away with the money. Al unfolded it. *Stay safe, son* was written in his dad's neat script. Below it, his mom had added her own blockier letters: *We're sorry.*

Tears blurred Al's vision and he wiped them away fiercely. They were sorry? *Sorry?* What good did that do?

Al's tears continued to flow as he balled up the parchment and threw it into the trees. His parents were sorry. He shoved the money back in the bag. Wasn't that nice. He was alone in the wilderness, on the run from people who wanted to kill him, and they were *sorry*. He leaned his head against the cold bark of a tree and closed his eyes.

He still couldn't believe he was a zero, had always been a zero.

CHAPTER 6

POWERLESS

The next morning, Al unwrapped himself from his blanket and groaned. His back and legs ached, and his backside had a bruise from pressing against a root all night. Most of all, though, he was hungry. He downed three biscuits, chewed hurriedly between gulps from his waterskin, and then stuck a piece of dried meat in the corner of his mouth while he repacked the leather bag.

Mist rose from the ground, and no breeze stirred the branches around him. The woods felt peaceful and quiet. He wondered what Wisp or Trillia would say about his situation. *Probably tell me to hurry up*, he thought, or at least Trillia would. She'd tell him to get moving. Wisp was tougher to guess. He'd probably just tell him he was nuts, that he should go back and find a good hiding place.

Al put his bag on his back and tried to orient himself toward the east. Mr. Evanson had said it would take him three days to reach Brighton, but he hoped he could reach it sooner than that. Then what? He didn't know, but with the money his parents had left him, he should be able to rent a room for several weeks, plenty of time for him to figure out what to do next.

The morning slipped by as he hiked through the hills. He stopped to refill his waterskins twice in the cold streams that bubbled and burbled their way through the trees, but otherwise kept a good pace. By noon, he had already crested his first peak and seen the folds of forested hills ahead of him. The sight had been discouraging at first, but then Al thought about the Cullers, and how much land they'd have to search to find him. It would take them months to comb through these hills. They would have no idea that he was heading for Brighton.

Shortly before sunset, Al unpacked the tarp. He'd worked with tarps like this before, helping the farmers tie them down over bales of hay to keep them dry, but he wasn't sure how to make a shelter out of it. He settled on putting one edge on a small boulder, with rocks stacked on it to hold it in place. Next, he stretched the opposite edge as far from the boulder as he could and piled rocks on it too, then wormed his way into the space beneath the tarp. The ground and air were cold, but with the blanket around him and the tarp to keep the wind out, his little space felt warm enough. He pillowed his head on his leather bag.

Alone, in the dark, his tears started to come back. He had just spent a whole day without seeing another living soul, without hearing another voice. Tomorrow would be the same, and probably the day after that. Even when he reached Brighton, he'd have to keep to himself. *That's what being a zero means*, he thought. *Nobody will want me around.* He tried to picture Wisp and Trillia, to imagine what they'd say to him if they were there, but the thoughts wouldn't come, or at least not the ones he wanted.

Al's eyes drifted closed and he fell asleep.

The rumbling of thunder woke him hours later. Rain tapped on the tarp over his head, and blackness surrounded him. He stared at it for a while, then rolled over to go back to sleep. As he moved, his shoulder hit the tarp. It pulled off of the boulder, and the rocks that had been weighing it down came with it. One thunked into his shoulder. Another rolled into his ribs.

Shouting in pain, he scurried out from under the tarp, only to have the cold rain soak his hair and clothes. He shivered as he kicked the rocks off the tarp, then crawled back under it. His teeth chattered with cold, but the blanket was still dry. He curled into a ball and closed his eyes.

The rain lasted through the night and into the morning. Al woke, bleary-eyed and hurting. He picked up his pack, stuffed his blanket in it, and started hiking, keeping the tarp wrapped around him like a poncho. It dragged on the ground behind him, collecting leaves and small branches.

As he walked, Al decided he hated his parents. It was their fault he was walking in the rain, covered with bruises. He sniffled and wiped his nose with the back of his hand. At least they could have left him a horse.

When the rain cleared, he folded the tarp up and carried it under his arm. It was heavy and cold and wet, but he didn't want to soak everything else in his bag. That night, he found a branch to hang the tarp over. The arrangement worked much better than the boulder and rocks had.

The next evening, as he trudged over a hilltop, he spotted smoke through a break in the trees. A long lazy smudge on the blue sky, it drifted up from behind a fold in the hills: Brighton.

Al laughed with relief, and slipped his pack off his back to stretch. He'd been starting to wonder if he'd ever make it out of the trees. *I can't wait to tell Wisp*, he thought. *He's never going to believe I walked across the Thumb.*

A branch cracked nearby. Al jumped in surprise, then ran to a tree and climbed up as high and as fast as he could.

The Cullers couldn't possibly have tracked him through the mountains, he thought. He clung close to the tree's trunk, frozen with fear. *Could they?*

Moments later, a man appeared among the trees.

Not just a man, Al realized as he watched the figure. It was an earther. He had never seen one before, but he had read about them.

The earther was impossibly broad-shouldered, with arms so long that his hands almost reached the ground as he walked. He wore layers of mismatched clothes and carried a canvas sack over his shoulder, patched in several places. Al squinted at him, searching for any images of the sheaf of wheat the Cullers used as their insignia. There were none.

The earther stopped next to Al's pack and bent down.

"Hey!" Al shouted. "That's mine!"

The earther turned. He had the spare, angled features that Al had read about, with a face that looked as though its skin had been pulled too tightly over the skull. There was no facial hair, not even eyebrows, but thick black hair hung from his head to his shoulders, a vivid contrast to his pale white skin. He crossed his oversized arms on his chest.

"I mean," Al said, climbing out of the tree. "I'm sorry. I just . . ." His voice trailed off. The earther was more than a head shorter than Al, with hands unlike anything Al had ever seen — each had two thumbs and two fingers, and was covered by some kind of segmented shell.

The earther touched his fingertips together. "I wasn't going to take your stuff."

"Okay." Al stepped around him to pick up the bag. He wasn't sure what the whole fingertip-touching thing meant, but it didn't seem threatening. "I'm sorry," he said. "I didn't mean to say — oh, never mind." He held out his hand. "I'm Al."

The earther took Al's hand and shook it. "Nice to meet you, Al. Happy Darkenday."

"Um, yeah." Darkenday was some kind of earther festival, but that was all Al knew about it. He had learned about earthers from his tutor, but hadn't paid much attention. He'd never dreamed he'd actually meet one. "I should get going," he said.

"Going where?"

"Brighton." Al nodded toward the smoke. "How about you?"

"Checking traps. Caught some kind of ground bird yesterday that tasted great. You're welcome to join me. Be good to have the company."

"You live out here?" Al asked.

"For now," the earther said. "How about it? I'll cook if you pluck."

Al looked back toward the smoke of Brighton. The city looked to be at least several hours' travel away, more than he wanted to try with the sun so close to setting. "Okay," he said. "That would be great."

The earther led him through the trees to a box made out of branches lashed together. A plump blue and white bird sat inside, blinking at them. The earther whistled. "He's a big one, isn't he?"

Four stops later, the earther had three birds hanging from a rope over his shoulder. He chuckled as he led Al to his camp. "Never dreamed I'd catch so many in one night. Lucky thing you showed up to help me eat them."

The earther's camp was a firepit in front of a cave so shallow that Al could have reached in and touched the back without stepping inside. A blanket hung from nails pounded into the rock, forming a curtain that the earther could pull over the opening.

"Nice place," Al said as he lowered his pack to the ground. It made sense that an earther would have found a cave. Earthers had been created by the dragons to collect Earth Potentia, just as humans had been created to collect Life Potentia.

"There's not enough room inside for both of us," the earther said, "but I don't think it'll rain tonight. You're welcome to sleep here if you want." He dropped the birds. "After you're done plucking, that is. I'll get the fire started."

The birds tasted delicious, not as spicy as his mom's cooking, but rich and flavorful. Al ate all the earther offered, savoring each bite. When he was done, he looked around for a branch to toss his tarp over, then sat on a rock by the fire.

The earther lounged on the other side of the flames, picking his teeth with a piece of bone. "That was good."

"It was," Al said. "Thanks." After three days without speaking, Al had thought he would be talking nonstop. Instead, he was having trouble thinking of anything to say. "You never told me your name."

The earther pulled the bone out of his teeth and looked at it. "How about Bird? You can call me Bird."

Al snorted. As solid and square as the earther was, "bird" was about the last thing he would have picked. "Thanks for dinner, Bird."

Bird tossed the bone into the fire. "My pleasure. No one should be alone on Darkenday."

"That's the second time you've mentioned that. What is it?"

"The story is that when the dragons created the first earthers, they left them encased in stone for an entire day, to teach them to be one with the rock. Darkenday is when we remember that day."

"How?" Al asked. "What do you do?"

"At the end of Darkenday, after the last light of the sun has faded, we extinguish all lights and stretch out on the stone floors of our caves. It's an amazing time."

"Okay," Al said. It didn't sound that amazing to him.

Bird smiled. "My people's skin is very sensitive to vibrations. The first thing you feel when you're lying naked on the stone is the echo of your own heartbeat. Then you start to sense other heartbeats." Bird closed his eyes. "As time passes, you feel more and more of them, until the heartbeats of thousands echo through your body." He sighed and opened his eyes. "Some say they can feel the breathing of those around them. Others that they feel the heartbeats of family long dead, as though they live on in the rock."

"Wow," Al said.

Bird stretched his long arms and yawned. "How about you? What do lifers do to celebrate their creation?"

"Nothing," Al said. "Not that I know of. We have lots of festivals, but the only one we all share is Testing Day." He tried to keep the bitterness out of his voice. "That's when we learn our rank."

Bird's face stilled. "Ah. That's not a celebration for us. We call it the Dividing."

Al looked into the flames. "Good name."

Bird's voice was very quiet. "Yes."

They sat without words for several breaths, watching the crackling fire. Finally, Al spoke. "Were you going to take my pack, back there, when you first saw it?"

Bird laughed. "Of course." .

"What changed your mind? I mean, you're a lot bigger than me."

"No." Bird shook his head. "We're both *uldi'iara*. Our lives are hard enough without us stealing from each other."

Al struggled to remember his language lessons. He hadn't heard *uldi'iara* before, but it sounded like the diminutive of *iara*, which meant *threat*. "Threatless?" he asked.

"Close. It's more about power than threat. The *uldi'iara* are not threats to anyone because they don't have the ability to be threats." He smiled. "It's not that we don't want to, but that we can't."

"Powerless," Al said, his heart speeding up. "You're saying I'm powerless, that I have no Potentia, that I'm the lowest rank."

"Am I wrong?"

Al slumped on the rock. "No."

Bird turned his head and lifted his hair out of the way, showing Al the rank mark on the back of his neck. It looked like a jagged pile of rocks, dark and threatening, with the number one emblazoned in silver. He was rank one, the lowest Al had ever heard of before his own Testing Day.

Al stared dully at the tattoo. "Is it really that obvious?"

"Hiding in a tree, covered with dirt and bruises?" Bird shook his hair back into place. "Not at all."

"It's been a rough few days."

"That's what being *uldi'iara* means. No friends, no family, no money. Every day is rough when all you can do is run and hide. Believe me. It's been ten years since my Dividing Day, and it hasn't gotten any easier."

Al picked up a stick and poked at the fire. Being called *uldi'iara* felt even worse than *rank zero*. It was like he had no chance, like there was no point in even trying. He shook his head. He had to stop thinking that way. Otherwise, he'd never want to move again. "Who are you running from?" he asked the earther.

"No one now," Bird said. "I left the caves months ago and have slowly been working my way south."

"Why'd you leave?"

Bird sighed. "There was a girl. I thought she loved me, but she was just using me to make her parents angry." He smiled. "Boy, did they get angry." He stood. "I'm glad to have met you, Al." He grabbed a handful of dirt from the ground and tossed it on the fire.

Al watched the fire sputter. He didn't want to be alone again. "Where are you going from here?"

Bird paused. "I don't know."

"Why not come to Brighton with me?"

"Brighton?"

"It's a city just east of the Thumb," Al said. "I don't know if there are any earthers there, but it's got to be better than this."

Bird finished burying the fire without speaking, and then nodded. "Okay. I'll do that. Right now, though," he stretched and started pulling off his layers of clothes, "I need to get ready for Darkenday." He nodded toward his shallow cave. "I don't know if I'll be able to feel anyone through that rock, but I hope so."

"Good luck," Al said.

With the fire out, the cold air had him shivering. Al finished setting up his tarp, pulled out his blanket, and settled down for the night. As he closed his eyes, though, all he could think about was being *uldi'iara*. The thought made him feel hollow inside, and frightened.

CHAPTER 7

BRIGHTON

"Wait," Bird hissed. "There's a cabin up ahead."

Al sighed in frustration. They had been hiking most of the day, moving at Bird's pace, which was much slower than Al's. If he'd been traveling alone, Al would have been at Brighton hours ago. He was frustrated and cold, and ready to find a nice warm inn. "So? It's a cabin. Let's go. It's going to be dark soon."

"I don't think there's anyone in it."

Al peered through the trees at the house. It wasn't very big, and built entirely of logs laid on top of one another. A stone chimney jutted out of the roof at one end, but despite the cold, no smoke came from it. Bird was right. It didn't look like there was anyone inside. "Maybe they're visiting friends. Who cares? Come on, let's go."

"No. Wait here."

"Why?" Al asked.

"Because I saw it first." Bird pushed through the branches and strode to the cabin.

Al followed him. "What are you doing?"

"Shh!"

"But —"

Bird put both hands on the cabin's front door and pushed. The wood splintered under his claws.

"What are you doing?" Al asked.

Bird tore through the rest of the door. "Seeing if they have any decent food, or a hat. I could really use a hat." He stepped into the cabin. It had only one room, with two beds in the far corner and a cooking rack in the fireplace.

Al stayed on the front step. "You can't just take their stuff!"

"Of course I can." Bird opened a wooden box that sat at the base of one of the beds.

"It isn't right!"

"We're *uldi'iara*," Bird said. "Do you think any of these people would help us if we asked? Would give us a job, or let us live near them? No. To them, we're no more than animals."

"But that doesn't —"

"All we'll ever have," Bird continued, "is what we can take when people aren't looking."

"No," Al said. "That's not right."

"You'll understand someday. You'll see." Bird reached under the bed and pulled out a long, heavy scarf. It was dyed deep red, with a green border. He wrapped it around his neck. "They don't have anything, anyway. No food or money at all."

"You're a thief."

Bird walked past him. "You will be too. Just give it time."

"No I won't!"

They passed two more houses on the way out of the hills, both empty. Bird broke into both of them. He found some money in the first, and a heavy jacket in the second.

He ripped the sleeves off the jacket to fit it on over his other clothes.

Al followed, feeling frustrated and helpless. Since he couldn't stop the earther, he knew he should leave, but if he did, he'd be all alone again, and he just couldn't bring himself to do that. More important, though, he'd grown to like the earther. *It doesn't make sense*, he thought. Bird had seemed so reasonable. How could he not see that what he was doing was wrong?

At the fourth empty house, Al put a hand on Bird's shoulder. "Stop. There's something wrong here."

Bird shoved his hand off. "No there isn't. This is just the way things are."

"Not that," Al said. "Where are all these people? Why are all the houses empty? There should be people here. Something's wrong."

Bird shrugged. "Who cares?" He tore his way through the front door of the house.

Al watched him go. Now that he'd thought about it, he was convinced he was right. Something was seriously wrong here. These houses shouldn't be standing empty, and why did none of them have food in them? The hairs on the back of his neck stood up. There were no plague warnings marked on the doors, no signs of fighting. These people had simply left their homes. Why?

When Bird returned, this time wearing a hat with gray fur on its brim, Al breathed a sigh of relief. "Let's get to Brighton before dark. You can come back and steal more stuff tomorrow."

"Not much here, anyway."

"Good." Al took the lead, walking so fast that Bird had

to jog to keep up. They followed a footpath that wound down out of the hills and to the edge of the fields. Once there, Al stopped, confused. None of the fields had been harvested. Even stranger, the land was crisscrossed by long gashes that cut deep into the earth. Al had never seen anything like it. The ditches were wider than a man could jump, and so deep he couldn't see the bottom of them.

Bird stopped beside him. "You were right. Something is wrong."

Al turned to him. "What is it?"

"Rockeaters." Bird's eyes were wide, his nostrils flared. "We've got to get to Brighton before full dark. It won't be safe out here then. It might not be now." He pointed at the sky, to the column of smoke they'd been following. It was coming from their left, along the tree line, and Bird started running in that direction.

Al followed, jogging easily along behind him. "What are rockeaters?"

"Just hurry."

Al stole glances at the fields as he ran. Even though it was late in the season, much of the grain could still be harvested, but they had to do it soon. Otherwise, it would all be lost, and that would mean a hard winter for the people of Brighton.

Bird and Al passed more empty houses as they ran along the edge of the tree line. Abandoned buildings stood in the fields, quiet and dark against the setting sun. Finally, they arrived at the source of the smoke. It billowed out from behind a ten-foot-tall stockade of sharpened logs. Wood and stone buildings stood behind the fence, and men carrying crossbows patrolled its top.

Al's eyes widened. Brighton looked like a city under siege.

The ground around the stockade was trampled flat, and the road leading up to it had several of those gashes cut straight through it.

Muted voices and the rich smell of roasting meat drifted in the air.

Al and Bird hurried to the open gate. Five guards stood at its entrance, but they didn't pay any attention to Al or Bird. Instead, they kept their eyes on the fields.

As they entered, Al was hit by the musty smell of livestock. Cattle, sheep, and goats were everywhere, penned between white stone buildings. Those streets that hadn't been turned into animal pens were filled with people. They huddled against the buildings, under blankets, some talking quietly, others fast asleep. Children ran in the streets, playing some kind of tag, as best Al could tell.

"It's not as bad as it could be," Bird said. "Come on."

Bird led Al to the center square of town, where a huge bonfire roared. Several soldiers rotated cows on spits over the fire, while others handed out chunks of cooked meat to people waiting in a line.

"They'll keep this burning all night," Bird said. "If they have any Magisters here, they'll use the fire to fight the rockeaters."

Al nodded. The Magisters were the chosen of the dragons. Always rank six or higher, they were trained in the use of Potentia, and both governed and protected the people. Al had read stories about them, but never met any. They were the heroes of the world, the best that mortals could aspire to be.

Bird tapped him on the shoulder. "Good. It looks like

they're not using any tickets. Let's go get in the chow line and get some food."

"You go. I'm good."

"Suit yourself. I'll meet you over there." Bird gestured with his chin to a fenced-off street filled with cattle. "Keep your head down, and remember what you are. Don't talk to any of the soldiers. Like as not, they'll try to make you a soldier, and then you'll be stuck here."

"Stuck?"

"We can't stay here, Al. The rockeaters are going to tear this place apart. First thing tomorrow, we head back to the hills and climb as fast as we can."

Al nodded without speaking. He still didn't know what a rockeater was, but Bird was right. There wasn't anything he could do to save Brighton. Even if the soldiers wanted a zero, he wouldn't do them any good. He'd never fired a crossbow, and he still didn't know how to attack with his sword. He didn't think he could fight off rockeaters just by parrying.

After Bird left, Al sat by the fence Bird had indicated and opened his bag. It was much lighter than when he'd started, with only a few biscuits left and a handful of the strips of dried meat. He dug out a biscuit and started chewing.

A little blond-haired girl watched him eat, her eyes wide. Al smiled at her. "Hi."

The girl ran behind the legs of the man walking beside her. The man wore black leather boots and a green jacket of brushed suede. He glanced at Al and then quickly away. "Come on, honey." He took her hand and sped up. "Mommy will be worried about us."

The smile on Al's face disappeared. He recognized the look the man had given him. He had used it himself when walking past beggars at the Testing Day festival. Al focused his eyes on the cobblestones of the street. Did he really look that bad? He guessed he did. There had been no way to keep clean hiking across the hills, not with the streams as cold as they were. It was no wonder the man had mistaken him for a beggar.

Bird returned after the sun had set, a steaming wedge of meat in his right claw. He was easy to spot in the light from the fire at the center of the square. "Good news." He sat down next to Al. "They used to have earthers here."

"Why's that good?"

"Two reasons," Bird said around a mouthful of food. "First, they all left, which means word is out about the rockeaters. If they don't already have a Magister here, one will be on the way." He chewed and swallowed. "The other thing is that the earthers told them all about the rockeaters. That gives them a better chance."

"You still haven't told me about them."

"It's an old story." Bird sighed. "And not a happy one. Generations ago, one of the dragons took a tribe of my people and changed them." His voice dropped. "It was trying to make them better fighters. What it ended up with was rockeaters. They're small and quick, and hate everything that's not a rockeater, but they weren't smart enough for the dragon's purposes and it abandoned them. Since then, the rockeaters have flourished. They live underground in complex warrens, and have their own society, completely separate from the rest of us."

"Why are they called rockeaters?" Al asked.

Bird shrugged. "I don't know. I only saw them once, when they attacked our village." He wiped his hands on his sleeveless jacket. "If the Magister hadn't shown up, they would have killed us all."

"What do they look like?"

"Like my people, but smaller, and much quicker. Also, their skin is very thick. It's said they can't feel the rock anymore, that that's what drives them to kill." Bird took off his stolen hat and put it on the ground in front of them, open side up. "Don't worry, though. We're leaving at first light." He fished in his pocket and dropped a penny into the hat.

Al stared at the hat. Pennies were the least valuable of all the coins. It took a hundred of them to equal a drake, and Al had over a hundred drakes in his pack. "What are you doing?"

"People don't have much during a siege. This lets them know we need money, and that it's okay to put even small coins in."

"I thought maybe we'd get a room at an inn. You know, sleep inside, where it's warm."

Bird laughed. "Sure."

"What?"

"Even if we had the money, there aren't any rooms. Look around, Al. The streets are packed with people. This is why all those houses are empty. Everyone's here, trying to stay safe. The city is full."

Al looked back down at the hat with its lonely penny, his heart racing. Was this the kind of poverty Bird was used to? What would he say if he knew how much money Al was carrying? A drake dropped into the hat next to the penny, and Al looked up to see a soldier walking quickly away. He turned his attention back to the hat, too embarrassed to look anywhere else.

CHAPTER 8
MAGISTER LUNDI

Al woke to the sound of a horn. The bonfire still burned, but now the streets were filled with people running back and forth. Half-dressed men stumbled out of buildings, pulling on clothes as they ran to the stockade. Others ran to the bonfire to light torches. Al jumped to his feet and peered down the street. People were swarming up the scaffolding that lined the inside of the stockade. Most didn't have any sort of armor, and many were groggy-eyed and fumbling.

A man holding a bugle and wearing the purple and yellow flower of Lord Archovar sat astride a horse near the gate. Men in chain mail surrounded him, shouting orders and directing the villagers to different parts of the stockade. The man blew the bugle again, and then hung it from a hook on his saddle. He cupped his hands around his mouth and yelled in a clear tenor that carried over the din: "Torches! Set the torches!"

People ran to pass lit torches up to the men on the scaffold, who grabbed them and threw them into the night.

"That's to help them see the rockeaters," Bird muttered, "and to make it harder for the rockeaters to see. They have trouble with fire."

Al watched the torches spin into the night. Men continued to climb the scaffold until they filled it, standing shoulder to shoulder with each other, peering out over the stockade.

"Crossbows!"

The people who had been carrying torches now started handing crossbows and bolts up to those on the scaffold. Al couldn't see where all the weapons were coming from, but guessed there must be storage buildings.

"Now is the time," the man on the horse shouted as the crossbows were distributed. "Now is the day!"

Al started to stand, but Bird grabbed his arm. "Stay."

A low rumbling rolled over Brighton, like the warning growl of a thousand angry dogs. Al's skin prickled with the sound. He tried to pull his arm away from Bird, but the earther held him firm.

"Stay here," Bird hissed. "If you go to help, you'll be stuck on the wall."

On the street, everyone was awake, their eyes wide and frightened. Al didn't see a single man or boy among them, just women and small children. "But, Bird," he said. "I have to help!"

The man on the horse drew his sword and held it high over his head. The blade flickered red in the flames. "For Archovar!" he shouted.

Another voice answered. This one was deeper, but every bit as resolute. "For Brighton!"

The people in the city erupted into noise, shouting and clapping and stomping, drowning out the growl of the rockeaters.

"Here it comes," Bird whispered. He sank to the ground, dragging Al with him.

Al yanked his arm away and looked back to the wall. As he watched, three men fell backward off the scaffolding. They didn't scream, just fell limply to the stones below. Their comrades roared and fired their crossbows, then ducked down to reload. A wave of loud *thud*s and the *crack* of splintering wood sounded. Something metal spun through the air over Al's head and slammed into a building across the street.

It landed heavily on the stones, a metal ball that was only slightly bigger than Al's fist, but covered with spikes. Al turned back to the wall. More people were pulling themselves up onto the scaffolding, grabbing for the crossbows dropped by those who had fallen.

"Man the wall!" the horseman shouted. "Keep those crossbows firing!"

Al's blood pounded in his ears. Down the street, a woman screamed her husband's name. "I have to help," he hissed.

"Help do what?" Bird said. "Sit down, *uldi'iara*."

A wave of frustration washed through Al. "No! I can't just sit here. I have to help!"

Bird's claw locked around Al's wrist. "The rockeaters won't attack for real until they think the city is helpless. Until then, they'll just keep launching their *rikahts*."

"What?" Al looked down at the earther.

"The rockeaters are trying to beat down the city from a distance. Once they think the defenders have been weakened enough, they'll attack for real. Those men aren't fighting.

They're just buying time. From this distance, their cross-bow bolts can't even penetrate the rockeaters' hides."

"But —"

"Use your eyes! Tell me what you see."

Al examined the stockade. The men on the scaffolding ducked to load their crossbows, then stood to fire. There was no coordination to their movements, no organization. They were simply shooting as fast as they could. Below them, the horseman in Lord Archovar's colors paced back and forth, shouting encouragement. His men hadn't drawn their swords. They stood in formation and watched the walls.

While Al watched, a boy roughly his age swung onto the scaffold and picked up a crossbow.

"On the wall," Al whispered. "They're not soldiers." He looked down at Bird. "The real soldiers are hiding inside the city."

Bird nodded. "Now you've got it."

"Why don't they fight?" Al's fists clenched as he glared at the armored men. "They're sacrificing the people they're supposed to be protecting!"

"You can't ride against rockeaters," Bird said. "Remember the gashes in the field? The rockeaters control the ground. If anyone charges out there, they'll be buried alive. They have to keep the soldiers alive for when the rockeaters attack in earnest."

Al tugged weakly at his hand, but it didn't come free from Bird's grasp. He couldn't see the boy on the scaffolding anymore. A man had taken his place.

"That's it," the man on the horse bellowed. "Stand

strong! Today is the day we stand! Today is the day we show them the honor of Archovar!"

Al sank down to the stones, his stomach roiling. Across the street, a woman stared at him, naked hate in her eyes. He didn't blame her. He put his head on his knees and his hands over his ears. Bird was right. There was nothing he could do, but that didn't make it any easier. He gritted his teeth. *If the rockeaters do attack*, he thought fiercely. Then he would draw his sword and fight, would do everything he could to help these people.

Wave after wave of the metal *rikahts* slammed into Brighton's walls and buildings. Beneath the onslaught, the shouts of the city's people faded and died, until only the unwavering growl of the rockeaters could be heard. Over time, even the horseman's voice grew ragged and hoarse. Al huddled miserably next to Bird. Angry eyes glared at him from the darkness. He did the best he could to ignore them.

"Where are the dragons?" Al whispered. "Where's Archovar?" Castle Surflienne was under Lord Gronar, who bowed to Lord Archovar. Al didn't know who ruled over Brighton, but whoever it was should be here to protect its people.

"The dragons?" Bird barked a laugh. "What do you know about dragons?"

"I don't know," Al said. The truth was that he had never actually seen one, except high overhead when it was too far away to notice if he was bowing or not.

"We are so far beneath them," Bird said. "They barely even know we're here."

"They *should* know," Al said.

"Well they don't, and that's the best we can hope for."

"What are you talking about? They created us."

Bird's eyes turned bitter. "The dragons are evil, Al. Pure evil. I wouldn't be surprised —"

"Shh," Al interrupted. "What are you doing? Someone might hear!"

Bird laughed bitterly. "See? You're afraid to even talk about them. Huddling in a city under siege by creatures *they* created, and you're scared to even consider they might be at fault."

Al opened his mouth to answer, but stopped. Bird was right. He and Wisp had talked to each other about dragons, but never to criticize them. Even hidden away in their houses, they'd known it was too dangerous.

"That kind of fear will cripple you," Bird continued. "It's the fear of the *uldi'iara*, the fear that even speaking a thing can destroy you. Believe me." He crossed his arms across his chest. "I know."

Al pressed his lips together and stared at Bird's hat sitting on the stones. More *rikahts* crashed through the city. More people screamed and shouted. He put his forehead on his knees and closed his eyes.

The attack lasted for hours, until, just as the sky was starting to lighten to dawn, the *rikahts* stopped coming and the roaring stopped. The city held its breath for a heartbeat, then erupted with cheering.

"Collect the torches!" the man on horseback shouted.

Bird stood and brushed off his pants. "We've got to get out of here."

Al nodded numbly, then jumped in surprise as the woman from across the street grabbed his arm. She wore a heavy cloak, and her face was streaked with tears. "Why? Why didn't you help?"

"Coward!" a girl behind her hissed, her cheeks flushed with anger.

Al backed away. "I — I'm sorry. I'm not from here. I didn't know —"

Bird handed Al his bag and shouldered the woman away. "Come on."

Al took the bag and followed the earther, his eyes down.

"Coward!" the girl yelled again. She was around Al's age, and wearing a blue dress. "You can't even look at us, can you?"

Al hunched his shoulders.

"There are riders approaching," a deep voice shouted from the wall. "Humans!" Al remembered that voice from the previous night. It was the one that had shouted the city's name, and Al could see its owner standing on the wall. He was a large man and square, with blond hair that hung to his shoulders. His left arm was in a sling. "How many?" the horseman croaked. He spurred his horse into the open gate and drew his sword. His men ran after him.

"It's Magister Lundi!" the deep voice bellowed.

Al's mouth dropped open. Magister Lundi was the most famous of Archovar's Magisters, the highest of the high, a perfect rank seven. If anyone could defeat the rockeaters, he could.

Shouts of excitement raced through Brighton, creating a stampede toward the city's gate. Al and Bird followed the crowd out of the city. In the distance, armored men on horses galloped toward them. Al watched in fascination.

The five horses formed a narrow V, but only four had riders. As they grew closer, Al saw why: the fifth man floated in the air above the riders, keeping pace with them. Despite the cold, he wore only loose pants, with no shirt or shoes. Skincarvings covered the man's torso and bald head. Even his bare feet were swirled with tattoos.

The horseman in Lord Archovar's colors dismounted and knelt. His soldiers did the same, waiting for Magister Lundi to arrive.

Bird grabbed Al's arm and tugged in the opposite direction, toward the tree-covered hills.

"Wait," Al said. "He's almost here. Then we can go."

"I've seen it before," Bird said. "We'll get caught up in it. Come on!" He pulled Al's arm.

Al stumbled backward and bumped into a man leaning on a crutch. The man grabbed Al to keep from falling. "Careful, boy! Watch where you're going."

"I'm sorry," Al mumbled. "I didn't mean to." He picked up the man's crutch and handed it to him, then hurried after Bird.

"Hey!" The man pointed at Bird. "That's my hat. You took my hat!"

"And that's Emma's scarf," the woman next to him said. "She hid it under her bed before we left."

"You're thieves!" the man said.

Bird ran for the trees, barreling through people as he went. Al leaned forward and sprinted past him.

"Stop!" the man shouted. "Someone stop them!"

"Help!" the woman screamed. "Help!"

Al looked back at Bird. The earther had broken free of the crowd, but three men from Brighton were closing in on him, their tired faces grim and angry. Al slowed. Even at top speed, Bird wouldn't make it to the trees. The earther's mouth hung open as he ran, and his eyes were wide with fear.

Al stopped. "It's not what you think," he said to the men. He shrugged his bag off his shoulder and held up his hands. "Let me explain."

Bird passed him, tossing the hat and scarf as he ran.

One man grabbed Al. The other two ran past him to cut Bird off from the trees.

Bird stopped, panting, his hands on his knees.

The woman picked up the scarf. "This is my daughter's," she shouted. She held it up and flipped it around to show everyone where the word *Emma* had been embroidered on one end. "See? It's Emma's!"

"You robbed us while the rockeaters were attacking our city?" the man holding Al growled. "You're worse than a thief." He shoved Al to the ground. "You're a traitor."

Al sprawled in the dirt and rolled over. More people had turned to face the commotion. They all looked angry. "No," Al said without standing. "We didn't know what was going on. We came here looking for a new home, and found the houses empty. We didn't know . . ." He trailed off.

The growing crowd looked tired and dangerous. Al knew he was in trouble. At the very least, he'd be tossed into prison. The thought sent a jolt of fear through him. If he were arrested, they'd find out he was a zero, and that would bring the Cullers. He grabbed his bag and scrambled to his feet. "Please," he said. "We didn't mean to steal anything."

The man who had grabbed him shook his head. "It's too late for that."

Hands shaking, Al opened his bag. He couldn't go to prison. He couldn't face the Cullers. He lifted the flap, slipped off the leather strap, and drew his sword.

The woman with the scarf screamed.

"L-Let us go," Al stammered. "You have your stuff. Now let us go." He turned a slow circle, keeping his sword up. The men backed up several paces. Two of them had Bird's arms locked behind his back. Al tried to catch the earther's eyes, but Bird was squinting at the sky behind Al, his upper lip curled back in a snarl.

Al followed the direction of his glare to see Magister Lundi floating above the crowd. The Magister was close enough now for Al to make out the details of his skincarvings. The top of his head was covered by a complex pattern of interlocking black triangles. On his chest, a stylized dragon spread its wings, blasting red fire up to his left shoulder. The fire twined together and ran down his arm to the tips of his fingers. In contrast, his right arm was carved with blue and green waves that crested and crashed in white foam against his shoulder.

"You're not going anywhere," Magister Lundi said quietly.

Beneath him, the people of Brighton parted to let the Magister's men through.

CHAPTER 9
HOW TO STAND

Al gripped his sword tightly in his right hand. "I can't go to prison," he whispered.

Magister Lundi's men spread out between Al and the people of Brighton. They wore chain-mail vests and heavy leather pants, and had swords hanging in scabbards from their belts. Instead of boots, however, they had strange low-sided shoes that Al had never seen before. As he watched, the men took off their gloves and kicked off their shoes, revealing hands and feet covered with colorful skincarvings.

Al swallowed. Those skincarvings meant that all five of the men were Magisters, masters of Potentia. He tried to catch their eyes, to see some sign of compassion, but their faces were passive and expressionless, as though they were staring at a blank wall. Al forced himself to breathe.

Whatever happened, he couldn't let himself be caught. Once the Cullers had him, they'd force him to identify his family. He drew in a shaky breath and blew it out to try and steady himself. "I'm not going to prison."

"You said that already," Magister Lundi said. He spoke clearly and distinctly, but his voice sounded sad. Despite how old Al knew he must be, his skin was without wrinkle or flaw, as though he were only twenty years old. He landed gracefully behind his men. "Unfortunately, I agree. Stealing from a besieged city is a capital offense. So is threatening Lord Archovar's Magisters."

The four armored Magisters in front of Lundi drew their swords. They were rapiers, longer and thinner than Al's blade, and much faster.

Al fell back a step, keeping his sword between himself and the Magisters. His eyes darted around the crowd, looking for somewhere to run, but there was no sympathy left in the people of Brighton. They were exhausted and angry, and not about to let a thief get away, not even one as young as Al.

"Is there anything you'd like to say?" Magister Lundi asked in his gentle voice.

Al felt his throat constrict. There was nowhere to run, nothing he could do. He didn't stand a chance against one Magister, let alone five.

Bird's voice rang out, heavy with derision. "*Five* mighty Magisters against one boy?" He heaved his body forward, tossing away the men who had been holding him. The earther stepped straight-backed into the ring of people surrounding Al, and flexed his claws. "How strong they look," he said with a sneer, "against one little *uldi'iara*. What's next?" Bird spat at the ground before Magister Lundi. "Will you amaze us with how many insects your men can kill?"

Magister Lundi's eyebrows raised. "Do I know you?"

"No," Bird said, "but I know you." He turned his head and spat again. "And I know the story of the Third. Five thousand strong, Magister. Five thousand loyal. Five thousand *dead*."

Magister Lundi lowered his eyes, and a confused hush fell over the crowd. The Magister straightened, eyes fixed on Al. "Which of you did the stealing?"

"What?" Al asked.

"Which of you did the actual stealing? There are two offenses here. The first is the stealing. That is against these people and cannot be commuted. The second is raising your blade against the Magisters. That is a matter that I can show leniency on, and offer prison time instead."

Al couldn't believe it. Magister Lundi was giving him a way out. All he had to do was say that Bird stole the clothes, and he'd go to prison instead of being killed. He looked back at Bird. The earther nodded slightly, his expression grim.

Al shook his head. Even if he could bring himself to abandon Bird, prison meant the Cullers, and interrogation. Eventually he would crack, and his family would be found out. Then they'd all be killed. The alternative might mean death for him, but his family would be safe, and Bird would go free.

"It was me," Al said, staring at Bird. He felt light-headed, almost nauseous with fear. "I stole those clothes for my friend. He'd missed Darkenday and I thought they might cheer him up. I didn't know I was stealing. The houses were empty. I thought they were abandoned."

Bird's eyes widened. "Al —"

"No," Al interrupted. He turned back to Magister Lundi. "It was me. All me."

The Magister's head tilted to one side and his eyes narrowed. "Interesting. Captain, secure the boy. The earther is free to leave."

"No!" Bird shouted, but before he could take more than a step, the earth rose up around him, encasing him to his chest.

Al shifted sideways as the ground beneath his own feet surged upward. His movement kept him out of the earth's grasp, and Al felt an unlikely thrill of victory. Maybe those three months of learning footwork had been worth something, after all. He faced the Magisters with his sword slanted toward them.

"You're going to fight?" Magister Lundi asked, incredulous.

Al didn't answer.

"Primus," Magister Lundi said quietly. "Can you take care of this?"

The armored Magister standing in front of Lundi shrugged, raised his sword in a salute, and stepped forward. He was bigger than Lundi, and looked sterner, with a hard set to his jaw and narrow eyes.

An excited murmur ran through the crowd.

Al didn't move. Primus was taller and stronger, and held a longer blade, but the man carried his weight all wrong. Al watched as the Magister approached, waiting for the telltale shift in the man's balance that would precede an attack. He timed it perfectly. Just as Primus started to extend, Al stepped in to slide his blade under his attacker's, then shoved hard straight up, driving the man's hilt against his thumb. Before the Magister could recover, Al jerked his sword sideways, knocking Primus' weapon out of his hand.

A rush of excitement surged through Al, quickly tempered with frustration and fear. He'd just disarmed one of the most powerful men in the world, but what did that matter? It would take a straight, powerful stab to penetrate the man's armor, and Al didn't know how to do that. He stepped backward and nodded to the Magister to pick up his sword.

It seemed insane, but unless Primus attacked him, Al couldn't do anything. Besides, he was pretty sure the man was more dangerous without the sword.

Primus retrieved his weapon without taking his eyes from Al's. "Why?"

Al shrugged, not sure what to say.

The Magister feinted a lunge, but Al didn't move. It had been too obvious — the man's point hadn't even been in line. Primus raised his eyebrows and glanced over his shoulder at Magister Lundi.

"I believe you have other weapons at your disposal?" Magister Lundi said drily.

Primus faced Al and gestured with his left hand. As with the sword, Al had seen the motion before it started. He stepped sideways, expecting a thrown knife. Instead, a blast of water burst out of the Magister's hand. It smashed into a townsman behind Al, encasing him in a block of ice as he fell backward.

Bird exploded with laughter. "You're beating them, *uldi'iara*. You're beating the Magisters!" He tilted his head back to the sky. "A boy is besting Archovar's finest!"

Magister Lundi sighed audibly. "That's enough."

Not sure what to expect, Al moved to his right, sword up and ready to parry. When no attack came, he let out a relieved breath. He was doing it. He was actually standing up to the Magisters. He inhaled again, but no air came.

Instead, the breath rushed out of his chest. Al dropped his sword and clutched at his throat as his lungs emptied themselves of air.

Magister Lundi nodded sadly.

Sparks filled the corners of Al's vision. He fell to his knees, then tried to force his fingers down his throat, to stop whatever was happening to him. His chest heaved with the effort to suck in air, but none came.

Bird screamed at Magister Lundi, but Al could barely hear the words. His eyes closed, and he curled on the ground, gasping for breath. Bird's screams grew fainter and fainter in Al's ears, and then stopped altogether.

Al lay motionless on the cold ground.

CHAPTER 10

AWAKENINGS

Al woke in complete darkness, curled up on a rough wooden floor that was bouncing and tilting beneath him. He sat up shakily, then put a hand to his neck and sucked in a breath. His throat was dry, his lips chapped and cracked, and his tongue was stuck to the roof of his mouth. The floor lurched again, tossing him sideways, and then was still.

Feeling around with his hands, Al found a wall. He crawled to it and tried to stand, only to bump his head on the ceiling. Crouching, he followed the wall to another wall, and then felt a door handle. He turned it and pushed.

Bright sunlight dazzled his eyes, and he raised a hand to shade them. He was crouching in the back of a wooden wagon.

"See?" Magister Lundi's voice said. "How many of them have just started screaming? The Evan was right. He kept his head and found his way to the door."

Al squinted. Two men stood facing him, several steps away. The sun was high in the sky, just left of the road, and blindingly bright.

"Believe it or not," another voice said — Al recognized it as belonging to Primus, the Magister who had been so bad with his sword — "basic problem-solving is not that rare."

"So *you* say," Magister Lundi answered.

As Al's eyes adjusted, the men came into focus. He had been right, it was Magister Lundi and Primus.

"What happened?" Al rasped. The words burned coming out of his throat, and his lips cracked and bled when he moved them.

"It's from the Air effect," Magister Lundi answered. "It sucked the breath out of your body so fast that everything dried out. It's uncomfortable, but you'll heal."

"No," Al croaked. "Not that." He stepped down the stairs onto the packed dirt of the road. "Where am I? What's going on? Where's Bird?"

"You are a zero," Primus said sternly. "We are taking you to the Cullers, as is our duty."

Al froze. "You can't," he said. "They'll kill my family."

"See?" Magister Lundi said to Primus. "I told you he was trying to make you kill him." The bald Magister clucked his tongue. "You never should have tried to disarm him."

Al put his left hand on the side of the wagon. Behind the Magisters was blackened ground, without even a clump of grass to hide behind, but to his left was a river, not too far away. If he jumped fast enough, he might be able to swing around the wagon and sprint for the water.

"Ul!" Magister Lundi said sharply.

Without him wanting it to, Al's hand lifted off the side of the wagon and dropped limp at his side. Al's eyes widened with fear. The Magister was controlling his body!

"There's a fine line between ingenuity and stupidity, Ul. I'm not going to let you cross it now."

Al sagged against the wagon, out of ideas. "What did you call me?"

"Ul. Isn't that what the earther called you?" A smile played at the corners of Magister Lundi's eyes. "Short for *uldi'iara*, right?"

"Oh, right. Yeah. That's what they call me: Ul."

Primus rolled his eyes. "We need to be moving, Magister. The rockeaters may have fled from Brighton, but they'll resurface nearby soon enough. Duty calls."

Magister Lundi raised his right hand. "Not quite yet." He touched his lips with his forefinger and then pointed it at Al. "Are you familiar with people who like to watch animals fight? People who set their pets to tearing each other apart?"

Al licked his lips. Was the Magister threatening him? "Yes."

"What do you think of them?"

"It's disgusting."

"What about those who kill without even the excuse of entertainment?"

"Magister," Primus whispered. "You go too far."

Magister Lundi nodded. "Probably." He took a breath. "Still. He asked where we are. It's only right to answer him."

"No," Primus said.

"We are standing," Magister Lundi continued, looking at Al, "in what used to be Stelton, before it burned."

Primus threw up his hands and turned away.

Al looked around. He'd never heard of Stelton before, but based on the sizable area of blackened dirt, it had been at least as big as Brighton. The ground was completely lifeless, all the way to the river and a short distance across it, but now that he looked more closely, he could see that much of it was cobblestone.

"No." Al shook his head. The Magister was teasing him. He had to be. "Even if there had been a fire, there'd still be stones left from the buildings. No fire is hot enough to burn stone."

"*No* fire?"

"Well, maybe dragon —"

"Enough!" Primus said firmly. He glared at Magister Lundi.

"Because of a bet," Magister Lundi whispered. His gaze was distant, out of focus. "A bet between dragons that a certain all-powerful Magister wouldn't be able to get here in time."

Al's breath caught. It couldn't be true. It just couldn't.

"The people here never did anything wrong," the Magister said. "Other than trust in my protection. Now they're gone."

"Magister," Primus said more gently. "You must be silent. Speaking of such things is not appropriate."

"No," Magister Lundi shook his head as if to clear it. "No. You're right." His eyes met Al's. "I should not have told you that. It puts you in even more danger. Here's another thing I should not speak of: I am truly sorry that you are a zero. If someone of your talents were to show up at my home with any other rank mark, that person would be welcomed into my household. I always have need of people who can find resources where others see none, and I pay very well. Do you understand? I pay very well."

Al opened his mouth, but couldn't think of anything to say. Had Magister Lundi just offered him a job?

"I have such an opening, currently," Magister Lundi added, "but it will only remain open for three weeks."

"It is irrelevant," Primus said. "He is a zero. He will be delivered to the Cullers."

"Yes." Magister Lundi sighed. "Believe it or not," he said to Al, "even we Magisters must answer to the Cullers."

Primus nodded. "Allowing a zero to live would be to sacrifice all our lives."

"Wait!" Al said. "I could get my rank mark changed. I could find a skincarver, someone who —"

"It is time for you to get back into the box," Magister Lundi interrupted.

"And changing your mark would not change what you are," added Primus.

Al tried to leap away, but instead his body climbed calmly back through the door and pulled it shut behind him. The door fit snugly into position. Once it had closed, Al was again in complete darkness. He heard a click from the door's handle and realized that it had just been locked. Then his body crawled across the wooden planks until it bumped into a leather bag and collapsed to the floor.

All at once, Al felt control of his muscles return to him. Quivering, he ran his hands along his discovery. It smelled and felt exactly like his bag, the one that Mr. Evanson had given him. His shaking fingers found the laces at the top and untied them, then felt deeper inside, pushing aside the leather flap to grasp the hilt of his sword.

The weapon slid silently out of its scabbard, and Al crawled with it to the center of the cart. Now that he was paying attention, he realized that the wood floor felt slightly moist beneath his hands, as though the planks were still alive. The thought unnerved him, but he shoved it aside.

As the cart lurched into motion, he found a crack between two planks and worked the tip of his sword between them. Once it felt far enough in, he threw his weight against the hilt. The plank creaked and groaned, and a chunk of wood flew free. The sword banged against the floor.

Disappointed, Al felt for the split he'd made in the wood, then slammed the metal pommel of his sword against it. The impact jarred his arm and set his shoulder tingling, but he lifted the sword and hit it again. On the third try, the wood cracked wide enough for light to leak into his little prison. Al wedged the point of his sword into the crack, and this time he was able to lever the end of the beam up. More light shone into the cart, revealing the heads of the nails holding down the other beams.

The cart swayed and bounced as it traveled over the dirt road. Al steadied himself as he selected which nails to dig out with his sword. In no time, he had a hole big enough to drop through. He slid the sword back into his bag and tightened its straps around his chest.

Underneath the cart, the road sped by. Al heard the jingle of harness and tack, and the steady rumble of galloping hooves, but couldn't tell if there were more horses than just those pulling the cart. Even if no one followed directly behind the cart, what were the odds that he could drop out without being spotted by the Magisters?

Al squatted by the hole and watched the mud go past. Based on where the sun had been earlier, the cart had either been traveling northwest or southeast. He couldn't know which without knowing if it had been just before noon or just after.

Not that it matters, he thought. Even so, not knowing bugged him. He stared at the ground beneath the cart. It seemed impossible that the horses had maintained their gallop for this long, but they clearly weren't slowing down. More of the Magister's magic, he thought. If they could control his body, they could probably make a horse run forever.

A shiver ran through him at the memory of his body moving in spite of him. He hadn't realized that Magisters could do that, although maybe only Magister Lundi was that powerful. *And dragons*, he thought. Dragons had so much Potentia they could do practically anything.

Even burn a city.

The thought came without him wanting it to. Had they really done it? He crossed his arms tightly, feeling cold. Had they burned an entire city to ash? It would have had to have been a complete destruction, with no witnesses and no survivors. People were scared of dragons, but they didn't feel threatened by them. If they knew Lord Gronar was letting dragons burn entire cities, there would be panic.

Bird's words about the dragons being evil came back to him. Even as cynical and jaded as Bird had been, the earther had seemed to have a special hatred for dragons.

And Magisters, Al thought. Bird hated them too. Al blinked, remembering his friend. He really hoped the earther was still alive, and not trapped in some wagon heading off to a Culler prison.

The dirt slid past, mile after mile. Al fidgeted, not sure if he should jump or not. If he waited too long, they would reach the Cullers. If he moved too soon, they might spot him and put him in shackles. He adjusted the weight of the bag on his back. It seemed crazy that they would have left it in the cart. Maybe they'd counted on him not exploring?

He remembered what Magister Lundi had said. Maybe other prisoners just sat screaming in the darkness.

The floor of the cart creaked and swayed beneath him, turning to the right, then bounced and jostled over deep ruts in the road. *It's an intersection,* thought Al. They had just turned from one road onto another. The galloping hooves clopped on wood, and Al saw the wooden slats of a bridge slide past. He tensed. They must be crossing the river he'd seen, but what did that mean? Where were they taking him?

His mind worked at it as the light beneath the cart slowly changed from daylight to dusk. The cart reached another intersection and turned right again. Al tried to calculate distances in his head. How far would a horse gallop in a whole day if it never slowed? They'd turned right twice since he woke up. If they'd been traveling southeast before, what direction were they going now? North?

A sick feeling settled in Al's stomach. They were taking him back to Castle Surflienne. It was the only thing that made sense. That way, if the Cullers couldn't make him tell them who his family was, they'd just parade him around until someone recognized him. Once that happened, it was just a matter of time before they realized his parents were lying about having adopted him. He clenched his jaw. How long had he been unconscious? Had he been out for a whole day? Were there any roads through the hills, or would they have had to go all the way around the Thumb? He didn't know. They could be arriving at the castle at any moment.

Below the cart, dusk faded into night. Al gripped the sides of the hole. He couldn't risk staying put any longer, but he'd never done anything like this before. Placing one forearm on either side of the hole, he lowered himself slowly down, until his boots were inches from the ground and his chest was even with the wagon's floor. He closed his eyes, took a deep breath, and let go.

His feet hit first, and then his backside. The leather bag cushioned his back somewhat and kept his head from hitting the ground, but the hard scabbard dug into his spine. The wagon passed over him and continued down the road. Al lay motionless on the dirt for several ragged breaths, and then opened his eyes and rolled to his stomach to watch his prison roll away.

Two horses pulled the black wagon at a gallop, and there was no sign of the Magisters. A single man sat on top of the square box that had held Al. The man held the reins in both hands, his attention focused on the road ahead. Al let out his breath and stood slowly, trying not to hurt any bruised muscles.

Harvested fields surrounded him. Night had fallen, but a bright moon overhead revealed farmhouses clustered together with smoke drifting out of their chimneys. Al opened his bag. The food was gone, but the blanket, tarp, and empty waterskins were all still there. He dug into the folds of the blanket and pulled out the money pouch his parents had left him. The coins were all still there too. Whoever had tossed his bag into the cart must not have searched it very thoroughly.

Al smiled. He had escaped the Cullers again, and had more than enough money to pay for an inn. He hitched his bag over his shoulder. Judging by the stars, the road headed almost straight north. Al walked across it and to the west. If he was right about where he was, the river Flienne would be in that direction, and he remembered his dad talking about staying at inns along the river.

As Al walked, he felt more and more nervous. He had no way of knowing when his escape would be discovered, when the black wagon and its horses would come racing back to find him. He sped up to a run but quickly gave it up. His hip hurt from hitting the road, and his throat burned with each breath. Better to conserve energy, he thought, and put as much distance between himself and the road as possible.

Al shifted his bag to his right hand. He still couldn't believe they'd left it in the wagon with him, especially with the sword. He stopped. On the wagon, he'd guessed they must have just tossed the bag in after him, not realizing it held a sword, but that didn't make sense. He had fallen with the sword in his hand, not in the bag. Someone had to have put the weapon back in the bag. How could they have forgotten about it? It didn't make any sense. Al shook his head, and kept walking.

The thought that Magister Lundi had somehow engineered his escape bothered him. Why would he have done it? Why would Magister Lundi, the highest of the high, care about a zero? No, it didn't make any sense. Whoever put that bag there must have done it simply so the Cullers would have it when they arrived.

By the time the sun peeked over the fields behind him, Al was too exhausted to continue. He spotted a fallow field and made his way to it, then slid his pack off his shoulder and sank down among the tall weeds. The night of walking and thinking had left him no closer to figuring out what to do next. Whatever else had happened, he was still a zero, still one of the *uldi'iara*. He wrapped himself in his blanket and lay down, pillowing his head on his bag. Thinking of *uldi'iara* brought Bird to mind. He hoped the earther had escaped, even if it was just to go back to the hills.

Al woke to a cold, wet nose sniffing his face. He scrambled away. The dog followed, licking his face. "Stop it," Al rasped, standing up.

A man carrying a forked snake stick stood behind the dog, a collection of dead snakes hanging from his belt. "You can't sleep there."

Al straightened. Every muscle in his body ached. From the look of the sun he'd only been asleep for an hour or two. "I'm sorry," he said. Fresh blood seeped out of his lips, and the words that came out of his dry throat were barely more than a whisper. "I just fell asleep."

"Can't sleep there," the man repeated. He wore high leather boots and canvas pants, with a loose shirt and a wide-brimmed grass hat. "Too many snakes."

"What?"

"Got an infestation." The man stretched out one of his dead snakes. "See?"

Al blanched. He recognized the red stripes on its back. Anyone who'd ever spent any time on a farm did. One bite would lay you out for a week, if it didn't kill you. At this time of the year, the snakes would be looking for burrows to hibernate in. They were slower in the cold, but still deadly. Al slung his bag over his shoulder. "Thanks," he croaked. "Could you tell me where the nearest inn is?"

The man pointed with his stick. "There's a place just over that rise there. Next to the river."

"Thanks."

"Be better to stay out of the tall grass," the man said. "Those boots don't look thick enough."

Al waved and made his way carefully to a harvested field, then walked as quickly as he could in the direction the man had indicated. As he crested the gentle rise, he saw the river gleaming in the sun, wider than he could see across. A dirt track ran along beside it, with a lone cart making its way south.

On the other side of the road sprawled a long low building with brick walls and multiple chimneys. A wooden pier jutted out behind it into the broad, slow-moving river, where boats of all sizes were moored. There were people fishing on the pier, and more boats moving in both directions on the water. The scent of fresh bread and cooking grease filled the air.

Al almost cried with relief. Digging in his pack for some coins, he walked down the hill.

CHAPTER 11

THE RIVER

Before Testing Day, Al had never been more than half a day's hike from his house. He'd read about inns and heard about them in his dad's stories, but had never actually seen one.

People filled the building's front porch, eating breakfast at tables underneath an off-white canvas roof with green stripes. Al slowed as he approached. This looked more like a restaurant than an inn. He stopped at the edge of the porch, not sure what to do. A small white sign at the edge of the road had the words *The Water's Blessing* painted on it in blue letters.

A lady carrying a tray of plates stopped in front of him. She was much bigger than Al, and wore a deep green dress with a white apron over it. "No begging."

"I'm not —"

"Then get along. Fishing's out back, if that's what you're here for. One crown for the day. Pay at the pier. Keep what you catch."

"No," Al said. "I'm —"

"I've got no time to waste, boy. You here to watch the boats? They're out back too."

"I need a room," Al said as fast as he could.

She looked him up and down. "You?"

"Please, ma'am." Al pulled two nuggets out of his pocket and held them out. Each one was worth ten drakes. He hoped they would be enough to pay for a night.

"Well," she huffed. "I never! Where did a ragged thing like you get so much money?"

"I worked for it, ma'am," Al said, thankful he'd thought up a story on his way down the hill. The harvest had just ended, which meant there were plenty of workers who were moving on to other things. "I helped my dad in the fields every day this past summer. Now that the harvest is over . . ." Al shrugged. "Well, he said I could spend my pay however I want, and what I want is to sleep in a nice soft bed, and wake up to a hot breakfast."

The lady's expression softened. "You do look like a farm lad, and that's the truth. Okay, follow me."

Still carrying her tray, she wove between tables, through an open doorway, and into a kitchen bustling with activity. She lowered her tray onto a stone counter and continued out the far side of the kitchen and into another room filled with wooden tables and chairs. A man was setting silverware out on the tables.

The lady in the green dress stopped and waited for Al to catch up. "What's your name?"

"Al, ma'am." As soon as he said it, he realized he should have used a fake name. *Too late now*, he thought. Besides, there were plenty of Als out there. A fake name would have just made it more likely for him to mess up.

"Okay, Al. You can call me Miss Sarah."

Al nodded. "Thank you, ma'am."

Miss Sarah guided Al to the man setting the table. "This young man would like a room for the night."

The man looked down at Al and harrumphed. He was wearing a burgundy brushed short coat with a white shirt underneath, and smelled vaguely of flowers. "You know we're all full up."

"I know," Miss Sarah said, "that number seventeen is empty. I cleaned it myself this morning."

"That room is behind a chimney and costs at *least* fifteen drakes a night."

"Good thing he has twenty, then, isn't it?"

Al opened his hand with the two nuggets in it. "If I could have a bath also, I'd really appreciate it."

The man in the burgundy coat took his money with a thin smile. "I think we can manage that. Please follow me. That'll be all, Sarah."

Miss Sarah arched her eyebrows at him, then spoke to Al. "You tell me if you need anything else, honey. Okay?"

When Al reached his room, he locked the door and collapsed onto the mattress. The room had no windows, but the back of a chimney dominated one wall, and the heat radiating from it filled the room. A tall pitcher of fresh water sat on a table by the bedside. Al drank deeply, then sighed and kicked off his boots. *Safe at last.* Closing his eyes, he let out a deep breath. He didn't remember ever being so tired, or being in a bed that was so comfortable. He slept for the rest of the day and all through the night.

The next morning, Al woke up with the dawn and explored the inn. He found the baths and scrubbed himself pink, then enjoyed the kind of breakfast he hadn't had since leaving home: eggs, biscuits, and sizzling meat.

Miss Sarah stopped by his table as he ate. "How was that? Worth all those months of hard work?"

Al smiled and swallowed the mouthful of food he'd been chewing. "Yes, ma'am," he said. It didn't hurt to talk anymore. His voice still sounded raspy, but the water and rest had done miracles for his throat.

"I'm glad." She turned to leave.

"Wait," Al said. "Are there any . . ." He hesitated, embarrassed. "That is, do you have any work for me? This place is so amazing. I'd love to get out of the fields, and with winter coming. . . ."

Miss Sarah cocked her head. "We might have something for a pair of hands to do, especially if they're cheap."

"I just need room and board," Al said. "Maybe a drake a week?"

"I'll have to see, but I think we could manage that." She paused, considering. "What are you, a two or a three? If you're a three, we might be able to use you in the front. That would mean more money."

Al's heart sank. "I'm, uh, not, um" — he looked at the table — "not quite a two."

Miss Sarah's eyes widened. "Oh, honey," she said sadly. "You know we can't hire any ones here. I'm sorry." She started to pat his hand, then stopped and wiped her hand on her apron. "I really am." She dropped her voice. "But don't worry. I won't tell anyone. You can still stay here."

Al nodded miserably. "Yes, ma'am. Thank you, ma'am." He picked at his breakfast for a few more bites as she walked away, then stood up. He should have known better. Nobody was going to hire a one, let alone a zero. On his way back to his room, he saw the man in the burgundy coat.

"I trust your stay with us was enjoyable?" the man asked.

Al clenched his jaw. Zero or not, that bed had been the most comfortable he'd ever slept in, and he was going to enjoy it while he could. "Perfect," he said. He reached in his pocket. "In fact, I'd like to stay another night."

"Very well," the man said as he took Al's money. "But since you'll be staying with us for the whole day, might I suggest you make use of the laundry?"

"No thanks," Al answered. "I —" He stopped at the sight of two men getting off their horses in front of the inn. They wore pants dyed a deep green, and white silk shirts. Rapiers hung from their hips. "Actually," Al said. "Yes. Which way to the laundry?"

The man pointed down the hall, and Al walked as casually as he could in that direction. As soon as he was out of sight, he turned and sprinted for his room.

Miss Sarah was inside, making the bed.

"Excuse me," Al said. "I just need to get my bag."

"Don't worry," Miss Sarah said. "It'll be safe here." She patted her pocket. "Only you and I have the key."

"I know," Al said. "It's not that. It's just that I need to get going. I —" He paused, searching for a good lie. "My dad will be worried."

Miss Sarah put her hands on her hips. "You're in trouble, aren't you? Some kind of runaway?"

"No," Al said, picking up his bag. "Not really. Well, maybe. I don't know. I just have to go. I'm sorry. Thanks for everything!"

Outside the room, Al fumbled in his bag for his money. With the Cullers on horseback, he wouldn't stand a chance on the road or fields. That left the river. He shoved a fistful of money in his pocket and sprinted for the pier. The carpeted halls and rich colors of The Water's Blessing rushed past him in a blur as he pushed through doors and jumped around startled patrons.

The back of the inn looked out over the Flienne and a well-kept wooden pier that jutted into the wide river. Only a few boats were moored, with the rest out fishing in the river.

At the entrance to the pier, a man with a wide-brimmed canvas hat leaned on a post, yawning. As Al approached, the man stepped in front of him. "One crown."

Al dug in his pocket for the appropriate coin. A crown was worth half a drake, but with the Cullers after him, it didn't matter how much the man had asked for. "Are any of the boats leaving soon?"

"Sure," the man said. "But the fishing's just as good from the pier."

"Thanks." Al handed him the money, trying to figure out what to do next. The pier had several boats tied up at it, many with people working on them. "Which one's leaving soonest?"

The man's eyebrows raised. "In a hurry?"

"Please," Al handed him a drake. "I need to get out of here. Can you help?"

The man looked at the coin for a moment, then raised his head and whistled sharply. A white-haired man stopped scrubbing a sailboat and looked in their direction.

"Hey Martin," the man next to Al bellowed. "You got a fare. Double time!"

The man at the boat waved. Despite the cold, he had no shirt on, just tattered gray breeches. His skin was wrinkled and tanned to the shade of old leather, making the gray hair on his face and chest stand out.

Al hesitated.

"Better get a move on," the man next to him said. "Martin's old, but he'll get you where you need to go."

"Thank you." Al dug another drake out of his pocket and handed it to the man, then ran to the boat.

By the time Al reached him, Martin had tossed his brush and bucket onto the boat and was untying the rope that connected it to the dock. The boat was made of three huge logs floating parallel to one another. They were connected by wooden planks that left about four feet of open water between each log. The center log was the longest and had been hollowed out. The space wasn't much wider than Al's shoulders, though, and shallow. It had a center mast, but its sails weren't up, and the bottom was filled with ropes and nets. The whole thing stank of old fish. Al stopped on the dock, not sure where to go.

"Don't be shy, boy!" Martin jumped past him, his tanned bare feet landing on the tangle of ropes, and held out a hand. "The current'll carry us free and then we'll put the sails up."

Al took the man's hand and stepped carefully in, then slipped and fell with a splash into the rancid water pooling at the bottom of the boat.

Martin laughed. "That's it. Just stay down there while I handle the rest. Mind the boom!"

Al ducked as the wooden beam swung over his head. Over the edge of the boat, he saw the Cullers striding along the back of the hotel, talking to the man in burgundy. They were joined by Miss Sarah.

The boat rotated as it floated away from the dock. Al stayed on his hands and knees to keep from being seen. The sail unfurled overhead, and Al glanced over his shoulder to see Martin hauling on a rope, his lean body contorting with the effort. Back on shore, the Cullers had reached the man in the canvas hat. He shrugged and stepped aside to let them onto the pier. Miss Sarah stayed behind to speak to him, her balled fists on her hips. The man's shoulders hunched, and he shook his head.

Al ducked back behind the side of the boat and let out a long breath. There were dozens of boats in the water, some anchored, others sailing, and no way the Cullers could check them all in time. He peeked over the edge again and watched them jog up the pier, stopping to search each boat along the way.

The sail rattled and snapped as it filled with air, and the boat sailed farther out into the river. Neither Al nor Martin spoke until they were too far away to see the people on the pier.

"Looks like we made it," Martin said at last. "Who were those guys, anyway? Never mind. Better if I don't know."

The boat wasn't wide enough for Al to sit sideways, so he faced backward, kneeling on the ropes in the cold water. The boat had two triangular sails: a large one pointing backward and a smaller one pointing forward. Al thought about moving forward to sit on the front, but didn't know how to get past the mast.

Martin sat on the back of the boat, where the two sides of the center log came to a point, one hand on a big wooden handle. "Eventually, you should probably tell me where we're going."

"I don't know where," Al said.

Martin laughed. "That's going to be expensive. How much money you have, anyway? Never mind." He smiled. "Better if I don't know."

Al shifted uncomfortably on the ropes. A thin layer of water swished around the bottom of the boat, with bits of dead fish floating in it. "I just needed to get away," Al said. "Now I have to find somewhere to hide, someplace they'll never look for me."

"That's easy," Martin said. "Just go where they've already looked."

"Where they've already looked?"

"It's the best place. No one looks in the same place twice." He gestured with his chin. "You might want to sit up on the edge there. Not quite as smelly as down with the ropes."

Al lifted himself to the side of the boat, holding tight with both hands. *Someplace they'd already looked.* He swallowed. There was only one place that he knew the Cullers had already looked for him, but he wasn't sure he had the guts to go there.

Martin leaned forward and held out a hand. "Name's Martin. Nice to meet you."

"Oh," Al shook his hand. "I'm Al. Nice, uh, nice to meet you too."

"Sure is beautiful weather." Martin looked up at the sky. "Look how clear that sky is. Don't get skies like that in the summer."

"Yeah." Al said. He stared out at the sky, thinking about what Martin had said. Maybe hiding where they'd already looked was a good idea. It would buy him some time, maybe even give him a chance to find Wisp. "Dockside," he said at last. "Up by Castle Surflienne. How much to get there?"

Martin shook his head. "In this little boat? That's against the current the whole way. Sure, the wind'll be with us in the mornings, but —"

"A hundred drakes?"

Martin whistled. "That'd do it. You got that kind of cash in there?"

Al opened his pack and fished out his coins. It would leave him with only thirty-five drakes, but if it got him away from the Cullers, it was worth it.

"Dockside it is," Martin said. "I hope you like raw fish, 'cause this trip's gonna take a while. Matter of fact, grab a net and hang it off the back. Might as well start trying to catch our lunch now."

Al stood up. Now that he'd decided, he felt excited. Dockside was big enough that he was sure to be able to find work there, even if he was a zero, and with the Cullers searching downriver, he should be safe enough. At least for a while.

CHAPTER 12
THE PERFECT HIDING PLACE

The trip to Dockside proved to be harder work than Al ever could have imagined. When the wind was blowing north, they made decent time. When it wasn't, the current was too strong for them to effectively tack against it. Instead, they furled the sails and used long paddles, with Al kneeling in the front and Martin in back. Close to the shore, the water moved slowly enough that they could at least make some headway.

They didn't sleep regular hours, but took it in shifts. When the wind turned north, whoever was awake would unfurl the sails and weigh anchor.

Al's skin burned, peeled, and burned again. His shoulders and back developed a constant ache from paddling. He lost weight and discovered a deep and abiding hatred for the taste of raw fish. The whole time, he kept a rag tied around his neck to keep his rank mark covered. He told Martin it was to catch the sweat, but was pretty sure the old sailor knew better. Whatever Martin thought his rank was, the man never brought it up.

Finally, after five long days and nights, Dockside appeared on the bank, with Castle Surflienne rising majestically behind it, silhouetted against the morning sun.

Martin tossed out the fish bone he'd been using to pick his teeth. "Well, I'll be. Looks like we made it."

Al stopped paddling and shaded his eyes. He'd never thought Dockside could look so beautiful. "You didn't think we would?"

"In this little boat?" Martin laughed. "No way. Why do you think we kept so close to shore?"

Al laughed. He'd come to appreciate Martin's sense of humor, though a part of him suspected it was due to eating so much fish. "What now? Do we just sail, er, paddle in?"

"No." Martin shook his head. "I'd like that, but the dock fees would kill us. Let's find a place to put in on shore. We'll tie her up and walk the rest."

With Al paddling, Martin steered the boat to a quiet stretch of grassy bank between two trees, then hopped out and waded to shore, pulling the painter behind him. While he tied it to the trunk of a tree, Al stowed the paddles and shouldered his bag. Just a few days ago, he thought with a smile, he hadn't even known what a painter was. Now the language of the boat was a part of his vocabulary.

Al and Martin climbed up the grassy slope and onto Riverway, the hard-packed road that ran alongside the Flienne and into Dockside. A horse and carriage rattled past. Behind it, a tired horse pulled a cart piled high with vegetables. The man walking beside the cart nodded at Martin and continued on his way. Al and Martin followed.

Dockside up close wasn't nearly as appealing as it looked from the river. The buildings appeared to have been built without any plan or vision, and all were either gray stone or faded whitewashed wood. They crowded next to each other, separated by crooked cobblestone streets and narrow alleys. Worse, the whole place stank of fish and smoke and sweat, and looked as though it had never been washed.

Martin stopped just outside. "Of all the places to hide," he said, scratching his belly. "You sure you want this one?"

Al shrugged as he untied the rag from around his neck. He'd forgotten how unpleasant Dockside was. Not that he had much choice. "Yeah."

"Okay, then." Martin shook Al's hand. "Good luck to you. I'm gonna catch the current back. Stop by if you're ever down my way again."

"You're not even coming in for a decent meal?"

"Nah. I don't mind the fish. At least it's fresh."

"But —" Al stopped himself before he could say anything embarrassing. The truth was that he didn't want to be back on his own again. Despite all the raw fish, he'd grown to like Martin.

"What is it?" Martin said.

"Nothing," Al said. "Thanks for everything. Have a good trip back."

Martin smiled crookedly and winked. "Don't worry," he said over his shoulder as he walked away. "I'll stay close to shore."

Laughing, Al hitched his pack over his shoulder and turned to the city. The smile left his face at how overwhelming the place looked. He took a breath and squared his shoulders. The last time he'd come to Dockside, he thought, he'd been a different person. Since then, he'd outsmarted the Cullers not once, but twice, and been places he'd never dreamed of seeing. Dockside wasn't much bigger than Brighton, and it certainly couldn't be more dangerous.

A cart loaded with crates of fall vegetables trundled past him on the road. Al stepped farther into the shadows. Hiding where the Cullers wouldn't think to look for him was one thing. Standing on the main thoroughfare was another. He ran across the road and entered the city through a side street.

The first thing he wanted to do was find an inn, preferably one close to the docks. That would let him get away quickly if the Cullers showed up. He followed his street until it turned left and dead-ended, then backtracked until he found another road that seemed to run parallel to the main thoroughfare. It dead-ended too. Al kicked a loose stone in frustration. Why would anyone build a city like this?

As the morning wore on, Al revised his plan. He just wanted some solid food, anything but fish, and a place to lie down. That was all. He spotted a building that had tables set up outside and ran over. It had no sign, and heavy blue curtains covered its windows, but it looked like it might be a restaurant or inn of some sort. He cracked open the door and peered in.

The smell of stale beer and old vomit filled his nostrils. In the dim light, he couldn't see much, just the impression of chairs and tables, and an oval-shaped bar with bottles hanging from the ceiling above it. A figure moved behind the bar, wiping a dingy white rag over its surface.

"You planning on standin' there all day?"

The voice was deep and rich, and not entirely friendly.

"I'm sorry?" Al said. His eyes were still adjusting to the darkness, but he could see that the rag had stopped moving.

"Don't usually get customers for lunch," the man said. "Can I help you?"

Al glanced over his shoulder at the bright street behind him, then stepped all the way into the room. "I" — he swallowed — "I need a room."

"Twelve drakes a night."

"Twelve? I only have —" Al stopped as he saw the man behind the counter grin. He could see better now, as his eyes adjusted to the gloom. The man was skinny and tall, with long greasy braids and dark skin. "How about seven and I buy some lunch?"

The man's smile grew wider. He threw the cloth over his shoulder and slapped the bar. "Deal."

Al reached into his pouch.

"But tomorrow," the man said, "we renegotiate."

"What?"

"Who knows?" the man said, taking the coins. "One of us may be richer by then." He held out his hand. "I'm Bull. Welcome to The Hook and Hand."

Al shook hands with him. "I'm Al. The Hook and Hand?"

"Didn't you see the sign out front?"

Al sat on a bar stool. There was no sign out front. If there had been, he never would have come in. Who goes to a place called The Hook and Hand?

Bull pulled a key from a pouch at his waist and handed it to Al. "Here's your key. Your room is up the stairs, third on the right. Latch the shutters after dark, and lock the door when you're inside. That's the warmest room in the house, right above the kitchen."

"Thanks." Al took the key. "You don't have a map I could look at, do you? I've been trying to get to the docks, and I can't seem to find them."

Bull burst out laughing, shaking his head so that his braids bounced around like snakes trying to escape his scalp. "First time, is it? Well, we get enough runaways through here. When you go out, turn left, go past three streets and turn right. Walk straight until the street ends. Then turn left and take an immediate right. That'll put you on Riverway. It's a nice wide street that the dockworkers use for loading and unloading, and it's right next to the Flienne."

Al examined Bull's face. Left, three streets, right, straight, left, right? Was he serious? "Don't the streets have names or something? I mean, wouldn't that be easier?"

"Easier for who? Sure, they have names. No signs, though, so the names won't do you much good."

Al sighed. "Okay, I'm gonna need you to give me those directions again. First, though, how about some lunch. And don't say fish. I'm sick of fish."

"Meat pie? Just like the ones at the Testing Day festival? Best in all Dockside. Only five drakes."

"Five drakes!"

"Comes with a drink and bread. Best bread in all Dockside."

Shaking his head, Al slid the coins across the counter. His money was going to run out quicker than he'd thought.

Bull finished cleaning the bar while Al ate, then started mopping the floor.

"Thanks," Al said as he licked his fingers. "You were right. That was the best meat pie in all Dockside."

Bull looked up from his mopping and winked. "Don't get too lost, now. If you're not back before we lock up, you won't be able to get back into your room."

"When do you lock up?"

"Dawn."

Chuckling, Al locked his bag in his room and left to explore. The meat pie had been hot and spicy and warm with fresh grease, and had tasted amazing after five days of raw fish and river water. On the street, Al reviewed his directions — left, three streets, right, straight, left, right — and started walking.

Half an hour later, he found Riverway, the same main thoroughfare he'd turned off of when he'd first arrived. The road was wide and straight, and was lined with unlit torches. Keeping as far to the shadows as he could, Al followed it to the docks, where ships were both loading and unloading.

Soldiers wearing the colors of Lord Archovar wandered between the ships, collecting fees. More soldiers lounged at tables on the street. Al sighed. If he'd been looking for an escape route, this most definitely was not it. He spent the rest of the day exploring the streets, finding restaurants and inns, and searching out places where he might be able to find work. As the sun started to set, he jogged back to the inn, finding his way without any problems.

The common room of The Hook and Hand was humming with people when Al returned. A singer sat at one end of the bar, pounding on some drums and belting out a song that Al had never heard before. Al stopped, stymied. The stairs to his room were behind that singer. He grabbed a seat at the bar and waved to Bull.

Bull looked surprised to see him. "Hey, kid! You made it back! How are you?"

"Great. I found the docks." Al paused. "There's a quicker way, you know."

"But then you wouldn't have seen our beautiful city. It's famous for its architecture."

"Oh yeah?" Al said.

"Yeah," Bull said with a smile. "Our most famous building is stone. Maybe you saw it? It's about three stories tall and gray, stands real close to the other buildings. It's a beauty, it is."

Al chuckled. That described most of the city. "Come to think of it, maybe I did see that one. Stained walls, smells like old fish?"

Bull slapped the bar. "Now you've got it!" He put a mug of cider down in front of Al. "This one's on — nah, you've got money, don't you?"

Al raised the mug and took a careful sip. The liquid inside was hot and spicy, with a warm aftertaste that felt wonderful on his throat. He started to ask Bull how much, but the bartender was tending to other customers. Al settled back on his stool and drank as slowly as he could.

As far as hiding places went, he thought, The Hook and Hand wasn't too bad. He'd start looking for work in the morning. If he could find something, maybe he could negotiate with Bull to get a longer-term rate, maybe even help out at the bar to reduce his rent. He sipped his drink, listened to the music, and watched the crowd around him. This wouldn't be such a bad life, he thought, working in town, spending nights at The Hook and Hand.

After the singer finished, another took his place, this one a woman with a lute, and much bawdier. Al's cheeks flushed with a few of the lyrics. He swayed on his stool, suddenly tired. Now that the excitement of being back in Dockside had worn off, all the built up fatigue from his time on the boat had caught up to him. He was looking forward to a good night's rest in a boat that didn't move with the current. He worked his way through the room and past the performer, ignoring the shouts of the people behind him.

Once upstairs, he made sure the door was locked before stretching out. The bed was soft and warm, but after so many nights on the water, Al couldn't help feeling like it was swaying. Even worse, the singing from downstairs carried up through the floorboards. Al closed his eyes and tried to force himself to sleep.

CHAPTER 13

OLD FRIENDS

Al woke the next morning with a throbbing headache. He groaned and rolled over, forcing himself to get up. He was in his room at The Hook and Hand, a wood-walled box so small he could walk across it in four strides. It did have a window, though, and that was something. He slid open the window, unlatched the shutters, and pushed them open.

Outside, rain was falling from an overcast sky, a slow, deliberate shower that Al remembered from countless autumns in the past. He stuck his arm out the window and shivered. Growing up, these rainy autumn days had been an excuse to relax by the fire. Yes, the chores piled up, but none were so pressing that they needed immediate attention.

Al wiped his hand on his pants and closed the window. Those days were gone. He couldn't afford to spend the day inside. If he was going to stay in Dockside, he needed some sort of income. Otherwise, he'd be sleeping on the street.

Bull was cleaning up the common room when Al staggered downstairs, one hand on his head.

"What's wrong?" Bull asked. "I thought all you drank last night was my famous cider."

"It wasn't the cider." Al rubbed his forehead. "It was the singing. It went on all night!"

"Told you we didn't close until dawn," Bull said. "But the cider was good, right?"

Al tried to muster a smile. "Undoubtedly the best in Dockside."

Bull put an arm around Al's shoulders and steered him to the bar. "Fortunately for you, we also have the best headache cure in Dockside."

"No," Al said weakly as he sat down. "I don't want anything to drink."

"Pff. What a stupid thing to say." Bull produced a collection of different-colored bottles from under the bar. "You're the first fisherman I ever met who didn't like a good drink."

"Not a fisherman." Al rubbed his eyes with the palms of his hands. "I'm a farmer."

Bull opened a bottle and poured two finger-widths into a cloudy glass. "With that burn?"

"Used to be a farmer," Al corrected himself. He watched Bull mix the different liquids in the glass and swirl them together. He had to admit that it smelled really good, fruity, but not too sweet.

Once he was done, Bull lifted the glass and poured half into a second, empty glass, then he slid one of them to Al. "There," he said, raising the other glass. "That'll do the trick."

The liquid inside looked murky brown, with surprising swirls of color. Al raised it to his lips cautiously.

"Not like that," Bull said. He opened his mouth and tossed his drink down his throat, finishing the whole thing in one gulp. "You've got to do it quick. Otherwise, you'll never get through it."

"You're trying to kill me, aren't you?"

"Trust me."

After another quick look, Al filled his mouth with the drink, then swallowed as fast as he could. The liquid tasted horrible, but felt smooth and cold on his throat, almost soothing. "Hey," he said. "That wasn't bad!" Al felt the pain behind his eyes slide away. Whatever was in the miracle mix, it was even more effective than his mom's soup at making him feel better.

Bull nodded. "So what brings you to Dockside, Al?"

"Looking for a job," Al said, picking at his sunburn. "Tried fishing, but it didn't work out."

"Thought you said you were a farmer."

Al smiled in spite of himself. "That didn't work out, either."

Bull laughed.

"You don't have anything, do you?" Al asked.

"There's nothing here a boy your age could do. My customers'd eat you alive. Besides, you smell like fish."

"Bath'd cost money, wouldn't it?"

"If we had one. Try Clock Street. Used to be one there."

Al resisted the urge to ask where Clock Street was. He had seen a big clock when he was exploring the previous day. It was an obvious place to start looking.

"How's the head?" Bull asked.

"It feels a lot better," Al said. He stood up. "Thanks."

"Not so fast," Bull said, leaning forward and looking serious. "You owe me three drakes for the drinks last night and a crown for the miracle mix you just drank."

Al dug in his pocket for the coins.

"And we still have to decide on a rate for tonight. It'll be five drakes."

"I don't have much left," Al said, putting Bull's money on the bar. "I don't know if — did you say five?"

Bull's expression didn't change.

"Deal!" Al slapped the extra drakes on the bar.

"Go get a job," Bull said with a smile. "Tomorrow's another day."

"It is. Isn't it?" Smiling, Al walked out the door and into the rain. He felt the best he had since leaving home. Somewhere between the fishing and the rowing and the previous day's exploring, he'd almost forgotten his rank. Now, all he had to do was find a job where they wouldn't bother to check, and he'd be starting a new life, one where people treated him like a person again, the way Martin and Bull did.

The street in front of the big clock did indeed have a shop with a picture of a bubbling tub of water on its front door. Al went in and paid two drakes for a tepid bath of murky water. It came with good clean soap, though, and Al washed himself and his clothes. By the time he was done, he was shivering with cold, but had lost his fishy smell. He asked the bathhouse if they had any work for him, but they turned him down.

Outside, the rain continued to fall. Al found a shop selling used clothes and picked up a rain slicker. Not that it mattered much with his clothes soaking wet from the bath, but it seemed like a good investment for the future. When he asked, the shopkeeper told him there was a job that paid three drakes a day, but he needed to see Al's rank mark. Al said he'd think about it.

The rest of the day repeated the same scene over and over. Al went from business to business, looking for work. Those few places that were willing to hire him at all wanted to see his rank mark. No one was desperate enough to hire a rank one, and most places kicked him out once they found out he wasn't a two.

By the time the sun was setting, Al was completely depressed. Hungry and out of ideas, he trudged back to The Hook and Hand.

Bull was behind the bar, talking to some customers. He waved to Al. "Any luck?"

Al shook his head and tried to smile. "Didn't work out."

"Keep trying. You'll find something."

"Yeah." Al went upstairs, hung up his wet clothes, and stretched out on his bed, grateful for the warmth seeping up from the kitchen below. While not as toasty as his room by the chimney, the room was still plenty warm.

It wouldn't last, though. Unless he found some way of earning drakes, he could only stay one or two more nights. He balled up a fist and hit the mattress. It didn't make sense. Why did it matter that he wasn't a rank two? No one ever asked the rank of the boy cleaning the dishes. It shouldn't matter.

Al stood up and started to pace, remembering how Bird had stolen from the houses outside Brighton. Morality hadn't been a part of the earther's decision. Stealing was just something that had to be done to survive. Without money, Al knew that he never would have been on that boat with Martin, or in this inn with Bull. The money he had now was buying him a temporary escape from the harsh truth that he was a zero, but if he didn't figure something out, he'd be back on the streets.

Small wonder Bird had felt like an *uldi'iara*. After just one day of rejections, Al was starting to feel the same way. He couldn't imagine how he'd feel after months or even years of no one wanting him around. He untied his bag and pulled out his sword. There had to be something he could do. He stood in his neutral stance. When he used to practice the sword, he imagined being in the army, leading brave warriors into battle. That wasn't an option now. The army was certain to check his rank mark, and then he'd be handed over to the Cullers.

Al practiced his parries deep into the night, trying to shake the feeling of desperation that was starting to overwhelm him.

The next morning, Bull was cleaning the common room again. "Are you sure there's nothing I can do to help?" Al asked. "You're always cleaning this place. I could do that."

Bull stopped mopping. "How much were you thinking I would pay you for this cleaning?"

"I don't know," Al said. "Three drakes?"

"Three? For something I do myself for free every morning?"

"But —" Al sighed. "Okay. How about two?"

Bull handed him the mop. "Let's see what you can do, then we'll talk pay."

Al took the mop. The room looked much bigger now that he was faced with the prospect of cleaning it. "For breakfast?"

"I can do that. You mop, I'll get us some breakfast."

Mopping wasn't new to Al, but he'd never been faced with anything like the common room of The Hook and Hand before. While the center of the floor was clean enough, the edges were sticky with accumulated spills. It occurred to Al that he'd never seen Bull clean anything but the one area in front of the door.

"Pump's in the kitchen if you need more water," Bull said.

"You have a well?" Al asked.

"No. Pipes from the river run below the city. They give us all water."

Al spent most of the morning working at the floor, first with the mop, and then with scrub brushes.

"Impressive," Bull said as Al finished up. "I'd forgotten about those blue tiles in the corner. Stash the mop and brushes and I'll take care of breakfast."

"Two drakes a day?" Al asked.

"Two drakes today," Bull said. "That means you owe me three drakes for tonight, but we may have to renegotiate tomorrow."

"How about breakfast?"

Bull handed him a meat pie. "Take it and go," he said. "You need a better job than this."

Al walked into the city. At least the rain had stopped.

Despite the improved weather, the search for jobs went no better. Even the jobs no one wanted, like mucking out stables or emptying chamber pots, were too good for any-one less than a rank two. By the end of the day, Al felt dejected and defeated. One more day like this, and he would be completely out of money.

As the sun set, Al pushed his way quietly into the raucous crowd filling The Hook and Hand. Bull was working the bar, alternating between serving drinks and bellowing out orders to the servers and cooks. Al slid onto a stool in the corner by the pile of coats and waved.

"That was quick," Bull said. "Got a job in just two days, huh?" He slid a plate of leftover ribs over.

Al smiled in spite of himself. "You know how it is. Everyone loves a guy that can mop." He nodded at the food. "How much?"

Bull dropped a half-finished tankard of cider in front of him. "Staff gets leftovers for free. Hook and Hand policy."

"But we may renegotiate tomorrow?"

Bull laughed as he glided down the bar to another customer.

After wiping off the rim of his cup with his thumb, Al stared into its depths, then fished his finger in to scoop out a piece of half-chewed fish left behind by the drink's previous owner.

"Al?" an astonished voice said from behind him. "Is that really you?"

Al flicked the fish quickly to the floor and turned. Wisp stood by the coats, his eyes wide. He held a brown suede jacket in one hand, but otherwise was dressed all in shades of black. The color made him look even taller, and highlighted the sharpness of his features. He'd also cut his hair to within a few inches of his scalp.

"Everyone thinks you're dead," Wisp said. "What's going on? Where have you been?"

"I . . . ," Al said, trying to come up with something to

say. "I just took a little trip." He paused. "You know, business for my dad."

Wisp snorted. "C'mon, Al. I know better than that." He dropped the coat and moved closer. "How'd you get away?"

Al's heart sped up. Did Wisp know he was a zero? Who else knew?

Before he could speak, a man wearing an orange tunic stumbled backward past Wisp and fell on the pile of coats. Trillia strode after him, her red braids dancing around her shoulders. She wore a dark blue tunic and leather pants. "When I said get your hands off me," she bellowed, "I meant it!"

Al laughed as the man scrambled away from her.

Trillia spun, eyes flashing, and then froze. "Al?" Her breath caught, and one hand raised to cover her mouth. "Al?" She stepped over the coats. "You're alive?"

"Sure am."

"You're alive!" Trillia yelled. She pulled him off his bar stool and into a hug. "You're alive," she said.

Al hugged her back, surprised at just how happy he was to see her. Suddenly, her body tensed under his arms and she shoved him away. He stumbled, tangled his legs in his bar stool, and fell. "What was that for?" he said.

"Oh, I don't know," she said. "Maybe for lying to us all those years?"

"Trillia," Wisp said quietly.

"Maybe for pretending to be the son of an Overseer," she continued angrily. "For lording it over us."

"I didn't —" Al started.

"You didn't what?" Trillia's face was flushed with anger. "You didn't tell us the truth? You didn't want us to know?

120

Why not, Al? Were you having too much fun pretending to be better than we were?"

Al sat on his stool, stunned. He'd never pretended to be better than them.

"Trillia," Wisp said sharply. "He didn't know. No one did."

"I didn't lord anything over you," Al said. "I thought we were friends."

"Friends don't just disappear," Trillia said. "Friends don't run off to Brighton and get themselves killed."

"Killed?" Al said. "Brighton?" How did she know about that?

"When you disappeared on Testing Day," Wisp said quietly. "Your father let everyone know that you weren't really his son, that you were an orphan he'd taken in out of the goodness of his heart."

"And to think I almost —" Trillia started.

"We looked everywhere for you," Wisp continued. "My dad said you'd probably headed south. Your dad said that you'd always wanted to visit Dockside, that you were probably here, so we came here."

"You almost what?" Al asked Trillia.

"Then we heard about Brighton," Wisp finished.

"How could you have heard about Brighton?" Al asked.

"So that *was* you!" Trillia said. "I knew it."

"Wait," Al said. "Slow down! I don't understand."

"An earther showed up," Wisp said. "He'd hiked all the way across the Thumb from Brighton, looking for your parents, to let them know what you'd done."

"What I'd done?" Al echoed weakly.

"About how you'd stood up to the Magisters," Trillia said, "actually drawn a sword on them. He said it like you were some kind of hero for doing it, like your parents should be proud."

"But they used Air magic to suck your breath out," Wisp said, "and then carried your lifeless body away."

Al drank from his cider to steady his hands. Bird was alive.

"Everyone said the earther was crazy, but he kept insisting, telling the story to anyone who would listen," Wisp said. "Then he started talking about fighting against the Magisters," Wisp said, "and they threw him in the dungeon."

"Do you know how much trouble you caused?" Trillia asked.

Al put his drink down. "Bird's in the dungeon?"

"Who's Bird?" Trillia said. "I'm talking about me."

Al blinked. "You?"

"Oh boy," Wisp said.

Trillia stepped closer to him. "Don't *tell* me you didn't know our moms were talking about us getting promised!"

"No," Al said slowly. "And I'm pretty sure I'd remember something like that." Getting promised was the step before getting engaged, an acknowledgment that the families involved approved of the match. Usually, the two people involved dated before being promised, but not always.

"Your mom said that if I was at least a three, she'd welcome the arrangement." Trillia leaned over Al, her face furious. "You want to know what rank I am?"

"No," Al said, raising his hands. "I really don't —"

"A three! But then it turns out you're not even a Pilgrommor." Trillia threw up her hands. "You're just some sort of waif the Pilgrommors took pity on. You're probably not even a three yourself."

"I'm sorry."

"*Sorry?*" Trillia grabbed the front of Al's shirt with her fist. "By the time we found out, there weren't any guys of rank left. You know who they promised me to?" She took a breath. "Leonard!"

"Leonard? But he's already seventeen, and he, uh, well, he smells."

"I know," Trillia grated, letting go of his shirt. "But he's also rank four, and his parents are desperate to get rid of him. They said I could court him, and when I became old enough, we could marry."

Al burst out laughing. "*You* could court *him*?"

"It's not funny," Trillia said, turning away.

"She had a major fight with her parents," Wisp said. "She lives in Dockside now."

Al's face fell. "Oh."

Wisp crossed his arms. "You still haven't told us why you're sitting here instead of lying in a grave at Brighton."

Al took a deep breath. He didn't know what his friends would say when they found out he was a zero, but now that he'd found them again, he didn't want to start off lying. "Okay," he said. "Not here, though. I've got a room upstairs."

CHAPTER 14
CATCHING UP

Bull stopped them on the way across the common room. "Everything okay, Al?"

"Sure, Bull. It's fine."

"I don't really like kids in my bar." He glanced at Trillia. "Especially not ones that shove the other customers around."

Trillia glared at him. "Our money is as good as theirs!"

"Yes," Bull smiled. "But there are more of them, and some of them don't like to see kids in a place like this."

"Then they should mind their own business." Trillia turned away.

Bull shook his head, then leaned closer to Al. "Are you really *that* Al? The one that popped the Magisters?"

Al sighed. He should have known Bull would overhear them. "Yeah, that's me."

"How'd you get away?"

"Cut a hole in the bottom of the wagon and just dropped out."

A grin spread slowly across Bull's face, and he burst out laughing. "Cut a hole in the bottom of the wagon!" He clapped a hand on Al's shoulder. "Boy, you just earned yourself a night's rent." The tall man shook his head as he walked away. "Drawing on the Magisters! Sure would have liked to see that."

Al led Trillia and Wisp up the stairs to his room, lit the lantern, and closed the door. Keeping things secret didn't seem so important now, but he would have felt silly just turning around and going back to the bar. He slid the window up and pushed open the shutters. "It started at Testing Day," he said. "When I found out I'm a zero."

"A what?" Trillia said.

"A zero," Al said. "You know, rank zero?" He couldn't quite keep the bitterness from his voice. "One less than one?"

Wisp had crossed his arms and was leaning on the door, his face serious.

"No way," Trillia said. "There isn't a rank zero."

"Not many, that's for sure."

"Show me."

Al's mouth dropped open. "You don't believe me? Of all the stupid things . . ." He turned and bent so she could see his rank mark. "Happy?"

"You're a *zero*." Trillia stepped back, eyes wide. "Wow. After all those years of being Alluencien Pilgrommor, the son of the Overseer, and now . . . I thought *I* had it bad."

"Thanks," Al said. "Really appreciate that."

"How'd you get away?" Wisp asked quietly. "Was it my dad's hat?"

Al sat on the bed. "Yeah. A guard spotted it and helped me get out through the catacombs. The weirdest thing was that when I tried to thank him, he said that if my dad knew an Evan, he was the one that should be thanking me."

"An Evan?" Trillia asked. "What does that mean?"

"Don't know," Al said. "I don't know anyone named —"
He broke off, looking at Wisp. "Your dad's last name isn't
really Evanson, is it?" Al stood, his mind racing, remembering the hat, and the feathers on its band, the same feather that
had been on Mr. Evanson's uniform. "And that hat wasn't just
a hat, was it? It was part of your dad's uniform. He was in the
military. He's the Evan the guard was talking about."

Wisp nodded. "First lieutenant in the Mountainfoot
Third."

Al leaned against the wall. The Third. That's what Bird
had shouted at Magister Lundi. "Five thousand dead?" Al
said, remembering.

"Yes," Wisp said. "Five thousand strong, five thousand
loyal, five thousand dead. That's what people remember of
the Third. Some people, that is."

"You knew?" Al asked. "You knew I was a zero? You
had to have. That's why you gave me the hat."

Wisp nodded. "I found out that morning. My dad wanted
me to be ready, to do what I could to help you, if it turned
out to be true." Wisp straightened. "I waited at the East
Gate all day and night, hoping you'd come out."

Al felt drained. "Thanks, Wisp."

"So you escaped the castle," Trillia said. "What next?
Why didn't you go home?"

"I couldn't." Al didn't feel right talking about Wisp's
dad. The fewer people who knew he'd helped, the safer he
would be. "The Cullers were after me."

"The Colors?"

"No," Al said. "Cullers, like people who cull the herd to
get rid of the sick animals. Except these Cullers cull *us*.
They kill off zeroes to improve our stock."

Trillia's face twisted with disgust. "That's not true."

"Yeah," Wisp said. "It is. They track down zeroes and eliminate them. They also go after people who have changed their rank mark. You've seen their insignia, Trillia. It's a sheaf of grain."

She sat on the bed. "I have seen that. Two soldiers came to the house a couple days after Al disappeared, asking if I'd seen a boy wearing a funny hat at Testing Day. I told them it was yours, Al, but that no one had seen you."

"They stopped by our place too," Wisp said. "I asked around. I think they checked with everyone."

"I was in the hills by then," Al said, "walking to Brighton. I met Bird on the way. When we got to Brighton, it was under attack by rockeaters and the Magisters showed up to help. But then Bird and I got accused of stealing, and, well . . ."

"You didn't really draw a sword on them," Trillia said, standing. "You did not. You don't even have a sword."

"Actually," Al said. He opened his leather bag and pulled out the sword. "I sort of do." He held it out hilt first.

"Wow," Trillia said. "And you can use it?"

Al shrugged. "Kinda."

"There's a feather on the pommel," Wisp said, peering at it. "That's the mark of the Third."

"So what happened next?" Trillia said, taking the sword.

"Magister Lundi sucked the breath out of me. I woke up in the back of a wagon, and found they'd left my pack in there too. I used my sword to get out, and made my way back here." He shrugged. "That's about it."

"Wow," Trillia said, swinging the sword. "You really know how to use this thing?"

Al and Wisp backed away.

"Yeah," Al said. "That's what I was doing all summer. If I could have it back now —"

She swung it around her head and crouched, then straightened. "Sure." She tossed it to him, hilt first. "Seems a little light, anyway. If you're going to use something that small, might as well just stick to daggers. Come on." She opened the door. "I'm not done dancing."

"You're going to get yourself in trouble," Wisp said, following her down the hall.

"Wait," Al said. He slid the sword back into its hidden sheath and tied the bag closed. Wisp and Trillia were already halfway to the stairs by the time he was done. "You haven't told me your stories!" Al hurried to lock his room and run after them.

Downstairs, the drummer was performing again, pounding out a rhythm with a fast beat. An area of the room had been cleared of tables, and people spun and whirled in time to the music. Trillia whooped and dove in, grabbing the hand of the nearest guy and dragging him after her.

Wisp maneuvered his way behind the drummer to a seat at the bar.

Al joined him there, watching Trillia. "We were really supposed to get married?"

"Can't believe you didn't know. She just about killed herself trying to figure out why you never brought it up."

"She is pretty," Al said.

Wisp laughed. "That ship has sailed, Al."

"Hey hero," Bull said, putting two fresh mugs in front of him. "Your friend buying?"

"For the best cider in Dockside?" Al said, clapping an arm around Wisp's shoulders. "Of course he is."

"Good man!"

Al leaned forward over the bar. "Could you keep the Magister story quiet? It's not exactly good for my health."

"Bartender's honor." Bull winked and was gone.

"Hey," Wisp said over his mug. "This *is* good." He took another drink.

"So what's your story?" Al asked, still watching Trillia. "Why aren't you with your folks? What are you doing in a bar?"

Wisp took another drink. "Apprenticed here in town to a skincarver. Trillia's working in a bakery. We're both living in the North End. We came down here tonight, just to explore." He shrugged. "Trillia's idea."

Al pushed his drink away, a sour taste in his mouth. He'd spent two days looking for a job with no luck. He could spend another two hundred, and he'd never get anything as nice as what his friends had.

"What about you?" Wisp asked. "What's your plan?"

"Just get by," Al said. Trillia had switched partners, and was twirling with a man who looked old enough to be her father, though to be fair, most of the men here looked old enough to be her father. "I've got a room here, and a job mopping up. If I can get another job, I'll have enough to pay the rent. Then, who knows?"

Wisp shook his head. "That's bleak."

"Yeah, well." Al turned away from Trillia and gestured with his hands. "It is what it is."

"It's not good enough," Wisp said. "That feather on your

sword means something," he said, suddenly intense. "You know that, right?"

"It's not that easy. When you're a —" Al stopped himself and took a breath. "Bird had a word for it: *uldi'iara*. When you're an *uldi'iara*, you don't have choices. Surviving is enough."

"You mentioned Bird before. Is he that earther they locked up, the one that walked clear across the Thumb for you?"

Al stared at his drink, feeling miserable. "Yeah."

"Was he *uldi'iara* too? 'Cause that hike sure wasn't about surviving."

Al nodded. "I know."

"And what are you going to do about it?" Wisp finished off his mug and reached for Al's. "Spend another day looking for a job?"

"What?"

"Listen, Al," Wisp said. "I was raised on stories of the Third, sworn to secrecy, always knowing my dad was part of something big." He drank deeply from Al's mug. "Now here you are, right in the middle of it, and all you want to do is get by."

"What do you want me to do?" Al said, his voice rising. "Don't you think I want to help Bird? But I can't save him. I can't even save myself!"

Wisp put Al's mug down. "You could try."

Al stared at him, his mouth open.

"You put my whole family at risk," Wisp said. "For what? No good-byes, no thanks, nothing."

"But I couldn't," Al said. "I had to leave."

"Yeah, sure." Wisp stood up and dropped some coins on the bar. "Listen, I gotta get going before Trillia starts another fight."

"I don't —"

"Stop by the shop if you get a chance. Maybe I can help find you a job."

Al slumped on his chair and watched Wisp drag Trillia away from the group of men she'd gathered. She smiled to him as they grabbed their coats and left.

"You okay?" Bull said.

"No," Al said quietly. "I'm really not."

He walked past the singer and upstairs to his room, then stretched out on the straw mattress. Wisp had always been his best friend, but now he didn't seem to like him anymore. Had being a zero changed him that much? He stared at the dark lantern hanging from the ceiling and watched a confused moth walk slowly across its glass. One thing was for certain: There was no way he was going to ask Wisp for a job. No way.

CHAPTER 15

BETRAYAL

Down in the common room the next morning, Bull had his feet up and was reading a book, a glass of the murky brown miracle mix on the table next to him. "One crown," he said. "Mop's in the kitchen."

"I'm okay," Al said. "Thanks."

Bull shrugged and downed the drink. "You can never have too much."

"I didn't know you liked to read," Al said. For that matter, Al didn't even know that Bull could read. Most people couldn't, not unless they'd had a reason to learn. Al's reason had been his parents.

"Don't get much chance." Bull smiled over the book. "Or I didn't, until a certain boy offered to keep my bar clean. Feels good to relax a bit." He paused. "While he cleans, that is."

"Okay, okay." Al found the mop and set to work.

"Did the singing keep you up again last night?" Bull asked.

"Nah. I slept with my head under my pillow."

Bull chuckled.

Al pushed the mop around the room, thinking about Bird. He couldn't believe that the earther had walked all the way back across the Thumb.

"Off to look for a job again?" Bull asked.

"Not today," Al said. "I was thinking about a visit to the dungeon. You know where that is?"

Bull put his book down. "There are two. One is under the castle. It's not used much. The other's on Canal Street."

"Hm," Al said. He'd spotted Canal Street during his previous day's search for a job, but had decided against walking down it. It was a canal that they had started building and then given up on. It had never been connected to the river, and now formed a street that was about ten feet lower than the rest of Dockside. "Which one do you think they'd put an angry earther in?" he asked.

"Whichever one they thought would catch them an angry boy."

Al stopped mopping. He hadn't thought of that. "Canal Street, then. No way such a boy would be stupid enough to go to the castle."

"Glad to hear it." Bull raised his book again. "I'd hate to lose my reading time."

After he finished, Al went to his room and counted out the last of his money: seven drakes and one crown. He transferred three drakes to his pocket, pulled on his rain slicker, and ran back downstairs. It wasn't raining, but the slicker was the closest thing he had to a disguise.

Canal Street was close to the northern end of the city, just one block east of Riverway. From above, it looked exactly like what it was: a dry canal, ten feet deep and three times as wide with walls all around it. Wooden stairs led down from the street level of Dockside, and a sloping ramp had been constructed on its south end.

Al pulled the hood of his rain slicker up and walked down the ramp. An open-air market filled the street's center, with vegetable carts, meat vendors, and craftsmen calling out to anyone who walked by. Homeless people huddled along the walls, using the relative shelter to stay out of the wind. Al found himself staring at them as he walked by, wondering how many were rank ones.

Probably all of them, he thought. What did that mean for a zero like him? He shook himself and looked around. He needed to stop thinking of himself as a zero, even if that's what he was. He spotted what he was looking for on the wall closest to the river: a wooden door with the flower of Lord Archovar painted on it.

Al leaned back to look up at the buildings above it. The dungeon had to have another entrance, be part of some structure up at street level. He looked around and counted blocks. From what he could tell, the dungeon was connected to a building that had its front on Riverway. He ran up the stairs. After three days, he was getting good at maneuvering around the dead ends that plagued the city.

Riverway, as always, was filled with people and wagons. Al walked quietly through the crowds, keeping his face down, until he spotted the building he was looking for. It was, like most of the rest of the city, three stories tall and made of gray stone. It stood separate from those around it, though, and its windows had metal bars on them. The flag of Lord Archovar was mounted above the door.

Al sighed and pulled his hood tighter over his head. At the very least, he'd thought he might be able to let Bird know he was still alive, but not now. There was no way he could go anywhere near the headquarters of the city guard. He walked away, frustrated. He couldn't stand the idea of Bird sitting in that dungeon, not even knowing Al was alive.

What he needed was someone who could ask to see Bird without getting arrested, someone the guards wouldn't care about. He paused. Maybe he did know someone like that.

A brick wall blocked off the most exclusive section of Dockside, an upscale neighborhood that Al had not yet explored. He walked up Riverway to its entrance, where an open gate had the words *North End* in the metal work. Al passed through it, uncomfortably aware that if the gate closed, he'd have no way out.

On the other side of the gates, the city was transformed. There was none of the gray stone and faded wood that dominated the rest of the city. Instead, the buildings were of brick and freshly painted wood, with plaster statues and elegant carvings. They stood apart from each other, with small gardens in boxes surrounded by white gravel walkways. Even the docks were absent, replaced with a fitted stone walkway for people to stroll along the Flienne.

Al had never felt more out of place. He walked nervously past the houses, knowing that the skincarver Wisp worked for would have a place of special significance. Though porta were illegal for anyone without an official document, decorative tattoos were very popular.

At last, Al spotted a group of white wooden buildings, set back from the river. Each was two stories tall, with green shutters and wide glass windows. Carriages were parked in front of the storefronts, their horses munching placidly from feedbags.

The center building's sign was unfinished wood with the word *Carver* burned into it. Wisp stood in front of it, talking to a tall, thin man wearing a leather apron. Al moved closer, his heart pounding. After the previous night, he didn't know how Wisp would treat him. He pulled the hood of his slicker down.

"Hey!" the man shouted.

Al's eyes widened. The man talking to Wisp was the skincarver who had given Al his rank mark.

"It's you," the man said, pointing. "It's the zero!"

Wisp's head jerked around and his eyes met Al's.

"Get him!" the skincarver shouted at Wisp. "He's the zero the Cullers are looking for!"

Al turned and ran. He couldn't be caught like this, not in front of Wisp, not after having come so far. Footsteps sounded on the gravel behind him. Al tried to sprint faster.

Wisp's shoulder slammed into the small of his back and the taller boy's arms wrapped around him, pinning his arms to his sides. Al shouted in surprise as he flew forward, then his head hit the cobblestones.

"I'm sorry," Wisp said. "I had to."

Al rolled over. Blood ran from his mouth and nose, and his eyes wouldn't focus. "Why?" He tried to sit up.

"Shut up!" Wisp hissed frantically, putting a knee on his chest and forcing him to the ground. His eyes looked wide and frightened. "He can't know that I know you."

"But my family! They'll —"

Wisp pushed down with his knee. "Shut up!"

The skincarver's tall, thin shape appeared behind Wisp. "Good work. This'll get us back into the castle for sure."

Wisp flinched when the man's hand touched his shoulder.

Al closed his eyes. His best friend in the whole world had just turned him over to the Cullers. He let the darkness flickering around his vision take him.

CHAPTER 16
THE DUNGEON

Al woke lying on cold stone in pitch-blackness. Blood had crusted his nose closed, and his head throbbed. He touched his mouth gingerly, feeling where his bottom lip had split from hitting the ground. His rain slicker and money were gone, but he still had his clothes.

"Hello?" he said. "Is anyone there?"

His hand brushed a wall, and he felt blindly along it, then used it to help him stand.

"Hello?" he called again.

Moving hand over hand, he followed the wall until he found the next one. It didn't take long to decide that he was in a stone cell, barely wider than he was tall, with one wall made of floor-to-ceiling metal bars. Al pressed his cheek to the cold metal bars and held on to them with both hands. He couldn't believe that Wisp had betrayed him.

Al and Wisp had been friends all their lives. They'd done everything together. Up until this past summer, when Al's dad had brought in his tutors, they'd been inseparable. Al closed his eyes. And now Wisp had tackled him, given him over to the Cullers to be killed. Why? Had he really been that angry about Al not saying good-bye?

A noise in the darkness snapped him out of his thoughts. "Hello," he called. "Is someone there?"

"Stop shouting," a familiar voice grumbled. "There's no one to hear. It's just you and me down here."

Al's heart thumped in his chest. "Bird?"

No one answered.

"Bird, is that you? This is Al!"

"Al's dead."

"No," Al said. "I'm Al! I escaped when the Magisters were taking me to the Cullers."

"What business do the Cullers have with Al?"

Al slumped against the bars. "I'm a zero," he said quietly. "Even more of an *uldi'iara* than you."

Bird's voice sharpened. "Who told you that word?"

"You did," Al said. "It really is me. I was the one that tried to stop you from stealing from the houses outside Brighton, the one you kept from going to the wall during the rockeaters' attack."

"Al," Bird said hesitantly. "You sound different."

"Having the air sucked out of your lungs messes with your voice. Magister Lundi says it'll get better."

"He talked to you?"

"Yeah, just before he loaded me in the wagon to send me to the Cullers. He said that he wished he could hire me, but that he could never hire anyone with a rank mark of zero."

"And then you escaped," Bird said.

"Yeah."

Bird sighed. "The Magister let you go."

"No, he didn't." Al said. "The inside of the cart was pitch-black. I dug my way through the floor and dropped out."

"Using the sword he'd left in the cart, and without the driver ever hearing you shatter the wood? He let you go, Al."

"Why would he do that?"

"Guilt," Bird said. "He finally feels guilty. After all these years, he's feeling guilty."

"About the Third?"

"The Mountainfoot Third," Bird said. "Five thousand strong, five thousand loyal. That was their motto."

"Who were they?" Al asked.

"A military division that reported directly to the Magister, until he turned on them."

"Five thousand strong," Al said, repeating the words he'd heard Bird shout at Magister Lundi. "Five thousand loyal, five thousand dead. Wait. You mean he killed them all?"

"Fourteen survived. The Magister attacked the army with air and fire, bathing them in flames, then crushing them beneath a mountain. Only one small group survived, saved by their captain. He was an Earth master, some say a failed Magister. When the fire swept across the army, he created a hole in the ground beneath the men. They dropped in, and he sealed the top over them. As Magister Lundi killed the army above, he moved the pocket of air through the earth, transporting them away from danger. In the end, though, the effort was too much. He couldn't handle the Potentia, and died. The fourteen survivors dug themselves out and fled."

"Evan," Al breathed.

"What?" Bird asked.

"I think that was the captain's name," Al said. It made sense now. The survivors, no longer able to use their own names, had taken the name of the man who had saved them. It was their tribute.

Bird was quiet for a while before speaking. "Maybe. All I know is that they went into hiding, afraid that Magister Lundi would hunt them down."

"Where did you hear all this?"

"I was in the army once, years ago. The story was common in the barracks back then, all the more so for being forbidden. No one really believed it, of course, but I was there when the Cullers came for one of our men. He called himself Evan, and he was a good friend of mine, had the mark of the feather tattooed on his shoulder. He didn't talk about the Third, but I knew he'd been one of them."

Al stared at the darkness, remembering Magister Lundi. Why would the man have killed five thousand men sworn to his service? And why hunt the survivors? He rubbed his rank mark. "You think he's feeling guilty?"

"Why else would he let you go?" Bird asked. "Or me?"

"We didn't get very far."

Bird laughed bitterly. "No."

Al picked at the blood scabbed over his nose, and wondered how long it would take before the Cullers came for him. The lack of a chamber pot in his cell certainly implied that they weren't expecting him to stay the night. "Have you thought about escaping?" he asked.

"Yes," Bird said. "I could dig through the stones, but I don't know which direction to go, or if the whole thing would fall on me once I started breaking walls."

"What about the bars?"

"I guess I could dig out around them, but what then? I can't fight the guards."

Al considered. "I was unconscious when they brought me in. You know which direction the river's in?"

"Don't even suggest it. We'd drown as soon as I broke through."

"No, the other way, toward the canal."

"I told you," Bird said. "I can't dig fast enough once water starts coming in."

"There's no water. It's dry. They never finished the canal, just turned it into a street instead. You break through the wall and we're in Dockside."

Al heard Bird moving in his cell, heard the soft click of horn on metal. "Are you sure about this?" the earther asked. "If they catch us, they'll kill us for sure."

"We just have to be quick enough. How often do they come down here?"

"Tough to tell with no windows," Bird said. "I think it's once a day, to change the chamber pots and leave water and food. It could be a while."

"Can you do it?"

Bird blew out a breath. "I can try."

Al heard a sound like a shovel hitting rock, then a shower of pebbles, followed by a scraping noise. He squeezed the bars in excitement. The sound repeated itself over and over, interspersed with grunts of effort. Al shifted his weight from foot to foot. He remembered watching Bird tear through the doors outside of Brighton. Was he going that fast? Or did rock take longer?

The sound of digging slowed down, and then settled into a steady pattern. Al pictured each of the earther's claws, tried to imagine them digging into the rock as easily as he'd lift a handful of sand. Time seemed to crawl by.

"Well?" Bird said. "You just gonna stand there?"

Al jumped. The earther's voice had come from inside his cell. He looked around, but still couldn't see anything. "Where?"

Bird chuckled. "I forgot that you *lifers* can't see like we do."

"Sure." Al didn't think he'd forgotten at all. "What can I do?"

Bird's claw closed gently over his wrist and pulled him down. "I'm going out the back wall, but we don't know how far it is. I need you to move the dirt back as I dig. You got a shirt or something?"

Al knelt down and took off his shirt, then passed it to the earther.

"Good," Bird said. "Now when I say, drag the shirt back and dump it, then put it back in front of me."

Al kept a hand on the shirt and waited. Then he heard the shovel sound again, followed by the shower of pebbles. Bits of rock landed on his hand.

"Here we go," Bird said. "I hope there aren't more cells on the other side of this wall, or a guardroom." He ripped another clawful of rock from the wall. "That would be really bad."

Ten shovel sounds later, the earther stopped, breathing hard. "Okay, take it away."

Al dragged the shirt back and dumped it behind him, then spread it back in front of Bird. He shivered as he moved back out of the way. The air in the dungeon wasn't as cold as outside, but without his shirt on it was cold enough.

The digging continued for longer than Al would have thought possible. After an initial layer of rock, the ground was hard-packed dirt. Bird continued clawing his way forward, until he reached rock again. He took a rest break before continuing, with Al shivering in the dark behind him.

Finally, one of the earther's claws broke through to daylight. He pushed his eye to the hole. "You were right, Al. There's a street there, lower than the rest of the city."

"Any guards?" Al asked.

"Can't see." Bird handed him his shirt and pulled back from the eyehole, letting light stream in. "What do you want to do? Wait till dark? From the shadows, I'd guess sunset's not far off."

Al pulled on his shirt. In the new light, he could see that Bird was soaked with sweat and thinner than Al remembered. "Any idea how long before they come down with food?"

Bird leaned against the wall. He was covered with rock dust. "No."

Al looked around. The hole was only about four feet deep, but if anyone came into the dungeon, they'd spot it right away. On the other hand, bursting out of a rock wall in broad daylight would be tough for anyone to miss. He remembered how slow Bird had run in Brighton. If it came to a footrace, Bird would lose.

"Could you dig out the rock without breaking through? Leave just a little bit so if anyone comes down here, we could break through and try to run? If they don't, we'll wait for nightfall."

"I can try." Bird sounded doubtful. "It's not clay, though. There's no telling if it'll collapse." He scratched the rock.

Al watched in fascination as Bird's claws shaved slivers of rock from the wall. It was made out of blocks of stone fitted together so tightly that no mortar had been used between them. The blocks were one foot on a side, and looked like solid gray stone, but they flaked away like butter under Bird's claws.

Bird grunted. "It's a lot harder this way."

"Wish I could help."

The block Bird was carving cracked and fell away into Canal Street, leaving a hole in the wall. Bird exhaled. "Whoops."

Al gasped. "Quick! Break through! We've got to get out of here."

Bird leaned into the stones next to the hole, shoving them out of the wall, then repeated the process with the stones around that bigger hole.

Al jittered behind him. "Quick, quick!"

"Shut up," Bird grunted again as he shoved two more rocks out.

Through the hole they saw people gawking at them. Bird heaved more rocks out of the wall, then wormed his way out and turned around to help Al.

"Cross the street," Al hissed as he squeezed himself into the hole. "Head for the nearest stairs and go south. I'll catch up."

The crowd parted before the earther, people falling over each other to get out of his way.

"Hey," Al called sharply to the crowd. He held his hand out. "Little help here!"

The crowd of gawkers turned away from Bird to face

him. One of them, an older woman carrying a bundle of greens, asked, "What are you up to?"

"Trying to get out of this rock," he said, trying to flash his most harmless smile. "Could use a hand."

She stepped forward, uncertain, then stopped herself.

"That's the dungeon," a man said, his eyes wide. "You're breaking out of the dungeon!"

A boy pointed at him. "Look at his face! It's all bloody."

"Stop him!" the woman shouted.

Glancing past them, Al saw that Bird had almost made it up the stairs. "That's crazy," Al said as he forced his way out of the rock. Before they could react, he put his head down and charged across Canal Street.

"Someone stop him!" the woman shouted. "Guards!"

A man pounded on the door to the dungeon. "Open up. There's been an escape!"

Al leaped up the stairs, taking them two at a time. At the top, he found Bird waiting for him.

"Why didn't you keep running?" Al said. He looked back down into Canal Street. No one had followed them up the stairs. Instead, the people were divided between pointing at him and trying to get someone to answer the dungeon door. A few were poking their heads into the hole Bird had made. The sun was low in the sky, but sunset was still a long way off.

"Let's go," Bird said.

The dungeon door opened, and Al ducked away from the edge.

Al and Bird ran east for as long as they could, with Al leading the way through the twisting, uneven streets. People gawked and drew away when they passed, but no one shouted or tried to follow. When they stopped to catch their breath, they were alone on a quiet street.

"I think we made it," Al panted.

Bird squatted by a street puddle left from the previous day's rain. "For now." He soaked his sleeve in the dirty water and used it to wipe the dirt and rock from his face.

"What do you mean? We're out. We can go anywhere."

"Yeah," Bird said. "A smashed-up boy and an earther. They'll never find us."

Al smiled. "Actually," he said. "I know a place we can hide."

CHAPTER 17

PAYBACK

Only a few people were in The Hook and Hand when Al and Bird reached it, but that was still too many for Bird. They stood against a wall, half a block from the inn. Overhead, the sky had faded to twilight, and in the shadows, with his claws behind his back, the earther could almost be mistaken for a human.

"The guard is looking for us," Bird said. "If I walk in there, I'll be spotted immediately."

"I know," Al said. They'd made it to The Hook and Hand before the evening rush, but not quite early enough to beat everyone. "We'll have to wait until everybody's left. I just hope no one sees us out here."

"Okay." Bird sat down and crossed his legs, still keeping his hands behind him. "How's your nose?"

"Still hurts," Al said as he sat down, "but at least I can breathe through it."

"You look terrible."

Al shrugged. He had wiped away as much of the blood as he could, but he knew he hadn't gotten it all, especially not the stuff stuck in his hair. The fat lip didn't help either. "It'll help keep people from looking at us," he said. "We're just two homeless *uldi'iara*. Who looks at them? I know I wouldn't have, once upon a time."

"True," Bird said. "I'd feel better with a hat, though."

Three men trudged along the street. Their pants were stained, their cloaks patched and ragged. Probably fishermen at the end of a hard day, Al guessed, or maybe dockworkers. They looked exhausted. Al kept his head down as they walked by. Once the street was empty again, he looked at Bird. "I've been thinking."

"Yeah?"

"I'm going to get my rank mark changed."

Bird raised his bald eyebrows.

"That's the source of all my problems," Al said. "If I were a rank three, or even a two, I could get a job, have a normal life."

"Until someone finds out and the Cullers come to kill you."

"They're already trying to kill me," Al said.

Bird didn't say anything.

"You could get yours done too," Al said.

"Costs money to hire a skincarver."

"Yeah," Al said. "But we can find a way."

Bird looked at him. "You mean stealing?"

Al shrugged. "Maybe."

Evening darkened to night, and more people walked by. Some looked like they were walking home from work, others like they were just starting out. At one point a guard strode by, face grim and determined, his bootnails clicking on the stones. But none of them seemed to notice Al or Bird. All the while, music and noise poured out of The Hook and Hand, first the familiar drumming, and then the lute music.

"But he's going to *kill* me," Wisp's voice hissed.

Al's head snapped up from the doze he'd fallen into. Wisp was walking up the street with Trillia next to him. Even in the darkness, Al could see how angry she was. "Good," she said tightly.

"For the thousandth time," Wisp said. "I didn't have a choice. Master Schion was right there. What could I have done?"

She slapped him on the back of his head, knocking him forward several steps. "You could have tripped."

"Trillia," Wisp pleaded. "You *know* how Schion is."

Heart racing, Al stared at the stones in front of him.

"You're lucky he escaped," Trillia said darkly.

"I wasn't trying to get him killed," Wisp said. "I didn't have any choice."

"He's your friend," Trillia shouted. "You should have picked him over Schion!"

Al watched Wisp's black boots walk past him, followed by Trillia's long brown ones.

"I'm sorry!" Wisp shouted back. "Okay? I'm sorry! I'd take it all back if I could."

Trillia huffed.

Al followed them with his eyes as they walked into The Hook and Hand.

"Friends of yours?" Bird asked.

Al looked back at the stones, not sure what to say. He hadn't thought about Wisp since the dungeon. Now, seeing him again, all Al wanted to do was punch him. Instead, he forced himself to look back at the stones of the street. He was tired of keeping his head down, tired of hiding, tired of being *uldi'iara.*

His earlier idea to change his rank mark solidified into rock-hard determination. The problem wasn't that he *was* a zero, he thought, but that other people *were able to see* that he was a zero. Once he changed his mark, no one would know but him.

Hours passed as Al and Bird sat unnoticed in the darkness. Gradually, the noise in The Hook and Hand quieted and its customers left. Bull emerged to clean up the tables in front of the inn and collect the lanterns. It took him several trips, but once he was done, he went inside and drew the curtain closed across the front window.

Al stood. He hadn't seen Wisp or Trillia come back out, but he also hadn't been awake the whole time. "Bird," he whispered. "It's time."

The earther opened his eyes. "You sure about this?"

"Come on."

Somewhat to Al's surprise, the front door of the inn was unlocked. He opened it and ushered Bird inside. Only the lantern behind the bar was still lit, leaving the rest of the room in darkness.

"Sounds like you had quite a day," Bull said from the bar. He dipped his rag in a bucket of soapy water and wiped it on the counter.

"You were right about that dungeon on Canal Street," Al said. "It also has an entrance on Riverway."

Bull smiled. "I didn't think you'd want to use that one." He gestured with his chin toward Bird. "You the earther from Brighton?"

"Yes," Bird said.

"No room sharing," Bull said. "It'll be twelve drakes each for tonight."

Al's mouth dropped open. "Twelve? But it was only five before!"

Bull shrugged. "That was yesterday, when you worked for me. Now you're on the run. I hide you here, I'm risking the whole place. Oh yeah, and I have to fire you."

"That's not fair," Al said. "You can't kick us out now!"

"Didn't say I was kicking you out," Bull said. He picked up his lantern and walked out from behind the bar to a table in the corner. Wisp and Trillia were slumped in the chairs, their heads on the table.

"What did you do?" Al whispered, moving closer. "Are they okay?"

"Just asleep," Bull said. "They came in here demanding to see you, then announced they were going to wait. I told them we had a two-drink minimum." He smiled. "I think they ordered the wrong drinks."

"You drugged them?" Al said.

Bull put his lantern on the table. "They're too young to be in here, anyway. It'll teach 'em a good lesson. They're just lucky I was the one that taught it." He walked back to the bar, where he lit another lantern. "Now get your rent and move 'em outside. I want to close up."

Bird reached into Wisp's pockets and pulled out three nuggets and four crowns, worth a total of thirty-two drakes. He pocketed them and moved to Trillia.

Al stopped him. "Not Trillia. She didn't do anything."

"We need the money," Bird said.

"No," Al insisted. "You get him. I'll get her."

While Bird lifted Wisp over his shoulder, Al grabbed Trillia's upper arms and dragged her out the front door. "Don't go too far," Al called. "She's heavy!"

Behind the bar, Bull chuckled.

"This'll do." Bird dropped Wisp in a pile just outside the door, then helped Al lower Trillia next to him.

Al straightened. "This isn't right. Something might happen to them."

"So?" Bird asked.

"I'm going to wake Trillia," Al said.

"Not with me here."

Al nodded. "Okay. I'll see you in the morning."

Bird went into The Hook and Hand, and Al listened to him pay Bull for two rooms. After it was quiet again, he knelt down and gently shook Trillia. "Trillia," he whispered.

Trillia groaned but didn't wake up.

Al slapped her lightly on the cheek. Her eyes fluttered. "Wake up," he said softly. He slapped her again. "Trillia!"

She pushed him away, eyes still not open. "Stop it. I'm up. I'm —" Her eyes opened and she scrambled to her feet. "Al?" Her eyes focused on his beat-up face. "You look terrible!"

"Yes, I do," Al said with a little laugh, "but I'm alive."

"What did you do? Where are we?" She looked down at Wisp. "Is he okay?"

Al's smile faded. "Better than me."

"Don't be mad," Trillia said. "You don't know what he's been through."

"Yeah," Al said, his voice tight. "I'm sure Wisp's had a really tough couple of weeks." He moved to the door of The Hook and Hand. "I'll see you around."

He stepped through the door and closed it behind him. Then he latched it.

Bull watched him from the bar. "You can use the room, Al, but I can't have you being seen around here. The guards in this town don't play around."

Al let out a deep breath. "Yeah."

"You know about the kitchen entrance and the back stair? There's a key in your room."

"Thanks."

"If anyone sees you," Bull said, his eyes level. "I'm going to tell them you stole the key. If I see you out front, I'll call the guard myself. Same for your friend."

"I get it, Bull. Thanks. We'll be out as quick as we can."

"Okay." Bull filled a metal bowl with water and dropped a towel next to it. "Take these with you, to help you get cleaned up."

"Thanks."

After scrubbing off as much of the blood as he could, Al stretched out on his mattress, unable to sleep. He was back on the run again. The Cullers would comb every inch of Dockside looking for him. He rolled over. And why had Wisp tackled him? Trillia had said he was going through something. What could possibly make him give Al to the Cullers?

Al rolled back to his stomach. Now he had Bird trapped in Dockside too, and even put The Hook and Hand in danger. Everything he tried just caused more trouble. He stood up with a frustrated growl and pulled out his sword. He was sick of running. All he'd done since Testing Day was run. Taking his stance, he went through his basic parries: down strong, up strong, up weak, down weak, sweep cross. Next he practiced counters, parries followed by quick stabs, slashes, or disarms. He stopped, shaking his head. Even with the sword, all he did was defend.

No more.

Returning to his center stance, he stabbed instead of parried. The tip of his sword touched the door, and he pulled back to his stance. The balance felt all wrong, he thought. He'd clearly felt his weight move before the attack had started, and if he could feel it he knew an opponent could see it. He tried again, keeping his balance centered. Without his legs behind the attack, though, it had no force.

The third time, he led with the point of his sword, shifting his weight as his arm extended. The motion felt counter-intuitive and awkward, so he tried moving the shift back to the moment his elbow started to straighten.

The tip of the sword *thunk*ed into the door. Al pulled it back with a grunt of satisfaction. He'd figured it out. Now he just had to practice it, make it as much a part of him as the parries. And while he was at it, he thought, he'd figure out how to start attacking the rest of his life. No more *uldi'iara*. He lifted his sword and glared at the door. No more being a zero.

CHAPTER 18

THE NORTH END

Al was still practicing his attack when Bird knocked on his door in the morning. Drenched with sweat, Al sheathed the sword and opened the door.

"You're up early," Bird said.

"Never went to sleep," Al said, backing up so Bird could come in. "I've been thinking, and I know what we need to do."

Bird sat on the bed. "What's that?"

"If there are any skincarvers in Dockside willing to do illegal work, Wisp will know who they are. As Schion's apprentice, he's got to know the competition."

"No," Bird said. "We need to leave. You can't fight the Cullers, Al. No one can."

"I've been thinking about that too," Al said. "Everywhere I go, the Cullers are there to catch me. I'm sick of running. I want to fight back, and there's only one person with the power to fight the Cullers: Magister Lundi."

Bird stood up. "You're crazy."

Al grabbed his arm. "Hear me out. Lundi said that even the Magisters answer to the Cullers."

"So?"

"So he also made it clear that he didn't like them. I think that might be the secret behind the Third. The Cullers must have been the ones that killed them. Why else would they be hunting down the survivors?"

"You can't trust Magister Lundi," Bird growled.

"It's some kind of power struggle," Al said. "And Magister Lundi wants me on his side. That's why he let me go. That's why he wants me to work for him. Something is happening that he needs me for."

"You're not thinking straight," Bird said. "You're a zero. What could the most powerful Magister in the world want with you?"

"I don't know." Al put his shirt on. "But I want to find out."

"So you're going to see the one guy in the city who had you thrown in the dungeon?"

"I don't like it," Al said, "but I have to. There's no other way. If I don't get it done quickly, I'll never get to Magister Lundi in time. He said three weeks, and that was over a week ago."

Bird folded his arms. "I'm not going with you."

Al nodded. He hadn't really expected Bird to go with him. "I know." He counted out the last of his money, four drakes and one crown. "If you have a few drakes left from last night, I'll stop by the kitchen on my way out and pay Bull to have the day's meals brought up."

Bird handed him three drakes. "You're going to get caught."

"Maybe," Al said. "But I've got to try." He picked up his bag and ran down the back stairs to the kitchen. Loaves of bread from the previous night were heaped in a basket on the counter. Al eyed them, wondering if his free leftovers deal was still in effect.

"You leaving?" Bull asked as he walked in.

"No." He handed Bull all of his money. "Could you send food up to Bird today?"

"Sure." Bull took the money without counting it and stuffed it in his pocket. "What will you be doing?"

"I need a new look. Know a place I can trade for some new clothes?"

Bull leaned on the counter. "I've been thinking about what you did, Al. I don't know many people that would even try to break someone out of the dungeon, let alone succeed."

Al hitched his bag higher on his shoulder. "He did most of the breaking."

"Even so, I wish things had worked out differently. I'd have been happy to have you working here."

"Me too."

They stared at each other for a moment, then Bull cleared his throat and tossed Al a loaf of bread. "Two doors down from the baths. It's got a picture of a red tunic painted on its door."

"Thanks." Al took the bread and turned to go. "If I'm not back tonight, tell Bird to start running and not look back."

"I'll do that. Good luck."

Al moved quickly through the streets of Dockside, chewing on his bread. It was crusty and dense, but it filled his belly. He finished half of it on the way to the shop. Once there, he traded his blanket and tarp for a gray pair of canvas pants, a threadbare blue tunic, and a wide-brimmed straw hat. He stuffed his old clothes into his pack, along with the remains of the bread, and headed toward the North End.

Instead of walking up Riverway, though, Al jogged east along the brick wall that surrounded the North End, broken only by decorative metal gates like the one Al had seen on Riverway. Guards stood at each gate, wearing the colors of Lord Archovar.

Al considered the closed gates. They had been open the previous day, and there hadn't been any guards. He watched the men open the nearest gate for a merchant pulling a cart filled with fruit. It was the same style of cart that Al had seen on his first visit to Dockside, with big wheels and two long poles jutting from the front for its driver to pull. Hiding in a cart would be one way to get in, but he doubted he could convince a driver to cooperate, and even if he did, there was nothing to stop the driver from turning him in once he was inside.

Al followed the brick wall north, hoping to find an unguarded gate. Instead, the street he was on ended in a gray stone wall. He narrowed his eyes, considering. Even for Dockside, this was weird. Unlike the wall around the North End, the wall blocking his way was only a couple feet taller than he was, with no gates whatsoever as far as he could see. And no guards. Al took a quick look around to see if anyone was watching, then pulled himself up and peeked over the edge.

Beyond the wall, the city was in ruins. Stagnant water filled the street, reaching partway up buildings that sat in various states of disrepair. Al pulled himself up to stand on the wall. It was over three feet thick, and solid. Below, all was still except for a gentle lapping of water against stone and the sudden movement of a rat as it scurried across a rotting door and jumped into the water.

It wasn't a wall, Al realized. It was a dike. The northernmost part of Dockside must have flooded at some point, and instead of fixing the river wall, they'd built a dike to keep the water out of the rest of the city.

The North End's brick wall turned west and ran adjacent to the dike, with no gates or guards along it, but still too high for Al to climb over. He walked along the dike next to the brick wall, looking out at the sunken city. Many of the buildings had collapsed, leaving mounds of rock and wood. Others were covered with vines turned brown by the cold weather.

As Al drew closer to the river, he saw that the docks were in ruin, with just a few wooden posts sticking out of the water. Riverway was nothing more than a rubble ridge between the city and the Flienne. Though he hadn't realized it before, from up on the dike it was easy to see that Riverway was actually higher than much of the city. It wasn't just a road, it also kept the river out.

Al knelt and peered at the water. Debris had collected against the dike, bits of wood furniture and other things he couldn't identify. Up the street, a rise of the road lifted out of the water, where it continued on above the waterline for several blocks.

Al smiled and lowered himself slowly down, until his boots touched the water. He let go and landed with a splash. The water was cold, but it only reached up to his knees. Keeping an eye out for rats, he waded up the hill until he was on dry land again.

The abandoned city was eerily quiet around him, with only the occasional distant splash to emphasize its stillness. He walked until he found a building with a drawing of a fork and knife on its outer wall, then peered into its darkened doorway. As he'd hoped, it was a restaurant, and the room was filled with a jumble of tables and chairs. Al grabbed two chairs and carried them to the dike, then tossed them up onto its surface. He turned and waded back to the restaurant for more chairs. This time, he just tossed one up, and left the other one in the water to help him climb back up.

Al paused to survey the ruined city again and take a bite of his bread. The morning sun cast long shadows across it, but the darkness didn't bother him. If he needed a place to hide, he thought, this was perfect. He wondered what kind of treasures lay forgotten among the broken buildings. Even if he didn't need a place to hide, he could probably find enough to pay for his room at The Hook and Hand, at least for a little while. He finished off his bread and wiped his hands on his pants. It was time to go find Wisp.

After carefully stacking one chair on top of another, Al put the third next to them and stepped up onto it. Steadying himself against the bricks, he climbed onto the stack of chairs, then reached up and grabbed the top of the wall.

Pulling himself up, Al hooked his upper arms over the wall and balanced. Below him white gravel walkways wound between flower gardens, with the nearest house a stone's throw away. No one walked in the gardens, or anywhere else, as far as Al could see. He kicked his foot up and swung over the wall, landing clumsily in the flowers.

Al brushed himself off and stood up, feeling pleased. He'd made it this far. Now all he had to do was find Wisp's shop without being seen. He looked around. What he needed was a disguise, some reason why he would be walking in the gardens in the middle of the morning. The flowers caught his eye and he smiled. The people of the North End couldn't possibly all know one another. If they saw a boy carrying flowers, they'd never suspect him to be anything more than that.

After he'd filled the top of his bag, he kept picking until he had a good-sized bouquet to carry in his hands. Taking a deep breath, he stepped onto the gravel path and did his best to saunter casually, and not gawk at the houses he walked by. He passed three houses without seeing anyone, then a woman wearing a fluffy yellow dress waved to him from a balcony. Heart racing, he nodded to her and smiled.

"After you're done with those flowers," she called, "could you trim the ivy by the back walk?"

"Yes, ma'am." Al ducked his head. "Soon as I deliver these."

As Al neared the center of the North End, he caught a whiff of the delicious smell of fresh baked bread. His mouth started to water. He hadn't had fresh bread since breakfast at that inn down south, and that seemed like a lifetime ago. A smile spread across his face as he remembered that Wisp had said Trillia worked in a bakery. He changed course to follow the smell.

More people were outside now, but none of them were paying him any attention. A couple of kids just a few years younger than him were throwing a ball back and forth on the path. A man carrying a sack of vegetables hurried past.

Guards paced along the walkway next to the river. Al did his best to ignore them. When he saw the row of stores where Wisp worked, he turned and followed a path that led behind them.

A guard stopped Al halfway to the buildings. "Where do you think you're going?" the man asked. He wore a spotlessly clean uniform with the purple and yellow flower of Lord Archovar gleaming on a white tabard over his chain mail. A rapier hung from his hip, and he sported a neatly trimmed mustache and beard.

Al kept his head down, trying to use the brim of his hat to hide his face. "Delivering these flowers."

"To who?"

"To mistress Trillia," Al said. "I'm to surprise her with them."

The man laughed. "*Mistress* Trillia? The bread girl?"

Al nodded.

"Someone has played a trick on you, my boy. Mistress Trillia doesn't take kindly to flowers." The man winked. "Believe me, I know. I've seen enough others show up with flowers."

"Please, sir," Al said. "My brother says I'm to deliver these to her and no one else."

"Your brother? Are you sure they're not from you?"

Al shook his head.

Chuckling, the man put a hand on Al's shoulder and steered him down the path. "By all means, then, let us go see Mistress Trillia."

Trillia was kneading dough on a wooden table in the back of the bakery when Al and the guard walked in. Her mouth dropped open at the sight of Al.

"Mistress Trillia," the guard said formally from behind Al, "this boy has informed me that he is delivering these flowers to you from his brother."

Trillia stared at them for a breath, then straightened, her eyes sparkling. "From his brother?" She stepped forward and took the flowers from Al. "But his brother is nothing but wind and noise." She buried her nose in the flowers and sniffed dramatically. "So beautiful. If only they had come from someone less like his brother" — she batted her eyes at Al — "and more like him."

The guard laughed and slapped Al on the shoulder. "Looks like you found the proper bouquet, boy. Best of luck." He nodded his head to Trillia and left, closing the door behind him.

Trillia shoved the flowers back into Al's hands. "For luck's sake," she hissed. "What are you doing here? You'll get caught!"

"I have to see Wisp," he said.

"After last night? After you left him sleeping in the street?"

"Let's call it even, okay? Dungeon for me, street for him."

Trillia sagged. "Why? What do you want with him?"

"I need a carver," Al said, gesturing to the back of his neck. "One that's not afraid to break some laws."

Trillia's eyes widened. "You can't do that. They'll kill you if they catch you."

Al raised his eyebrows without saying anything.

"He can't do it anyway," Trillia said. "He doesn't know how. He's only been an apprentice for a couple of weeks."

"He's a carver's apprentice. He must know someone. Please."

Trillia looked around the room, groaned, and took off her apron. "Okay. Stay here. I'll be right back."

Al leaned against the counter, trying not to think about what would happen if Wisp turned him in again. He adjusted the strap of his bag over his shoulder and waited in silence.

Minutes later, Trillia returned with Wisp right behind her. "What are you doing here?" Wisp asked as he walked through the door. "Do you know what they'll do if they find you?"

"Probably make you tackle me again," Al said, "then throw me in another dungeon."

Wisp winced. "I'm sorry about that, okay? I didn't have any choice."

"It isn't just me," Al said, his voice bitter. "They'll kill my family too."

Wisp's face was still. "I didn't know that."

Al's fists clenched. "But it wouldn't have changed what you did, would it?"

Trillia stepped in between them. "Ease up, Al. He's got something in his arm."

"He's got what?"

"Master Schion put a little black bead in my arm." Wisp pulled back his sleeve to show Al a bump on his forearm. "It lets him know where I am at all times."

"It does more than that," Trillia said. "Whenever *Master* Schion isn't happy, he burns Wisp."

"Burns you?" Al touched his friend's forearm. He could feel the bead just beneath the skin. It didn't feel any bigger than the one Schion had put into Al's arm on Testing Day.

"It burns from the inside," Wisp said. "Sometimes, the rock gets so hot that my skin bubbles."

"I've seen it," Trillia said. "The skin scorches from his shoulder to his wrist, and his arm swells and blisters. It smells horrible, like cooking meat."

"If he's really angry," Wisp said, "he waits until the next morning to heal me." He looked at Al, his eyes pleading. "It hurts so bad, Al, you can't believe it."

"How long?" Al asked.

"He put it in the day I started as his apprentice."

"Does your dad know?" Al asked.

"No," Wisp said. "Nobody does. Everybody likes Master Schion. When he's in public, he's so friendly, you'd never believe it." He swallowed. "Al, I didn't know he was the one that had ranked you. If I had, I never would have told you to come here, and I'm sorry I tackled you. It's just that when he shouted, all I could think about was not getting burned."

Al's mouth felt dry. He couldn't imagine living with that kind of fear. "You've got to tell your dad, or run away, or do something."

Trillia threw her arms up. "That's what I keep saying!"

"If I stick it out, I become a skincarver," Wisp said, rolling down his sleeve. "It's worth it."

The door to the main room of the bakery opened and a woman layered with makeup stuck her head through. "Trillia," she barked. "Get back to work. Your friends can stay and talk, but I need that bread in the ovens."

"Yes, ma'am," Trillia said, then stuck her tongue out as soon as the door closed. "I hate bread," she muttered as she started kneading again. "I think I'd rather be married to Leonard."

"You've got to get out of here, Al," Wisp said. "The Cullers are here. They already talked to me, and now they're searching the North End for you."

"I need a carver," Al said. "Someone to change my rank mark."

Wisp shook his head. "I can't do it. All I've done is clean Master Schion's shop. He hasn't even given me my Life porta yet."

"Not you, you idiot," Al said. "Don't you know anyone? You must have heard about Schion's competition. Aren't there any you can think of?"

Wisp shook his head. "Sorry, Al. He doesn't talk to me, except to tell me what to do and how to do it."

"Wonderful," Al muttered. He closed his eyes and took a deep breath, trying to think what to do next.

Trillia stopped kneading and looked at him, her eyes narrowed. "You don't have a way out, do you?"

"Flowers," Al said. "I'll walk them out the gate, say I'm delivering them to someone. No one will even see me."

"And what if they do?" Trillia asked.

"I run."

"That's stupid," Trillia said. "You couldn't even outrun Wisp."

Al shrugged as he gathered up the flowers. "It's not like I have a choice."

"Wait," Wisp said. "What are your plans?"

"I'm leaving Dockside," Al said. "I've got no money and no food, and with this zero tattooed on me, no chance. I'm going north. Sadraki's only a week or so away. With any luck, I'll find a skincarver there." Sadraki was also called Magister City. It was Magister Lundi's home, and where all Magisters went to be trained.

Wisp drew in a sharp breath. "You can't go there!"

"Sadraki?" Trillia echoed. "That's in the mountains, with the windwalkers, right?"

Wisp grabbed Al's shoulder. "The Magisters already know what you look like. Going there would be suicide."

"Actually," Al said, "Magister Lundi offered me a job."

"You can't," Wisp hissed.

"I can try," Al said.

Wisp let out an exasperated breath. "No. You don't — okay, listen. Hide in Trillia's room until tonight, then I'll take you someplace where you might be able to get your rank mark changed."

"In *my* room?" Trillia asked. "What's wrong with yours?"

"The stairs to your room are right there." Wisp pointed at a closed door that Al hadn't noticed. "He doesn't have to go outside to get to them."

"I like that idea," Al said. "I could use a nice nap."

"No," Trillia said. "Not on my bed. Absolutely not. Have you looked at yourself? You're filthy."

"Thanks!" Al ducked around her with a chuckle and ran up the stairs.

Trillia started to follow, but Wisp caught her arm. "It's Al," he said, closing the door. "You know he's not going to mess anything up."

Upstairs, Al stood in Trillia's room. It wasn't anything like the one at her home. That one had been filled with sketches of horses and pictures of her family. This one looked un-lived in, the only decoration a small painting of her parents on a table next to the bed.

Al felt his heart sink as the loneliness of the room hit him. He'd been so caught up in his own problems, he hadn't considered what his friends were going through. Now that he thought about it, though, he could see how alone Trillia must feel, living in a strange city, with no family and only one friend. He stretched out on the rug next to the bed and closed his eyes. No matter how much he teased Trillia, he wasn't going to ruin her only bed with the muck covering his pants.

The floor felt warm under his back. Probably from the ovens, he thought. The smell of cooking bread filtered up around him, and he smiled. As hopeless as everything seemed, it felt good to have his friends back. Together, he thought, they could find a way to get the lives they wanted.

CHAPTER 19

THE SIGN OF THE FEATHER

With Wisp on one side and Trillia on the other, a well-rested Al walked straight for the main gate out of the North End. The sun was setting over the Flienne, filling it with orange and pink clouds.

"Are you sure this is going to work?" Al asked.

"Keep your head up and pretend that you're having a good time," Wisp said. He was wearing his black clothes again, the ones that made him look years older.

"We do this almost every night," Trillia added. She was wearing her dark blue tunic and leather pants, the same outfit she'd been in at The Hook and Hand.

"Hey Wisp," a guard said. "Heading to the fights?"

"Not tonight," Wisp answered. "My cousin's in town." He wrapped an arm around Al's shoulder and gave him a squeeze. "We're taking him to Sid's."

"Looks like he could use a doctor, not a restaurant," the guard said. "That nose is busted up pretty good." He looked at Al. "You should take care of it before it sets that way."

"Yes, sir," Al said.

The guard pushed the gate open. "Have fun."

Al forced himself to smile, and they walked straight through, then took the first turn they could.

"Ha!" Trillia shouted. She threw back her head and spun a circle on the street. "We did it!" She punched Al's shoulder. "You should have seen your face! I thought you were going to puke right on that guard's shoes."

"What?" Al said. "No, I wasn't scared."

Wisp chuckled. "You did look a little green."

"It's from the broken nose," Al said. "It makes me look strange."

Trillia stuck out her bottom lip and made her eyes go big. "Oh, you poor wittle boy, with your poor wittle nose." She reached up and tweaked Al's nose, then skipped away.

"Ow!" Al grabbed his nose with both hands, tears springing to his eyes. "Don't *do* that!"

"Come on," Wisp said. "I don't know how long this will take."

"Where are we going?" Trillia asked.

"Not too far, just the other side of Canal Street. Al, you got your sword in that bag, right?"

"Yeah, but I'd rather not use it."

"You won't have to. Now hurry up." Wisp lengthened his stride. "We need to get there before dark."

They had to turn three times to avoid men wearing the deep green pants and white silk shirts of the Cullers. Finally, Wisp stopped them next to a wooden fence on a residential street. The fence hadn't had a fresh coat of paint in years, and people had carved initials and designs into it. Wisp double-checked that the street was empty, and then turned to examine the wall. "Let me know if you see anyone," he said.

Al and Trillia stood with their backs to him, trying to look casual. "What are you looking for?" Trillia asked.

"Something my dad showed me. Just be patient."

Al gingerly touched his nose. It still throbbed from Trillia's squeeze.

"There it is," Wisp said. He tapped the wall. "Al, I need you to see this."

"What about me?" Trillia said.

"You too. Hurry."

Trillia didn't move. "Why did you say Al needed to see it?"

"Because he is in the middle of this, just like my dad is. It's something he should have been told."

Al and Trillia crowded around Wisp, peering at the wall. Al sucked in a surprised breath. There, under the paint, was the faint impression of a feather, the symbol of the Third.

"Look at which way it points," Wisp whispered, checking around the street. "Then count the spines on its top. Each spine is a door. Got it?"

"Yeah," Al said, straightening and looking away. "I got it."

Trillia grabbed Wisp's shoulder. "What is this? Why haven't you ever shown it to me?"

"My dad showed it to me when he brought me to Dockside. He said it was for emergencies only, that I'd only be able to use it once."

"Come on," Al said, his heart pounding as he ran down the street counting doorways.

When they found the one indicated, they hesitated. The buildings on this street were a mix of stone and wood, some three stories tall, others only two. A few had fences separating them from the road. This one didn't, and was in no way distinguishable from any of the others.

"We're supposed to just walk in," Wisp said. "No knocking."

Al stepped back. "There's smoke coming from the chimney, but the shutters are closed. Are you sure this is the one?"

"Only one way to find out." Trillia twisted the doorknob and pushed. It swung smoothly open into a dark hallway. With a glance back at Wisp and Al, she stepped in. A fraying brown carpet covered the wooden floor, and a closed door stood at the end of the hall.

"Wait," Al said. "I think I should go first." He brought his sword out of his pack and moved past her. Wisp stepped in last and closed the door behind him.

"What now?" Al whispered.

"I don't know," Wisp said. "My dad never told me."

"Just go," Trillia said.

Al moved through the darkness, until his sword hit the door at the hallway's far end. Taking a deep breath, he pulled it open.

The room beyond was filled with warm firelight. A gray-haired woman sat knitting in a rocking chair by the fireplace, with a lantern on the small table beside her and a light green throw rug at her feet. Her dress reached from her neck to the wood floor, and it was a rich deep blue color, trimmed with white lace. Small metal toys sat on the mantle above the fireplace, soldiers and boats and small models of dragons. The walls held charcoal sketches of men, women, and children, all smiling and looking happy.

Al stepped into the room and lowered his sword, uncertain. Trillia and Wisp followed him.

The woman looked up from her knitting, and her eyes settled on Al's sword. She looked slender and frail, but there was nothing weak about her gaze as she raised it to meet Al's. A thin white scar, long healed, ran from the top of her left eye into her gray hair. "Most people," she said "knock before entering an old woman's house."

"Excuse us," Wisp said. "We must have the wrong house. We'll go. Sorry to disturb you."

Al reversed his sword and held it so the etching on its pommel caught the firelight. The woman's eyes flicked to it, then back to Al's face.

"I'm Orion Pilgrommor's son," Al said, "and this is the son of an Evan."

Her eyebrows raised. "Orion Pilgrommor doesn't have a son," she said. "The boy he'd been raising was an orphan, a waif he'd taken in out of the goodness of his heart."

"That's not —" Trillia started, but Al stopped her.

"No," he said. "She's right." He looked back to the woman. "If I were at all related to Orion, the entire Pilgrommor family would be hunted down by the Cullers."

The woman nodded and carefully folded her knitting, then set it on her lap. "And no son of an Evan would ever make such a claim, not without bringing the same doom on his own father."

"Please," Al said. "I need help. I don't know what to do."

The woman's eyes softened. "How can I help you?" she asked.

"I need to change my rank mark," Al said. "I'm hunted by the Cullers at every turn, and now I'm out of money. I've nowhere left to run."

"I'm sorry," she said. "I can't help you with that."

"But I've been offered a job by Magister Lundi," Al said desperately. "He said he needs me there in less than two weeks, but that he can't hire anyone who is rank zero."

The woman stood, letting her knitting slip to the floor. "Magister Lundi?"

"Tell him he's crazy," Wisp said. "It would be suicide."

"When did Magister Lundi tell you this?" the woman asked.

"It was after Brighton," Al said, "where I fought against his captain. I'd just escaped the wagon, only to find him and his captain waiting for me. They talked about how resourceful I was, then Lundi said he could use a boy like me."

"His exact words," the woman pressed. "Do you remember?"

Al closed his eyes. "I'm trying. First he apologized for me being a zero. Then he said that if someone of my talents were to show up at his home with any other rank mark, that person would be welcomed into his household."

The woman caught her breath. "Into his household? Are you sure he said that?"

"Yeah, pretty sure." Al glanced at Wisp and then back to the woman. "I mean a lot has happened since then, but I think that was it."

"Anything else?"

"There was something about people who could find resources where others see none. Oh yeah." He laughed. "He also said he paid very well."

The woman's eyes widened, and she stepped closer to him. "You must get to Sadraki as quickly as possible."

"What?" Wisp said. "No! That's exactly what he shouldn't do!"

"Hush, child," the woman said sharply.

"I can't go anyway," Al said. "Not with this rank mark."

"I'll arrange that. Can you be in the sunken city shortly after dawn tomorrow?"

"The sunken city?" Trillia asked.

"Go on," Al said to the woman. "I know what you're talking about."

"You'll find the mark of the feather four streets north from the dike and two from the river," the woman said. "It will guide you to a skincarver who will help you. After he's done, you need to get to Sadraki as quickly as possible. I'll arrange to have a horse trader meet you on the North Road. He will take you swiftly and in secret. You'll know him by the mark of the feather on his cart."

Al's eyes widened. He'd never dreamed of so much help. "What's going on? Why are you helping me? What's changed?"

"Everything," the woman said. Her eyes glittered as she leaned over him. "After seventeen long years, the men of the Third are finally going to be avenged." Her eyes focused in the distance. "My son is going to be avenged."

"But I don't understand —"

The woman held his gaze with hers. "I won't say any more. Secrets you don't know can't be taken from you. Go and sleep. You'll need it."

Al looked away, his heart pounding. He didn't know what was going on, but if it got the rank zero tattoo off of him, he couldn't afford to pass it up. "Thanks," he said. "No, wait! Can I take Bird? He's the earther that helped me break out of the dungeon. I don't want to just abandon him here."

"Take whomever you want," the woman said, turning away. She opened a drawer on her table, and pulled out a stylus and some paper. "The horse trader will have plenty of room."

"This is crazy," Wisp said to her. "He can't trust Magister Lundi!"

"For the son of an Evan," she said, looking over her shoulder at him, "you show remarkably little courage."

Wisp paled and his mouth dropped open.

"You have a choice to make," the woman continued, her voice hard and harsh. "Will you help your friend through this, or will you keep him a zero?"

Wisp blinked and closed his mouth. His fists clenched.

"What about me?" Trillia asked. "Can I go?"

The woman straightened, holding the stylus and paper in her hand. She looked frustrated. "I don't care who goes, just so long as he gets there." She gestured to the door. "Now go. I have a long night of preparations to make, none of them easy." She ushered them outside and closed the door. It locked with an audible click.

Trillia looked at Al. "Where's the sunken city?"

"Past the North End," Al said, "the city's flooded. There's a dike to keep the water back."

"A dike? A sunken city?" Trillia glared at Wisp. "I told you there was something to see past that north wall!"

Wisp's face was closed and angry. "I've got to get back."

"Wisp," Al said, "I know you don't want to keep me a zero. She doesn't know what she's talking about."

"That's right." Wisp turned on him. "She doesn't! But you're going anyway, aren't you? She doesn't care about you, or me, or anything but revenge. You think she'd care if Magister Lundi handed you to the Cullers?"

"I don't know." Al took a breath. "But this lets me start over. I get a new rank and a decent job. What's more, I get a chance to strike back at the Cullers."

"Strike back at the Cullers?" Wisp said. "You're crazy."

"No," Al said. "I think I've figured this out. It's not Magister Lundi that's the problem. It's the Cullers."

"You don't know what you're talking about."

"Yes I do! Listen. Magister Lundi and the Cullers don't get along. Lundi made that clear when he spoke with me. But if that's true, why are the Cullers hunting the Third? It doesn't make sense. They wouldn't be helping the Magister."

"Then why?" Trillia asked.

"I think the Cullers were responsible for what happened to the Third," Al said. "That's why they're hunting the survivors, and that's why the Third is helping Magister Lundi. They're working together against the Cullers."

"Don't be stupid," Wisp said. "I know you hate the Cullers, but it was Magister Lundi who killed the Third, and he'll kill you just as quickly."

Al crossed his arms. "I'm still gonna try."

Wisp sighed. "You're an idiot."

Trillia looked back and forth between the two boys, then put a hand on Al's shoulder. "We'll meet you on the dike just before dawn."

"You don't have to come with me," Al said.

Trillia laughed. "Are you crazy? Miss a chance to see the sunken city *and* go to Sadraki? I can knead dough any day. I want to see a windwalker."

"I have to talk to my parents first," Wisp said. "And you two should do the same."

Trillia stilled. "Yeah, okay. You're right. I should tell them I'm leaving. We better hurry, though. We're going to have to walk all night to be back by dawn."

"Don't worry about that skincarver," Al said. "Meet me on the North Road, right at the point where you can't see the castle anymore. I probably won't get there until noon."

"You're not going to see your parents?" Wisp asked.

"No." Al turned away.

"Why not?" Trillia asked.

"I tried that once already," Al said, remembering the sight of his empty bedroom. "They made it clear they don't want me back."

"But —" Wisp said.

"I'll see you tomorrow," Al interrupted, walking away. "Say hi to your parents for me." He broke into a jog, thinking about his parents. What did he have to say to them? Nothing they wanted to hear, that was for sure. He ran faster. There would be plenty of time to see his parents after he wasn't a zero anymore. Maybe then they'd want him back.

CHAPTER 20
GOOD-BYES

Al let himself into the kitchen of The Hook and Hand and ran up the back stairs to knock on Bird's door. The earther answered on the first knock. "What happened?"

Al stepped into the room. "You won't believe it," he said, closing the door behind him. "I'm going to Sadraki."

"Not the Magister thing again." Bird sat down on his bed. "You can't."

"I can," Al said. He told Bird about the sunken city, and the secret organization that Wisp's dad was a part of, then about meeting the woman and how she'd promised to set him up with a skincarver. The only thing he left out was the mark of the feather.

"You trust this woman?" Bird asked.

"Why not?" Al asked. Telling the story had left him feeling even more excited. Only one more night and he wouldn't be a zero anymore. "Listen," he said. "Worst case, she's setting me up for the Cullers. But why do that in the sunken city? You should see this place, Bird. There are a million places to hide. I'm going to get there early and scout it out."

"I'm happy for you, Al," Bird said, stretching. "But it's time for me to leave."

"You're still not coming with me?" Al said, disappointed. "Why not? It's a new city, a new start. You haven't broken any laws. The Cullers don't care about you."

"Because of *him*." Bird stared into Al's eyes. "Magister Lundi's a murderer and a traitor, and I'd kill him if I could. I can't live in the same city. I won't."

Al lowered his eyes. "Well, at least let me see if I can get you some food from the kitchen. Which way are you headed?"

"Back to the hills, then south."

Al opened the door and walked to the back stairs, with Bird following. "Okay," Al said. "Travel south a little ways first, though. That way you'll miss the swamp. There won't be many people in the fields. Just keep to the breaks, and you should be fine." He opened the door to the kitchen and stopped.

The kitchen staff was gone, the back door stood open, and none of the normal evening noise came from the front. Al stepped quietly into the room, looking around. Soup bubbled in a large black pot over the fire, and food sat on plates in a line on the counter.

"Something's wrong," Bird whispered. "We should get out of here."

"Wait," Al whispered back. He inched open the wooden kitchen door and peeked into the common room. The regular crowd was nowhere to be found. Instead, a single man sat at the bar. He didn't look remarkable, except for the sword at his side, and the dark skincarvings covering his left arm and hand. His face was grim, unshaven, and smeared with soot.

Bull walked among the empty tables, collecting mugs and abandoned plates of food. "Great business tonight," he said.

The swordsman barked a sound that probably would have been a laugh had it come from someone else's mouth. "This kid isn't just any runaway, Bull. This is serious. Orders come all the way from the top."

"No runaways here," Bull said lightly. He carried his tray behind the bar and scraped the food into a metal bin. "Never have been."

The swordsman's voice tightened. "I don't have time for this tonight. This kid made fools out of all of us. You know what they're saying out there? They're laughing at us for putting an earther in the Canal Street dungeon."

"Well," Bull said. "Looking back, it wasn't the smartest thing."

The man glared. "He was fine till that kid showed up."

Bull leaned his elbows on the bar and used his hands to push his braids behind his ears. "Relax. It's the same as always. I got no runaways here." His voice sounded tired to Al. "Never have."

"No," the swordsman growled. He tapped on the bar and a flame appeared at his fingertips, then spread sideways along the worn wooden surface.

Al's eyes widened. He bit his lip to keep from making any sound. The fire flared high as it licked up spilled alcohol.

Bull straightened. "That won't get you what you're looking for."

The flames flickered higher. "I got no choice."

"Everyone has a choice," Bull said. "So what now? You gonna burn me? 'Cause I'm not letting you up those stairs."

The swordsman's jaw clenched, and he stepped back from the bar.

"People saw you come in here," Bull said, his voice quickening. "If this place burns, they'll know it was you that did it. They know I pay you for protection. You burn this, and you'll lose your whole racket."

The man's hand dropped to the hilt of his sword. "I know he's here. I catch him, and nothing else matters, not your place, not you, none of it."

Bull held a bottle by its neck, almost casually. "Don't do this."

Al eased the door shut as quietly as he could and leaned against it, breathing hard. Bull was trying to protect him, facing a Fire master all by himself with nothing more than a bottle of wine in his hand.

Bird was already at the back door. "Come on," he whispered, gesturing.

Al looked back at the kitchen door, his jaw clenched. He couldn't just run out on Bull, not after everything he'd done. In all of Dockside, only Bull had taken him in. Fingers trembling, he swung his pack off his back and slipped the loop from over the hilt.

"Al," Bird hissed. "You can't win this."

Al slid the sword out, took a deep breath, and opened the door.

In the common room, Bull stood in front of the door to the stairs, holding his bottle in front of him. The fire on the bar was burning in earnest now, and had spread to the wooden tables and chairs. Smoke billowed along the ceiling as it worked its way to the chimney.

The swordsman stood a few paces from Bull, his hand on the hilt of his weapon. His eyes flicked to Al, then narrowed. He stepped back from Bull, his sword whispering out of its sheath, and turned to face Al. The weapon was the same that all the guards carried, a larger version of what Al held. Designed for stabbing, it was also capable of slashes.

"About time you got here," Bull bellowed.

Al looked at him, confused.

"What do you think I've been paying you for?" Bull roared. He pointed at the man. "Get him out of here!"

"Nice try, Bull," the swordsman said, "but the skin-carver that caught him has been sketching his picture all afternoon. They've got a dozen of 'em up at the station."

Al shifted his feet into his center stance and stepped forward out of the doorway. This man was bigger than the Magister captain, and he held his sword like he knew how to use it.

"They say you beat a Magister," the swordsman said. "You know what that'll mean for me when I skewer you?"

The smoke stung Al's eyes, making them water. He watched his opponent approach, but didn't see any flaws in his balance, no weaknesses in the way he held his sword. "Shouldn't you be arresting me?" he asked, trying to keep his voice steady.

"After the trouble you've caused?" the man asked. "Nah. Not when there's just the two of us here, and I'm not in uniform."

Al shifted sideways, stepping away from the door. The man followed his movement, turning his back to Bull, then lunged. Al parried the blade and tried to riposte, but the man blocked Al's blade so hard that Al barely managed to get back to his center stance in time to prevent another attack.

The man smiled. "You beat a Magister?" He barked his laugh again. "I don't think so."

Al circled to his right, away from the wall. He kept his eyes on his opponent, trying to ignore the sight of Bull walking silently across the room, the bottle in his hand.

"What have you been doing since Brighton, anyway?" the man asked. He thrust again, almost casually.

Al parried, but did not attempt any kind of counter. Instead, he smiled. "Practicing."

Seeing the man's eyes widen, Al performed his one attack. His arm extended in perfect synchronization with his shifting balance, the tip of his sword aimed straight for the man's chest.

The side of the man's blade slammed into Al's, knocking him off balance. Sneering, the man stepped forward and smashed the pommel of his sword into Al's face.

Sparks exploded in Al's vision, and he staggered backward, dropping his weapon.

The man laughed and stepped back, touching the tip of his sword to the base of Al's throat. "I can't believe you beat a Magister."

Al backed up, but the blade stayed with him until he was pinned against the wall.

"Good-bye," the man said, twisting his weapon.

Bull's bottle slammed into the back of his head. Swung with two hands, it had all of Bull's weight behind it. The man collapsed to the floor, unconscious.

Al sagged against the wall. Blood gushed from his ruined nose and broken lip.

"You okay?" Bull asked.

"No," Al said. His nose hurt so bad he thought he was going to be sick. "Why can't people leave my nose alone?" He tilted his head back.

"I've got to put out the fire." Bull ran to the bar, smacking at the flames with his rag.

Bird emerged from the kitchen. He had towels wrapped around his claws, and was holding the black kettle of soup from the fire. He tossed it over a burning table, drowning the flames, then ran back to the kitchen.

"Not the soup!" shouted Bull as he upended a table, squashing the flames on its top against the tile floor. "Water! Use water!"

Al staggered through the smoke to the kitchen and started pumping water into the mop bucket. The water didn't come out very fast, but it was better than nothing. Bird waited impatiently, then grabbed the bucket when it was half full. Al moved the kettle over and pumped as fast as he could. He heard the sound of more tables being turned over, and Bull shouting directions. Bird ran back to get more water, his face sweating.

After several more buckets went out, Bull came in to the kitchen. "That's done it," he said. "It's all out."

"What about the guy with the sword?"

"Your friend's dumping him in the street," Bull said, splashing water on his face.

"Won't he come back?" Al said.

"You look terrible," Bull said. "I thought you were supposed to be good with that sword."

"You're avoiding the question," Al said.

Bull sighed. "That's because you don't want the answer."

Al's eyes narrowed.

"The truth?" Bull said. "I'm not the only one the man's been charging for protection. Now he's lying on the street unconscious. . . . Let's just say that he's not going to be a problem anymore."

Al looked away. He didn't know how he felt about that.

"You," the earther said, walking into the kitchen, "are the worst *uldi'iara* ever."

"If *uldi'iara* means swordsman," Bull said, laughing, "I agree with you."

"Thanks," Al said, touching the sides of his nose. "I appreciate that. Are you still leaving?" Al asked.

The earther nodded. "Yeah."

"Take what you like," Bull said. He gestured to the food on the counters. "You've earned it. Not like I'm going to be doing any more business tonight. There's a sack for carrying vegetables too. I imagine you could use it." He grabbed the mop and left for the common room.

Al watched Bird fill the sack with food. "Good luck," Al said. "Are you sure you won't come with me?"

Bird slung the sack over his shoulder. "No, Al. I won't go anywhere near Sadraki." He met Al's gaze. "For your sake, I hope I'm wrong about Magister Lundi." He held out his hand. "Thanks for getting me out of that dungeon, and for standing up for me at Brighton. It's been a long time since anyone's done anything like that."

Al shook the earther's hand. "I hope you find a home."

"You too." The earther turned and walked away, pulling the kitchen door closed behind him. Al watched him go, then walked heavily up the back stairs to his room and laid down on his bed.

CHAPTER 21
THE SUNKEN CITY

Al crouched on the dike and looked out over the sunken city, trying to decide the best way to find the place the old woman had described to him. Four streets in from the dike was easy enough, but counting two streets from the river was a challenge. In order to do that, he had to go to the river and count backward, and Al was pretty sure that things were swimming down there.

Even crouching on the dike in the predawn darkness, he'd seen ripples in the dark water, heard larger splashes in the distance. It didn't help that many of the buildings had collapsed, and that in the darkness, things seemed to skitter and crawl across their rubble.

He shifted the pack on his back. It was heavier than it had been since he'd first gotten it, weighed down with food and blankets from The Hook and Hand. Bull had been generous, even if he had said that Al would have to pay him back the next time he was in Dockside.

Something tumbled from a window in the sunken city and landed with a splash. Al leaned forward, peering into the darkness. Whatever it was swam with a predator's grace, the water rippling from a ridge of scales that stuck into the air. Al shuddered as he watched it go.

Once all was still again, he lowered himself over the edge of the dike. The cold, dark water made it impossible to see anything past his knees. He swung his pack around and pulled out his sword, pushing aside the straw hat he'd tied to the top of the pack. Putting the bag back on his shoulder, he poked his sword at a floating piece of wood that looked like it might have eyes. It drifted harmlessly away. Satisfied, Al waded away from the dike.

The cobblestones were slippery beneath his boots, and they sloped down as he walked.

"Idiot," Al muttered as he remembered the high spot he'd seen the day before. Not only would he have been closer to the river if he'd started there, but he would have been drier. He rubbed the back of his neck. His nose and head had been throbbing ever since the fight in The Hook and Hand. Small wonder that he wasn't thinking clearly.

The water continued to deepen until it reached his hip. At the cross street, Al looked both directions in the gloom. Broken buildings huddled as far as he could see, covered by fuzzy brown vines. Something long and skinny brushed along his knee. He jumped and shouted, slashing his sword all around him, then slogged through the water as fast as he could.

At the next street, the cobblestones started climbing again. By the time he reached the third intersection, Al was on dry land. He took a moment to collect his nerves. Whatever happened with the skincarver, he thought, he was going to have to find a different way back. There was no way he was wading through that water again.

Al shivered. The water had been cold, but getting out of it felt even colder. He jumped a few times to try to get his circulation moving, then ran to the fourth cross street and turned left, toward the river. The road stayed above the water, sloping up as he jogged. As on the other streets, the windows in these buildings had no glass or shutters, and many of them were nothing more than jagged walls of stone jutting from piles of debris. Stringy vines covered the cobblestones, smaller and greener than the ubiquitous fuzzy brown ones that seemed to be doing their best to pull the buildings down.

As Al neared the river, he realized that he hadn't run into a single dead end. In the rest of Dockside, none of the streets ran this straight. Was this how Dockside had been laid out decades ago? He thought about it as he ran. What had happened to the city? Had there always been a dike there, or had they constructed it after the flood? He wished his history tutor had spent more time on things that were a little more recent.

The dry street continued to slope gently up until it crested at the pile of broken rubble that was Riverway. Al turned around and ran back the way he'd come, counting intersections. At the second one, he stopped to examine the fitted stone walls of the buildings, using the pommel of his sword to push the vines out of the way.

The sun rose while Al searched, streaking the sky red and orange. Al bit his lip. Looking for the feather had taken too much time. He wasn't going to be able to do any scouting before meeting the skincarver. For that matter, he thought, if he didn't find the feather soon, he'd never even meet the skincarver. The old woman had said just after dawn, but how long was that? Al put his sword away and leaned closer to the wall, using his hands to push back the vines. Several of the stones had cracked and dropped away, leaving uneven holes in the rock.

It was next to one of these holes that Al found the faint etching of the feather. It pointed along the dry street, toward the Flienne, with only three spines on its top ridge. Al backed up to count doors, then ran to the third one, a faded red wooden door that somehow still clung to its hinges. He pushed it open.

The smell of rotten fish and old charred wood wafted out. Al covered his mouth with his sleeve and stepped carefully through the opening. The inside of the building was just a shell, three stories of awful-smelling emptiness surrounded by old stone walls. It had no roof, and broken-off pegs on the walls showed where stairs and ceilings used to be. Rotting burned beams covered the floor in a crazy crisscross of shadows and soot.

Al climbed slowly across the wreckage, wondering if he'd counted the doors wrong. In the back corner, he found a trapdoor in the stone floor. He pulled it open, then paused to catch his breath. The fish smell was even worse down in the hole. Covering his mouth with the back of his hand, he peered down. A rope ladder hung from the edge of the opening down into a small stone-floored chamber with a door on one side.

Great, Al thought. He hadn't thought to bring a lantern. Holding his breath, he lowered himself down and pulled the trapdoor closed. Darkness enveloped him, and the air felt dense and oily. Eyes watering, he continued climbing down.

When his feet touched the stone, they slipped. He clung to the ladder to catch his balance, then turned carefully on the slimy surface to feel for the door handle he'd seen from above. His hand found the metal knob, and he turned it and pushed. A wave of light and odor washed over him, and he clamped a hand over his mouth against the sudden urge to vomit.

A voice chuckled. "First time down?"

Al nodded, squinting against the light. The room was small and low, less than six feet high and not more than ten paces across or deep. A torch burned in a bracket on the far wall, and in the room's center, the silhouette of a tall man sat cross-legged on a keg, positioned between a wooden crate and a hole filled with water.

Something moved in that water, but Al didn't pay it any attention. His eyes were stuck to the top of the crate, to the collection of knives and needles there. The torchlight danced across their stained surfaces, and Al felt queasy again.

"Stop that right now," the man said sharply. "This place is foul enough without you puking all over it."

"I'm sorry," Al said. "It's just —"

"I know, kid." He gestured with a hand that looked unnaturally long, "but we take every precaution here. Now come take a seat." The man's hand was covered with a swirling skincarving that reached all the way up to his shoulder. The tattoo was a green and blue mass of swirling waters and swimming fish. The porta wasn't the surprising part, though. Al had been expecting that. What caught his attention now was the thin membrane of skin that connected the man's fingers to each other.

Al moved closer, his eyes wide. The man wasn't wearing a shirt, just short breeches that looked like they were made of fish scales. His skin glistened gray and smooth in the torchlight, and his torso looked long and lean. Al's eyes focused on the gill slits that lay flat on either side of the man's throat.

"Okay," the man said. "That's enough gawking. Let's get started."

"I'm sorry," Al said again. "I've never seen a waterfolk before." He held out his hand. "I'm —"

"No," the waterfolk man interrupted. "No names. What we do here could get us both killed. You don't know me. I don't know you." He patted the floor in front of him. "Now sit down with your back toward me."

Al put his bag down and sank to the floor in front of the keg. Next to him, something splashed in the dark water. A tentacle jutted out to feel along the floor, but the skincarver kicked it back in with his foot. "Touch your chin to your chest," he said.

Heart pounding, Al did as he was told. He tried not to flinch when he felt the cold blade touch the back of his neck, but he couldn't keep the tears from coming as the metal peeled off his skin. He squeezed his eyes closed.

"Easy now," the skincarver rumbled. "We gotta get the old one off before we put the new one on. I was told you only want a rank two. You sure you don't want to go higher?"

Al's voice came out weak and raspy from the pain. "Please," he said, opening his eyes. "I just don't want to be a zero anymore."

The skincarver patted his shoulder. "I understand. Just thought you might want to aim a little higher. If anyone finds out, you're dead anyway. Why not try for something more?"

Al didn't answer. As the skincarver had been talking,

his knife had been working. Warm blood flowed down Al's back, and his vision was sparkling with the pain. The waterfolk tossed something into the water, and the tentacle grabbed it. Al locked his jaw, fighting a wave of nausea as the wedge of his flesh disappeared into the water.

Next, a coldness spread down his neck, taking the pain with it. It tingled and intensified, flowing around to his face and across the top of his skull. A loud crack sounded from the bridge of his nose, followed by a cold so intense it took his breath away; then the sensation faded.

Al slumped, breathing heavily. All the pain was gone, and not just from his neck. His head and nose felt better too. Even the rasp in his throat was gone.

"There now," the skincarver said. He patted Al on the shoulder. "That's doing better, isn't it?"

Al touched his nose, wonderingly. It felt straight again. He looked over his shoulder. "Life magic?"

The waterfolk nodded. "We got the old carving off. Now we just wait for the healing to finish, and then we'll start on the new one. Don't worry. The worst part is done."

"How many of these do you do?" Al asked.

"You're my first zero, but enough of the others. I don't change rank that often. People who want to change rank usually want the rest of the mark left intact, and just the number changed. I don't do that. Mostly I work with folks that don't like the dragons stealing their Potentia. They have me alter their carvings so the rank is still there, but it doesn't do anything else. Then they get a porta of some kind so they can do magic."

"Stealing Potentia?" Al asked.

"Yeah." The skincarver poked the back of Al's neck experimentally. "You didn't think these things were just for show, did you?"

"Um," Al said. "I hadn't thought about it." He'd known that the five races, including both humans and waterfolk, gathered Potentia for the dragons. But he'd never thought about how that gathering actually happened.

"You should. Everyone should. It's how the dragons get their power. We absorb the Potentia. They steal it." He tapped Al's neck again. "All healed up. Ready?"

Al nodded.

"Good." The skincarver reached into the water and pulled out a bag. "Just a moment while I get the inks ready."

Al watched him untie the top of the bag and unlock the box it held. "How do other people feel?" he asked.

"Feel? About what?"

"About dragons taking their Potentia," Al said.

"Oh." The skincarver lifted glass jars and set them on the crate. Each one held a different colored ink, all shades of blue and green. "Mostly angry, I guess. Without Potentia, you can't do magic."

"That makes sense, I guess. But if you don't know how to do magic, why does it matter?"

"The dragons don't own the Potentia. Why should they control it — or us, for that matter? Why are they in charge?"

"Well," Al said, "they did create us."

"Really?" The waterfolk smiled at Al, showing double rows of sharp teeth. "Many of my people feel differently." He pushed Al's head gently forward. "That's enough treason for one day. Let's finish this."

Al put his chin on his chest and closed his eyes again. The skincarver was right that getting the tattoo wasn't nearly as painful as having it removed. It still hurt, though, and Al heaved a sigh of relief when he felt the familiar coldness of Life Potentia spreading through his neck.

"All done," the skincarver said. "Tell Lady Sapphire it was a pleasure doing business with her."

"Who's Lady Sapphire?"

The skincarver smiled again. "Right." He collected his tools, put them in the box, and locked it. "How are you getting back?"

Al stretched and stood up. "I'm not sure. Hopefully some way that's dry."

"Follow the road away from the Flienne. It's dry all the way to the dike." He knotted the top of the bag around the box and slung it over his shoulder. "Good luck to you. Put the torch out when you leave."

"Thanks."

The skincarver stood up, but stayed bent over so his head wouldn't hit the ceiling. Al tried not to gawk. If the waterfolk straightened, he would be over seven feet tall. Like an earther, his arms were proportionally longer than a human's, but the difference wasn't so exaggerated. Where the earther looked awkward with his short legs and long arms, the waterfolk looked graceful.

He nodded to Al and stepped into water.

Al rushed to the hole to look, but the water was too dark. He remembered the tentacle collecting his flesh and shuddered, then turned away. A metal cap with a long wooden handle hung from the torch's bracket, and a bucket of pitch sat a few feet away. Al picked up the cap and put it over the torch, then hurried for the door, grabbing his bag on the way.

Back on the street, Al ran down the cobblestones. Just as the skincarver had said, the road stayed mostly dry, with only a few inches of water at its lowest point. Al followed it all the way to the dike and climbed out, looking around. He hadn't been to this part of Dockside, north of the North End but east of the sunken city. He untied his straw hat and put it on, pulling the brim low over his eyes. Hopefully, no one here would recognize him.

A cold wind blew down from the morning sky, but aside from the temperature, Al felt better than he had in days. Not only was his headache gone, but he was breathing clearly again. Add to that the new rank mark and the promise of a job in Sadraki, and he felt like everything was finally starting to work out.

CHAPTER 22
THE ROAD TO SADRAKI

"I can't believe you actually met a waterfolk." Trillia glared at Al, hands on her hips. She was wearing her heavy work clothes, just like Al, but also had on a long black coat that somehow made them look good.

"You mean in the hidden chamber under the sunken city?" Al smiled. "Yeah, sorry you missed that, but at least you got to see your folks, right?"

She crossed her arms. "I hate you."

Al laughed.

Trillia's meeting with her parents had not gone well. She hadn't told them about Al, but said instead that she and Wisp were taking a trip together. First they'd yelled at her, then forbidden her from leaving the house. She'd left anyway.

Al had found her sitting on the side of the North Road, right at the point where they couldn't see Castle Surflienne anymore. Now they were just waiting for Wisp. He picked up a rock and tossed it. Horse fields spread around them, rolling grasslands separated into nice, neat rectangles by split rail fences. "I'm going to miss this place."

Trillia sighed and sat down in the grass. "Think we're really going to see windwalkers?"

"That's the plan."

"With my luck," Trillia said, "they'll all have left by the time I get there."

Al tossed another rock into the field. "Shouldn't Wisp be here by now?"

Trillia plucked a long piece of grass and stuck it between her teeth. "He'll be here." She lay back in the grass and stared at the clouds.

"What's the story with you two?" Al asked. "Seems like a lot has changed since I left."

Trillia rolled her eyes. "We're not promised, if that's what you mean."

"No, I — hey, someone's coming!" Al pointed at a horse trotting up the road from Dockside. It carried two riders, with the larger one in front. Al ran for his bag. After his last fight, he had no desire to draw his sword again, but trying to outrun a horse across open fields was not an option. He slid out his blade.

Trillia moved next to Al. "Don't worry." She reached inside her coat with both hands and pulled out two long knives.

"Where'd those come from?"

"Straps inside the jacket," she said. "I sewed them in myself."

"No," Al said. "I mean where'd you get them?" The knives were a foot long, with edges on both sides and nasty-looking points.

"Nice, huh? One of the boys in the North End loaned them to me, said I shouldn't be walking around Dockside unprotected."

"*Loaned* them to you?" Al said.

She smiled. "Actually, they were sort of a bribe for me to pretend to be his girlfriend."

Now it was Al's turn to roll his eyes. He held his sword point down, but stayed tense and ready. If the horse did carry Cullers, he'd have to move quickly to get their attention, and hopefully buy Trillia some time to get away. Not that she would run, he thought, but it was all he could think of. The horse trotted closer.

"For luck's sake," Trillia said, blowing out her breath in disgust. "It's just Wisp and his dad."

Al squinted his eyes. Now that she said it, the shapes of the riders did look like them. "I think you're right."

Trilla put her knives away. "I miss out on *everything.*"

By the time Al had his sword back in its bag, Mr. Evanson had stopped the horse, a big bay mare, in front of them. Wisp sat behind him, looking glum. Just like Trillia and Al, he was wearing his work clothes and sturdy boots. He also wore a heavy woolen jacket and carried a backpack.

Mr. Evanson glared down at Al. "I thought I made it clear that you were to stay away from my son. And taking Trillia too? Her parents are beside themselves."

"I'm sorry, sir," Al said. "I didn't mean to —"

"Stop," Mr. Evanson snapped. "It's what you do that matters, not what you mean. Zero or not, you need to do better."

Al looked at the ground, his ears burning. It sounded exactly like the kind of thing his dad would say. "Yes, sir."

"Wisp will see you safely to Sadraki," Mr. Evanson said sternly. "I've given him a map in case you get separated from the horse traders."

Wisp slid off the back of the horse.

"Let me be clear," Mr. Evanson said. "If Lady Sapphire hadn't assured me of the importance of what you're doing,

Wisp would not be going with you. Do you understand? You will not involve him in whatever is happening in Sadraki. Once you are there, his part will be done."

"Yes, sir."

Mr. Evanson transferred his glare to his son. "I'd be going myself if I could. This whole idea is lunacy, sending kids to Sadraki."

Wisp bowed his head. "Yes, Dad."

"Good." Mr. Evanson's glare softened. "Now travel quickly and stay out of sight."

"Why?" Trillia asked. "No one knows we're out here."

"Lady Sapphire sent messengers last night, not only to me, but also to others. It was necessary, but what messengers carry, others may learn. Don't trust anyone without the mark of the feather. Our enemies may not know what we're doing, but they will try to stop you just the same."

"*I* don't know what we're doing," Al said.

"Join the club," Wisp muttered.

Wisp's dad laughed. "Few do. It's safer that way. Al, when you get to Sadraki, tell your new employer that the Third is assembling."

Al's head jerked up sharply. "Assembling? But there are only fourteen of you!"

"Yes, Al," Mr. Evanson said drily, "all fourteen are assembling." He turned his horse and pointed to Wisp. "You stay out of this, you hear me? I will *not* have your mother's heart broken. Do what you have to do and come back to us."

"Yes, Dad."

Mr. Evanson held them all with his gaze, and then nodded and rode away.

"Wisp," Al said. "What does that mean? How could fourteen people assemble?"

"Don't know," Wisp said tightly.

"But —"

"I don't know, okay?" Wisp yelled. "He won't tell me anything. All he does is tell me to stay out of it. That's all he's ever done."

Al blinked in surprise. Wisp and his dad had always gotten along great.

Wisp walked away. "Come on," he snapped. "Let's go."

Trillia grabbed her pack and ran to catch up. "Did you tell him about Schion?"

"That's where he's going now," Wisp said. "To get back the money he paid to have me become an apprentice."

"What about the thing Schion put in your arm?"

"Dad cut it out and stitched me up."

Al heaved the strap of his bag up over his head and across his shoulder. His pack was twice the size of the ones Wisp and Trillia were carrying, and not nearly as easy to put on. "Hey, wait up!"

"Walks all the way to Brighton, and he's still slow," Wisp said to Trillia.

She laughed and smiled over her shoulder at Al. "It's those short little legs."

Al hurried after them. "I am not slow!"

"How'd it go with your parents?" Wisp asked.

"Terrible." Trillia shrugged. "Like I knew it would."

"Sorry," Wisp said. "How about you, Al? How was the skincarver?"

"He was great. Want to see?"

Wisp stopped. "Can I?"

Al tilted his head forward so Wisp could look at his rank mark. "He healed my face too."

"I noticed," Wisp said. "For luck's sake! That's not a human mark!"

"What?" Al said.

"Trillia, check this out. See the waves and interlocking tridents? That's waterfolk. No humans do that."

"No way," Al said. "It is not!"

"Weird." Trillia brushed her fingers over the mark, sending shivers down Al's spine. "Does it matter?" she asked.

"I don't think so," Wisp said. "Not unless the person looking at it knows about skincarvings. Even then, I guess Al could come from one of the islands, been tested in a waterfolk city."

Al stepped away, disappointed. "I don't know any water-folk cities." In a strange way, he felt like his last tie to his home had just been cut. There was now nothing to connect him to Dockside or Castle Surflienne or even his family. *That's probably the point*, he thought morosely. *No one wants to be associated with a zero.*

The three of them walked until well past noon without seeing anyone. When the horse pastures changed into wood-lands, Al dragged them off the road. The autumn foliage hadn't completely fallen, and there was enough underbrush to hide them, even without the leaves.

"This is silly," Trillia said as they maneuvered through the trees. "I know what Wisp's dad said, but there's no one here, and we'll hear anyone coming way before they see us."

"Humor me, okay?" Al said, holding a branch out of the way for her to walk by. "We're hiding from the Cullers. I've done this before."

"But it's going to take twice as long!"

"He's right," Wisp said. "The road is too dangerous."

They walked through the trees, just close enough to the trail to be able to spot the horse traders that were supposed to be meeting them. An hour later, as they were hopping across the bed of a dried up mountain stream, they heard the sound of pounding hooves.

Al dropped to the ground, and Wisp and Trillia froze. Two horsemen galloped past on the road, wearing the dark green pants of the Cullers, with jackets to match. They leaned forward as they rode, their faces intent.

"Cullers?" Trillia whispered after they couldn't hear the hoofbeats anymore.

Al nodded.

"You think they were looking for us?" she asked.

"Me, at least," Al said, brushing himself off. "They always are."

She licked her lips, and Al saw her and Wisp exchange a worried glance.

"You can still go back," Al said. "You and Wisp aren't in any kind of trouble. You could get your bakery job back, and Wisp could —"

"Stop," Wisp said. "It was just a surprise, that's all. Let's have some lunch."

Relief washed over Al. He wasn't sure exactly why Wisp and Trillia were going with him, but he sure was glad they were. "Great idea. You won't believe what I've brought." He opened his pack and started lifting out the bundles of food Bull had packed for him.

"Wow," Trillia said as he handed her a broiled hen. "You sure know how to travel."

Wisp looked at his hen doubtfully. "Is this from the same guy that drugged me?"

"Enjoy," Al said around a mouthful of pulled pork. He chewed and swallowed. "Don't worry. If you fall asleep again, I'm sure Trillia can carry you."

Trillia laughed.

Wisp bit into his food. "Don't suppose you brought any of that cider?"

"No."

"Good," Trillia said. "Luck only knows what that crazy bartender would have slipped into it."

Al chuckled. "Bull's not crazy. You should have tried his miracle mix. Nastiest, most wonderful stuff I ever tasted."

Trillia was licking her fingers and leaned over, inspecting the rest of the food. "Can I have more, or should we save it?"

"I say we eat as much as we want. This stuff isn't going to keep —"

A man's shout interrupted him, echoing through the mountains. Al stood up. "That wasn't that far away, was it?"

Metal clashed on metal, followed by more shouting, the panicked whinnying of horses, and screams.

Trillia surged into a crouch, pulling out her knives. Al drew his sword. Wisp looked back and forth between them, his eyes wide. "We're hiding," he hissed.

The screams cut off, and the shouting and whinnying dwindled. Afraid to move and risk making any noise, Al looked at his friends. A yell of frustration echoed from up the trail, then the sounds of splintering wood.

Wisp grabbed Al's arm. "Come on," he whispered. "Let's get out of here!"

"What about the food?" Trillia whispered, sheathing her knives and picking up her backpack.

Al hurriedly scooped the leftovers back into his bag, then surveyed where they'd been sitting. He didn't think it looked too obvious they'd been there. At least he hoped not.

"Hurry!" Wisp urged.

Together, the three of them ran up the streambed, putting as much distance as they could between themselves and the road to Sadraki.

CHAPTER 23
THE HORSE TRADERS

"I still say that we don't know it had anything to do with us," Trillia grumbled as she climbed up the dry waterfall.

"We also don't know that it didn't," Wisp said from above her.

Al drank from his waterskin and watched Trillia climb. They couldn't have traveled more than a mile from the road, and Trillia and Wisp were already bickering again. "Guys," he said. "Could you keep it down? We're supposed to be hiding, remember?"

Trillia sighed. "Relax, already. There's no one out here but us." She pulled herself the rest of the way up and sat down.

"The bigger problem," Wisp said, "is what to do now."

Al climbed up the waterfall and found them crouched over a map. "Is that your dad's map?"

"Yeah." Wisp pointed to a line on it. "That's the North Road, which is what we were on, and here" — he moved his finger up it to where the line branched — "is where it splits. This branch is called the Uillian, and leads east to the earther cities. The North Road continues north, and then Mountainway peels off and heads west along the edge of the mountains. The North Road keeps going, though" — he

followed the line with his finger through the mountains —
"to Sadraki."

Al sat down. "That's a long way."

"And it's going to be colder up there," Wisp said. "Much
colder. Dad said the first snows have probably already fallen
in the mountains."

"Where are we?" asked Trillia.

"Somewhere down here." Wisp tapped the map. "If we
go north, we'll hit the Uillian. Then we could turn left and
get back to the North Road."

Al shook his head. "That's not safe."

"It's our only choice," Wisp said. "We can't get through
the mountains without a trail. Besides, if we don't meet up
with the horse traders, we're going to be walking for days."

All three of them stared at the map.

"I say we go back to the North Road," Trillia said.

"Are you crazy?" Wisp asked.

"No," Al said. "She's right. We have to find out what
happened. We need to know if something happened to the
horse traders."

Wisp looked back at the map, then sighed and rolled it
up. "Let's at least wait until dark."

Al cleaned out his pack while they waited, picking out
the pieces of half-eaten food he'd dumped in earlier, and
sorting Bull's contributions based on how long he thought
they'd stay fresh. Trillia took off her boots and stretched
out for a nap.

"Your watch," Wisp said, leaning against a tree. "We
were both up all last night."

Al nodded. He couldn't sleep anyway, not with the sun
still high in the sky. He picked up his sword and took his

center stance in the dry streambed. Without thinking, he started running through his parries. That man in The Hook and Hand had completely overwhelmed his attack. It had been too slow and too weak, and Al hadn't been ready for such powerful parries. In all his sparring, Al had never had his blade knocked so hard, nor had he thought about using his pommel to attack. He tried his attack again and again, focusing both on speed and balance.

As Al exercised, he lost track of time. Despite the cold, sweat dripped down his back and arms. He stared at the tree he'd picked to practice against, willing his attack to go faster. Speed was key, he thought. Against adults, speed was all he had. He had to move so fast that they couldn't parry, that they didn't have time to parry. His sword stabbed into the tree and withdrew. *Faster*, he thought. He wasn't fast enough.

"I guess you can use that thing, after all," Wisp said.

Al stopped, breathing hard. The light was fading from the forest. He'd been practicing for hours. "Not well enough. If it weren't for Bull, I'd be dead. Hey, can you do me a favor?"

Wisp stood up and brushed off his pants.

"Grab a branch and stand next to that tree."

"I'm not going to spar with you," Wisp said, looking around until he found a solid branch on the ground.

"No," Al said. "Just stand next to that tree. I'm going to try to stab it, and I want you to knock my sword out of the way."

Wisp smiled. "A penny a hit?"

"Sure."

Al returned to his center stance, then stabbed at the tree. Wisp's branch caught the side of the sword, knocking it away and pulling Al off balance. He swore.

"That's one," Wisp said. "Just forty-nine more, and you owe me a crown."

Halfway to that crown, Al hit the tree. Wisp nodded acknowledgment and switched to the other side of the tree. They continued practicing, with Wisp switching back and forth, until Al was hitting as often as not. Even better, Al thought, when he did get blocked, he was able to keep his balance.

They stopped once it was too dark to see. "You owe me two drakes," Wisp said.

"I'll pay you as soon as I have them." Al put his sword away. "I'm a zero, remember? No money."

Wisp groaned. "I liked it better when you were rich."

Al laughed. "Me too." He swung his arms to loosen them up. His shoulders ached, but not as much as he remembered from his tutoring. All those days paddling the boat with Martin, he thought. At least they were worth something.

Wisp woke Trillia, and the three of them crept back to the North Road, then moved as quietly as they could through the trees beside it. They slowed when they heard horses whickering and chuffing.

Wisp gestured to Trillia and Al to stop, then moved forward alone. Al didn't argue. Of the three of them, Wisp had always been the quietest. When he wanted to, he could move as quietly as his name, somehow ghosting over floors that creaked loudly when anyone else stepped on them.

Al and Trillia crouched in the darkness until Wisp returned.

"I think the Cullers ambushed the horse trader we were supposed to meet," Wisp said, "but there's no one around now."

Trillia stood. "What happened?"

Wisp led the way. "They were all killed," he said. "Their wagon smashed. The horses were cut loose, but some either came back or never left."

"Horses?" Trillia said.

Wisp pushed through the bushes and gestured.

Clouds covered the night sky, but even in the darkness, Al could see the shapes of three people lying motionless on the packed dirt. The broken remains of the wagon lay nearby, smashed beyond use. Behind it, the road was scattered with slashed feed bags, and four horses were eating from them. A fifth stared back at Al. Its ears were forward, its tail sweeping back and forth behind it.

"See how all the feed bags have been cut?" Wisp said. "They were searching for something."

Al stared at the bodies as he stepped onto the road, remembering how the Cullers had galloped past. It was hard to imagine that just two men had done all this. "Maybe it's not about us, then?"

Wisp shook his head. "Remember that my dad said our enemies don't know what we're doing? They think the Third is taking something to Sadraki, but they don't know what it is. They don't know it's you."

"Guys," Trillia called from next to the wagon. She pointed to a piece of broken wood on the ground. "It has the sign of the feather."

Al let out a breath, still looking at the bodies. Only one of them had a sword. He felt hollow inside. "So we're on our own."

"But with horses," Trillia said.

"All I've ridden are plow horses," Al said. "Somehow, I think these might be a little different." The animals were tall and sleek, with no saddles, just bridles with cut lead ropes hanging from them.

"Oh, don't be such a chicken." Trillia scooped a handful of grain off the ground and held it out to a chestnut brown mare with a black mane. The horse whickered and put her nose in Trillia's hand. "See?"

"One thing's for sure," Wisp said. "There's no way we can fix the wagon."

"What about," Al gestured toward the bodies, "you know, them? Shouldn't we bury them or something?"

Trillia looked at the bodies, her face still. "We don't have time. We should get to Sadraki as fast as we can and tell them what happened. They'll send someone to take care of them."

Wisp nodded.

"It doesn't seem right to just leave them here," Al said.

"We don't have shovels," Wisp said.

"And we don't know how long before the next pair of Cullers ride by," Trillia added.

"So what do we do?" Al asked, turning away from the dead men. "Tie the horses in a line or something?"

Wisp dug through the remains of the wagon. "They must have riding gear in here somewhere. They couldn't have been planning on walking the whole — aha!" He pulled a saddle out of the wreckage. "Trillia, give me a hand. You know how these things work better than I do."

Trillia's uncle worked in the castle stables. She knew more about horses than Al ever wanted to. He sifted through the remains of the wagon while she talked softly to the creatures, handing out grain, and luring them close. There wasn't much left of the wagon. Whoever had smashed it up had been extremely thorough.

"Dump out your bag, Al," Wisp said. "We need it to hold the feed."

"What?" Al looked over his shoulder. Trillia had saddles on three of the horses.

"It's the only one big enough," Wisp said. "All these are slashed."

Al tied his spare set of clothes in a bundle and put his straw hat on his head. They ate as much as they could of the food, and divided the rest between Wisp's and Trillia's packs. "What about my blanket?"

"Put it behind your saddle," Trillia said.

They dumped the feed into his bag, careful not to spill any into the hidden scabbard. Al drew his sword out, making sure that no grains were in its metal tube, then replaced it. "I hope you don't expect me to carry this thing. I can't even lift it."

Under Trillia's direction, they heaved it onto the blanket behind Al's saddle and tied it down. Once it was secure, Trillia swung onto her horse. "Mount up."

Al raised his eyebrows. "Sure."

"Just put your left foot in the stirrup and swing your right leg over."

Wisp tried, but the horse stepped forward as soon as his foot touched the stirrup. He hopped after the horse, swearing, until Trillia caught the bridle.

"See," she said. "It's easy."

Al managed it on the first try, but only because Trillia was holding his bridle. Once he was up, he picked up the reins.

"We're lucky. These are really well trained," Trillia said. "Sit up straight, keep your heels down, and hold your reins like I am. If you want to go fast, squeeze with your lower legs. Whatever you do, don't kick 'em. Even a little touch with your heels and you'll be running."

"We're riding at night?" Al asked. "Shouldn't we at least learn in the daylight?"

"No," Wisp said. "We should travel as far as we can in the dark, then get off the road."

Trillia clicked her tongue and shook her reins. Her horse chuffed and started walking sedately. The other horses, including Wisp's and Al's, fell into step behind it.

"What's happening?" Al called.

"They're used to following the lead," Trillia said. "Don't worry. It's a good thing. As long as nothing scares 'em, we'll get all five horses to Sadraki."

Al held the reins and concentrated on not falling off.

CHAPTER 24
THE SADRAKI GUARD

Al curled up under his blanket, remembering the bodies lying on the road. He'd never seen a dead person before, and the idea of leaving them on the road like that still bothered him. He stared at the horses. They had ridden until after midnight, then followed a stream away from the road to set up camp. Trillia looked like she'd never been happier, but Al hurt in places that he was pretty sure weren't designed to hurt.

"Still awake, aren't you?" Wisp asked.

"Yeah," Al said. "Can't stop thinking about those guys on the road."

"Me neither. I wish I knew what was going on."

Al nodded, though he knew Wisp couldn't see him. "You know what I realized back in Dockside? This isn't just about me being a zero. Something big is happening."

"I know," Wisp said. "Did you see how that old lady started being helpful after you told her about Magister Lundi?"

"The skincarver called her Lady Sapphire," Al said, thinking. "I think I was right about the Magisters and the Cullers fighting. Somehow, what Magister Lundi said to me was meant to reach Lady Sapphire and her friends. By the way, what should we call them? They use the feather for their symbol, but they weren't in the Third."

"Let's call 'em the Third, anyway." Wisp grinned. "It sounds better than feather people."

Despite himself, Al laughed. "Okay. So Magister Lundi thought I was in the Third and his message that he paid well was some kind of a secret message that Lady Sapphire understood. It let her know that it was important for me to get to Sadraki."

"And now my dad," Wisp said, "is assembling the Third."

"But the Cullers want to stop all this from happening."

Wisp nodded. "They know something is being taken to Sadraki, but they don't know what."

"What I don't get," Al said, "is what the most powerful man in the world could possibly need me for?"

"I still can't believe he's a good guy," Wisp said. "He killed five thousand of his own soldiers. I can't believe my dad's working with him."

Al didn't know what to say to that. He stared at the cloudy night sky and listened to the crickets chirp around him. In the distance, a night bird hooted. "Hey Wisp," he said softly, "you still awake?"

"Yeah."

"The waterfolk skincarver said something that's been bugging me," Al said. "He said people change their rank marks so that the dragons don't get their Potentia."

"Yeah," Wisp said. "When you get permission to get a porta, you also get permission to have your rank mark changed — not your number, but the mark itself. Unless you do that, you'll never be able to do magic."

"Why not?"

"Magic is just shaped Potentia." Wisp shifted under his blanket. "Here's how Schion explained it to me. Imagine that each person has a bowl inside them that can hold a certain amount of Potentia. Some people can hold more, others less, but everyone has one. As long as the bowl is empty, you keep absorbing it from what's around you. If you have a porta, and a lot of training, you can shape your Potentia and force it out through your porta to do magic." Wisp took a breath. "But with a rank mark, your bowl is always empty. All the Potentia that you absorb goes right to the dragons. A rank mark is kind of like a one-way Potentia door that's always open."

"But how can it go anywhere?" Al said. "I mean, if there's no dragon nearby, it can't leave, right?"

"Sure it can. Potentia can go all the way across the world, or even through it, if that's what its pattern calls for. Master Schion said that once I'm trained enough, I'll be able to see it, thin streams of power coming from each person's rank mark, well, as long as that person's rank mark hasn't been changed, and they're not a zero."

"Okay," Al said. "But if you don't know any magic, losing your Potentia doesn't matter, does it?"

"I guess not," Wisp said. "It is pretty creepy, though. It's like having someone cut off your hair without asking. I mean, it's *yours*. You shouldn't lose it just because you're not using it."

Al pulled his blanket tighter around himself, thinking. "But that's why the dragons created us, to gather Potentia for them. How could people be mad about doing what they were created to do?"

"Hey," Wisp said, "don't ask me. All I wanted to do was be a skincarver. You're the one causing all the trouble."

Al sighed. "I suppose."

After a while, Al did manage to fall asleep, only to wake at dawn, as he always did. Beside him, Wisp and Trillia were doing the same.

"So much for sleeping in," Wisp said. "I hate being a farmer."

Trillia stretched. "Being a baker's even worse. Let's get going."

"I've been thinking about the Cullers," Al said.

Trillia laughed. "Of course you have. Do you ever do anything else?"

Al ignored her. "I think they'll be waiting at the intersections."

"Huh," Wisp said. "You know, that's actually pretty smart. They can't cover the entire North Road. They'll probably be waiting where it meets the Uillian first and then Mountainway later. So we should be able to make good time on the road, just as long as we stop short of each intersection and work our way around."

"Sounds good," Trillia said. "On the way, I'll teach you two how to trot and canter. We'll go a lot faster if we mix it up."

Al groaned. "Do either of those hurt less than walking?"

"Not usually." Trillia flashed him an evil grin.

Al fell off three times before noon, which was two more times than Wisp. Trillia rode easily, calling out instructions as they traveled. The air became colder under the cloudy sky, and the hills grew steeper and more treacherous. The

North Road followed the contours of the land, climbing steadily as it went deeper into the mountains. Wisp used them to track their progress on his map, and called a stop well before they reached the Uillian.

"We're making great time," Wisp said, pointing out where they were. His breath puffed white in the air.

"These horses were trained to carry full-grown men and gear," Trillia said. "Not us. We could probably go faster if you wanted to."

"No," Al said. "No, this is good." He had decided that he hated cantering even more than eating raw fish, and that was saying something.

"Either way," Wisp said, "we've got to get off the road here and work our way around on foot."

Away from the road, the leafless trees grew tall, with little underbrush between them. Wisp led, leaving Trillia and Al to manage the horses. Al wore both his sets of clothes, and held his blanket around his shoulders against the cold. The ground sloped steeply up before them, and it wasn't long before Al's calves and thighs ached. "Don't most people ride their horses?" he asked.

"If we were better riders, maybe we could," Trillia said. "But if something were to spook them out here, there's no telling where we'd end up."

"Oh," Al said. It was hard not to think that he was the reason they were walking, the rider that wasn't good enough to ride.

They picked their way through the trees, splashing through icy streams and over high ridges. Finally, just as night was beginning to fall, they reached the road Wisp called the Uillian. It was broad and flat, and covered with crushed rock. They hurried across and into the trees on its other side.

"Let's find a place to camp," Al said. "My legs are killing me."

That night, as they lay shivering under their blankets, the broad-winged shapes of three dragons flew overhead.

"That can't be good," Trillia whispered after they had gone.

"No," Al said. The dragons had been flying south, toward Castle Surflienne and the gathering Third.

"I wish we could have a fire," said Trillia, shivering.

"Maybe tomorrow?" Al asked.

"Probably not," Wisp said, "but the night after that we should be in Sadraki."

After feeding the horses the next morning, Al discovered that his bag was empty enough to hang from his saddle instead of sitting behind it. He hung it on his left side, so he could reach down with his right hand and grab his sword if he needed to. Not that he knew how to use a sword from horseback, he thought, but it made him feel better.

Al, Wisp, and Trillia rode all the next day, pushing the horses as hard as they dared, until it was time to dismount and walk carefully around the intersection with Mountainway. Once back on the North Road, they tried galloping, but Al fell off before his horse had taken three strides, and they gave that up.

Night found them huddled in a tight circle, layered with every available piece of clothing. The trees were not much taller than the horses, gnarled evergreens that did little to block the wind. The rocks beneath them were frozen, with puddles of ice in every indentation.

"I sh-should have stayed at the bakery," Trillia said.

"At least it hasn't snowed," Al said.

"Hush!" Wisp hissed. "Don't tempt fate."

They woke before dawn, teeth chattering, and fed the horses the last of the grain, then hurried back to the road. It climbed steeply, up out of the trees, and along a barren wasteland of rock. The road was marked with cairns, four-foot-tall piles of rock. Behind them, the countryside looked distant and unreal. Ahead, peaks towered in the distance, disappearing into the heavy clouds overhead.

"It's like we're climbing into the sky," Trillia said. Her words sounded thin and small.

Wisp looked at the map he held against his horse's neck. "We've got to be close, but with these clouds, I can't tell."

They continued to climb into the clouds, until the air around them whitened and became so thick that they couldn't see the ground in front of their horses.

"Dismount," called Trillia. "We don't want any broken legs."

Al slid down gratefully. "Can you see the cairns?"

"I think so," Wisp said. "Follow me."

The road led steadily upward, over rock domes and across narrow ledges. Finally, they broke out of the cloud into dazzling blue sky. Al shielded his eyes. Ahead, the trail climbed steeply to a rock wall, where it passed through an arched opening. The mountain continued to rise behind the wall, and Al could see a road winding up it, with buildings huddling on either side.

"We're above the clouds," Trillia said. "Look."

Behind them, the clouds formed a cottony floor around the mountain. Overhead, the afternoon sky was a bluer blue than Al had ever seen.

"We have a problem," Wisp said, shading his eyes. "I think I see guards in front of that gate."

"So?" Al asked. "Let's mount up. We haven't done anything wrong."

"What if they're Cullers?" Trillia asked.

"I'm not a zero anymore," Al said, "at least not so they can prove it."

"I think Al's right," Wisp said as he swung into his saddle. "We're twelve-year-olds returning horses we found on the North Road. As long as some of those guys are town guard, they won't let the Cullers take us, not without reporting it to their superiors."

"You're crazy," Trillia said.

Al pulled himself up onto his own horse. "We don't have much choice."

Trillia mounted her horse. "We can't just walk up to them!"

Al twitched his reins and set his horse to walking. "Like I said, we haven't done anything wrong."

Trillia clucked and trotted past him.

As they drew nearer, Al spotted the guards. There were six of them, and four of those stood taller than anyone Al had ever seen, taller even than the waterfolk, and much more massive. They wore thick white furs under their breastplates, and were so huge that the men next to them looked like children. Two horses stood with their heads down, huddling against the wind.

"Windwalkers," Trillia breathed. "Look! You can see the fur!"

Al nodded his head. Trillia was right. Those men weren't *wearing* fur. That was their natural fur that he was seeing.

Beside the windwalkers, one of the humans pointed, then both of them mounted their horses and trotted toward Al, Wisp, and Trillia. The men wore heavy jackets, the same green color as their pants, and swords hung from their hips.

"Al," Wisp said tensely.

"It's okay," Al said. "They're the only ones wearing the green of the Cullers. Once they dismount, gallop past and get to the windwalkers as quickly as you can. They must be the town guard."

"What are you going to do?" Trillia asked.

"Not gallop," Al answered. "That's for sure." He opened the flap of the bag hanging from his saddle and unhooked the leather loop from the hilt of his sword.

"Al," Wisp said again.

"Just get there, okay? The quicker you get the guards, the better my chances." He twitched his reins and trotted in front. "As soon as I get off, you go."

They continued walking until Al could clearly make out the Cullers' faces. They were the same men he'd encountered in Dockside on Testing Day, the first Cullers he'd ever seen. One had green eyes, the other brown. Both looked like they wanted to kill him.

Heart pounding, Al dismounted and raised his sword in his center stance.

The brown-eyed man sneered as he swung out of his saddle and drew his own sword. "You going to fight us, boy?"

Wisp and Trillia kicked their horses into a gallop. The two extra horses, along with the one Al had been riding, followed, thundering past the Cullers.

"Help!" Trillia shouted. "We're being attacked!"

The green-eyed man glanced over his shoulder at the windwalkers and swore softly. He looked down from his horse at Al. "Why did the Third send you? What are you bringing to Magister Lundi?"

Al didn't answer. He was picturing the tree, wondering if his attack could possibly be fast enough.

"Listen, boy," the brown-eyed man said softly. "You tell us what it is and we'll let you go. No more being hunted. No more hiding. You'll be off our books. The first zero we ever let go."

"You have the wrong guy," Al said tightly. "I'm not a zero."

The green-eyed man laughed. "Oh, yes you are. Think we wouldn't recognize you just cause you lost some weight? Most zeroes lose weight on the run. We're used to that. This is your last chance."

Al kept his eyes focused on the man on the ground. He didn't know what to do about the horseman. Nothing he'd learned could help him with that.

"I'm sick of this," the green-eyed man said to his companion. "Kill him and take the body. We can search it on the road."

His partner nodded and lunged, his blade circling under Al's. Al spun his blade in the opposite direction, smacking the Culler's out of line, then whipped it across the man's chest. It pulled through the startled man's jacket and left a line of blood behind it.

Al returned to his center stance. As long as the Culler kept attacking, he thought, he should be okay. The Culler was stronger than he was, but not as fast, and nowhere near as good as the guard he'd faced at The Hook and Hand.

"Ow!" the man shouted. "You little maggot!" He lunged again, this time going for Al's chest.

Al parried. "Not used to fighting people who fight back, are you?" he taunted. "Much easier to kill helpless horse traders."

The man attacked again, and Al parried. This time, though, the man followed his attack with a second and a third, blocking each of Al's counters with his own. Al fell back. His heart pounded in his ears. The Culler was better than he'd thought. Now that the man was taking him seriously, it was all Al could do just to parry. Behind his opponent, he saw the town guard loping toward them. Trillia and Wisp followed, still on their horses.

"For crying out loud," the Culler on the horse said, "will you stop playing around? Finish him already!"

"Why don't you finish him?" the brown-eyed man growled.

Al jumped back, keeping himself well away from the horse. The Culler on the ground followed his motion, stabbing. Al batted the sword away and circled the other direction, trying to put the swordsman between himself and the horse.

The green-eyed man drew his sword. "You can drop your sword," he said, guiding his horse with his knees, "or I can ride you down."

Al faked a lunge at his opponent and jumped back again, keeping both the Cullers in front of him. The windwalkers were too far away to do anything, but Wisp and

Trillia had kicked their horses and were galloping straight for him.

The green-eyed man spurred his horse forward, leaning over and swinging his sword. Al dove sideways across the rock, barely managing to keep hold of his sword. He scrabbled to his feet, and blocked a slash by the swordsman more by luck than any sort of skill.

The brown-eyed Culler pressed the attack, stabbing and slashing. Al parried and dodged, backing away as he fought, concentrating on his balance and on turning the other man's attacks.

Hooves thundered on the rock and Wisp's horse barreled past. Without warning, he flung himself from the saddle and onto the green-eyed man's back. As the two of them tumbled from the saddle and onto ground, the Culler's sword skittered across the hard rock. Wisp scurried away, and Trillia was there, her horse rearing and kicking. The green-eyed man rolled away and came up in a crouch, his hand holding his dagger.

Al straightened and faced his opponent. They both still had their blades.

"You can't win this," the man said. "I've been a Culler for longer than you've been alive."

To Al's right, he saw that Trillia was off her horse. She had drawn both her knives and was standing between the other Culler and Wisp. Her eyes looked wide and frightened, but her hands were steady. The man was in a fighting crouch, his back to Al.

"Killing unarmed twelve-year-olds," Al said, "doesn't exactly hone your skills." He shifted as though he was going to attack, but when his opponent started to parry, he spun and slashed his blade down the back of the Culler facing Trillia. He would have preferred a stab, but couldn't have brought his blade back quickly enough. The man screamed in pain.

The brown-eyed Culler launched a furious sequence of attacks and Al fell back, parrying and stumbling. As the man pressed his advantage, Al's world narrowed to the tips of their blades. He didn't have time to try any counters, and all his attempts to slow the man's momentum failed. It was just a matter of time, Al realized desperately, before he was run through.

"Enough," a voice bellowed.

The Culler and Al didn't break their stances. White breath puffed out of their mouths, and their swords stayed up. Out of the corner of his eye, Al saw a windwalker raise a two-handed sword that was almost as long as Al was tall. The windwalker was well over nine feet tall, and covered with thick white fur. His breastplate bore the insignia of a flying bird in black. "I said enough!"

Al backed carefully away. When the Culler did not pursue him, Al lowered his sword.

"Captain Stani, this boy is mine," the Culler said without turning his head away, "an escaped zero. It is my duty to take him."

Captain Stani turned his gaze on Al. The windwalker's face had human features, but was covered with short white fur. The fur grew thicker and longer over his head, giving the impression of human hair. "Show me your mark."

Moving farther away from the Culler, Al turned to show the back of his neck.

"He is rank two," the windwalker said.

"No," the Culler said, sheathing his sword. "He is not. It's a fake. I have spoken with Master Schion, the skin-carver that ranked him at Castle Surflienne."

"The mark's not from Surflienne," Captain Stani said. "It's waterfolk."

"What?" The Culler's voice cracked. "That's impossible!"

"We will hold him here until you can obtain verification."

"No," the other Culler said. His face looked pale and determined, and he held the reins of their horses in his hand. "You will not," the Culler said. "It is our duty to take him with us. You have no right to keep him."

"It's a long trip to the islands," the windwalker said. "You better get started."

"No!" The green-eyed Culler dropped his hand to the hilt of his sword.

Captain Stani laughed. "You're already bleeding from injuries a *twelve-year-old* gave you, and now you want to draw on a captain of the Sadraki Guard?"

Face burning, the Culler took his hand from his hilt.

CHAPTER 25

A NEW JOB

Past the wall, the North Road narrowed to a single lane track. It curled around the mountain until it reached a hole in the rock of the mountain itself. Captain Stani led them through the hole and to the other side, where they dismounted. He passed their horses to a guard, saying something in a language that Al didn't know.

Trillia caught her breath. "It's beautiful."

The city of Sadraki lay on the inside of a caldera, a giant bowl where the top of the mountain should have been. Unlike the outside of the mountain, the caldera was filled with plant life, and the ground felt warm beneath Al's feet. He sighed as the warmth traveled up his legs.

"How's this possible?" Wisp asked.

Sadraki was a paradise of gardens and small wooden houses painted white, with slanted blue roofs. Aside from a single stone tower sitting on the far side of a lake at the caldera's center, there were no buildings larger than two stories. Footpaths wound between gardens, connecting the different buildings. On the other side of town, Al saw fields laid out in familiar patterns, with horses and livestock grazing beyond.

"It's amazing," Al said.

"Heat from the magma beneath our feet keeps us warm," Captain Stani said. "Though it snows often, it quickly melts."

"Magma?" Trillia asked.

"If you were to dig deep enough, you'd find this old volcano still has some life left. The Magisters value Sadraki because it is the juncture of all five elements: Life, Air, Earth, Fire, and Water. The elements are in balance here, a perfect harmony. That's why the Magisters put their school here. Come. Magister Lundi has been waiting for you these past two days." The windwalker lengthened his stride.

Al, Wisp, and Trillia hurried to follow. On either side of the path, plants of a kind they had never seen before grew lush and green, their leaves broader than Al was tall, many with bright blossoms that simply shouldn't be visible in the fall. They also passed windwalkers, earthers, and humans, all reading intently as they sat or lay on benches among the flowers.

"Look." Trillia tapped Al's shoulder and pointed at two of the windwalkers. They wore human-style clothes and had skin so dark it seemed blue. Their only remaining fur grew thick and white from atop their heads.

Captain Stani harrumphed when he saw the shaved windwalkers. "No respect," he muttered, "but at least they haven't dyed it." He turned his head back to Al. "Most of the people you see are training to be Magisters. Once they've achieved their full rank, they'll be given their assignments. If they don't make it, they're sent away. A lot of those join the Sadraki Guard, or some other military. The armies are always happy to hire people who can work Potentia. Except for the Cullers, of course. Magister Lundi refuses to let them have any trainees, failed or otherwise."

Captain Stani led them between buildings to a low wooden house with the same white walls and bright blue roof as the others. He stopped just off the front porch and coughed politely.

Magister Lundi opened the door a few seconds later, dressed exactly as Al remembered: no shirt or shoes, just loose trousers. Every inch of his skin was covered with vibrant skincarvings, the porta that allowed him to interact with Potentia. He held a book in his hand, with his finger marking his place. "Al," he said. "Welcome. I trust you had no trouble getting here?"

Trillia laughed.

"Not too much," Al said. He was not at all surprised that the Magister knew his real name despite seeming to get it wrong back at Stelton.

"Sir?" Captain Stani said.

"Thank you, Captain," Magister Lundi said. "I'll take them from here."

"Sir," Captain Stani repeated. "There was a problem with Cullers at the gate. Two were injured, and left at a gallop."

"Injured by you?"

"No, sir, nor my men, but I did send them away. They were going to kill the children, sir."

Magister Lundi let his breath out in a whoosh and ran his hand over his tattooed head. "I understand, but it puts us at great risk. If they bring Archovar here to help them get Al, everything could fall apart." He stared at the sky for several breaths. "All we can do is prepare. Tell Primus to go to Surflienne with all speed. Tell Lady Sapphire to move as many people as she can into the catacombs. I should have thought of this earlier. Hurry, Captain. Time is of the essence. I want Primus out of Sadraki before the sun falls. Tell him he is free to use any and all means to speed his travel."

"And if he sees the Cullers?" Captain Stani asked.

"Avoid them, as well as any dragons, for that matter. If we fail here, he is the only hope for Surflienne."

Fear jolted through Al at the Magister's words. The only hope for Surflienne? That's where his family was! He glanced at his friends and saw his own alarm mirrored in their expressions.

The captain saluted and ran back up the trail.

Magister Lundi watched him leave, his eyes narrow. Then, with a visible effort, he smiled and gestured for Al, Wisp, and Trillia to enter. "Come in, please."

Ink drawings covered the walls of his sitting room, mostly of birds, but with a few of plants as well. A table stacked with books dominated the room, wooden chairs all around it, right next to a blue woven throw rug.

"Magister," Al said. "What did you mean about Primus being the only hope for Surflienne?"

The Magister put a finger to his lips. "Not here."

"But —"

"Wait." Bending over, the Magister pulled the rug aside to reveal a metal door in the floor. The Magister inserted a key and pulled open the door. Below it, a stone stairway led into darkness.

When Al hesitated, the Magister handed him a lamp. They all walked silently down the stairs to a landing with two wooden doors. Magister Lundi unlocked the one on the left and led them into a room no bigger than the one Al had stayed in at The Hook and Hand. The chamber had no furniture, just a large wooden chest in its center. Its floor, walls, and ceiling were all made of unfinished wood. Magister Lundi pulled the door tightly closed behind them and locked it with the key, then lifted a second lantern from a hook.

"Now," the Magister said as he lit the lantern and walked to the wooden box, "we can talk."

Al, Wisp, and Trillia followed him. "Why here?" Al asked. His voice sounded different, thinner, and his ears felt like he was swimming deep underwater.

"We're surrounded by dead wood," Magister Lundi said, "with no element connecting us to the outside. Does the air feel different? It's a bubble. We're in an air bubble, inside a room that is completely isolated from the five elements. If there is any place safe to talk, this is it."

"So talk," Trillia said, looking across the box at him. "Tell us about Surflienne. What did you mean that Magister Primus is its only hope?"

Magister Lundi's expression was grave. "The dragons are going to war. If our business here is not successful, Castle Surflienne and its surroundings will be obliterated."

Wisp folded his arms. "I don't believe it. You're a liar and a killer. I don't believe a word you say."

"*Wisp*," Al said.

"No," Wisp said. "I don't care what you say. I know the truth." He glared at Magister Lundi. "I'm the son of an Evan. I know about the Third. I know you killed them."

"The son of an Evan," Magister Lundi repeated, resting his hands on the box. "That's a phrase you don't hear too often." He met Wisp's gaze. "It sounds like you need to hear the story of the Third."

"I already —" Wisp started hotly.

"Do you know who the Third were?" Magister Lundi interrupted.

"A division of the Mountainfoot militia," Wisp spat. "The Magisters' army, used to help protect the people when magic was not enough."

"Close," Magister Lundi said. "The Mountainfoot militia was *my* personal military, and answered only to me. I recruited them because I wanted people to see non-Magisters as their heroes, to give them something besides Potentia to respect."

"But you can't be that old," Al said. The Mountainfoot militia had been around for more than a century.

"Life magic." Magister Lundi smiled sardonically. "It can do amazing things."

"Enough with the history lesson," Wisp challenged.

Magister Lundi held up his hands as if in surrender. "I'm sorry. Even all these years later, it's still not easy to talk about." He took a deep breath. "The story starts in the mountains east of the Fingers. The Mountainfoot Third and I had just eliminated a warren of rockeaters that had been raiding our cities. During the battle, we had found a renegade Magister fighting for the enemy. With the Third camped outside the rockeaters' caves, I took the man a short distance away to question him in private. Before we could start speaking, though, Lord Archovar swooped out of the sky and burned him to a crisp."

"Why?" asked Trillia.

"Archovar refused to explain. Instead, he commanded me to send the Third back underground." Magister Lundi gazed at his hands. His face looked tired and sad. "I knew something bad was going to happen, but I didn't know what."

Quiet filled the little room as Al and his friends waited for him to continue.

"I tried to question him, but he refused to answer." The Magister swallowed. "As soon as the men were inside the mountain, Archovar filled the caves with fire. Then, as I stood frozen in horror, he collapsed the mountain on top of them."

"Why?" Al asked. "Why would he do that?"

"He said that no one who might have talked to the Magister could be permitted to live."

"That doesn't make any sense," Trillia said.

"No. I screamed at him, even threatened him." Magister Lundi shook his head. "He told me to pull myself together, lest he kill me as well. I didn't care. I had just sent my closest friends to their death."

Al and Trillia looked at each other.

"I managed to stop myself from screaming, but not crying." He paused to gather himself before continuing. "Archovar was satisfied. He flew away."

"You should have known," Wisp grated. His fists were clenched and his eyes narrowed. "You shouldn't have sent the men into those caves."

Trillia put a hand on his shoulder.

"Yes." Magister Lundi nodded, his eyes watery with tears. "After Archovar left, I collapsed again. For a long time, I lay broken on the mountainside. Shock eventually gave way to anger — without even thinking about it, I pounded at the rocks with my hands until they were bloody, and then . . ." He looked up to meet Wisp's angry gaze. "Then, I sensed life moving underground.

"It was like a light shining in the night. Half crazed, I ripped a hole through the earth, and discovered that some three hundred men had survived Archovar's attack. They'd been dropped into a cavern by an ingenious captain, one who had worked the Earth and Air to protect them, but died from the effort it cost him."

"Evan," Al guessed.

"Yes."

"Wait," Wisp said. "My dad said that only fourteen survived."

Magister Lundi's eyes gleamed. "That was my idea. I had served Lord Archovar for over a century, but my time on that mountainside seared away all my devotion and love, and replaced it with hate. I knew then, more clearly than I'd ever known anything in all my life, that the dragons were evil, that we had to be rid of them."

"That's impossible," Al said. "They created us."

"Perhaps, but when I found those three hundred men, it was all I could think of. I threw myself to the ground before them, begging for their forgiveness, and explained all that had happened. I told them that they would never be safe again, that as soon as Archovar heard even a hint that someone might have survived, he'd send the Cullers."

"Don't the Cullers answer to you?" Wisp asked. "I thought the Magisters were in charge of everything."

"No," Magister Lundi said. "Both groups answer to the dragons. We govern and protect. They cull" — his expression twisted — "and perform whatever other assassinations the dragons require."

"So what happened with the Third?" Trillia asked.

"We crafted a story to tell: only fourteen survived

my treacherous attack. No mention would be made of Archovar's role. If word of what really happened had spread, Archovar would have known that I was involved. He would have killed me. Instead, I was able to pursue my new ambition."

"To kill the dragons," Al said.

Magister Lundi nodded. "Though all three hundred agreed to the story, not all agreed to fight. But enough joined the cause. They wanted revenge as much as I did. They organized and recruited, built a secret network ready to move the moment I found a way to strike back at Lord Archovar."

"And you found it?" Trillia asked.

"Yes. I reasoned that whatever that renegade Magister had been up to, he must have left some clue behind in the tunnels. Archovar, having collapsed the entire mountain, would assume that no one could pick up the trail. But I spent months searching in secret, excavating the tunnels, collecting everything that seemed even slightly out of the ordinary. Finally, after years of research, I figured out what it was that Archovar had tried to destroy." He lifted the lid of the box and shone his lantern into it. An old iron key gleamed dully in the light, next to a silver bowl filled with grainy black powder. "There it is," he said triumphantly, "the one thing Archovar fears."

"What is it?" Al asked. The bowl was tarnished, and not much bigger than the ones his mom used to serve stew in. The powder in it was coarse and uneven. To Al, it seemed like nothing more than black salt.

"Poison," Magister Lundi said.

"For a dragon?" Trillia asked. She laughed. "Good luck getting him to eat it."

Lundi shook his head. "It's not that kind of poison. Do any of you know how a rank mark works?"

"Yeah," Wisp said. His face had lost its anger now, and he was staring at the black powder. "As a person absorbs Potentia, his rank mark sends it to the dragons."

"Not exactly," Magister Lundi said. "All that Potentia flows to a single place. From there, it streams constantly to the dragons, a never-ending fountain of power."

"You want to poison that fountain," Al guessed.

"Actually, Al," Magister Lundi said. "I want you to."

"What?" Al said.

Wisp snorted. "Told you he was crazy."

"No mortal can approach the fountain," Magister Lundi said. "The power flowing through it would burn them out. Maybe a dragon could survive, but one of us couldn't even get close enough to see it. Except for Al, that is."

"Me?" Al said.

Magister Lundi nodded. "You are completely powerless, devoid of any connection to the Potentia around you. While the rest of us are sponges, you are like a rock in a stream. It doesn't matter how much water flows past, it doesn't affect you. You are inert."

Al didn't know what to say. Was being inert any better than being a zero?

"Your rank is not a measure of your worth," Magister Lundi said.

"Yes it is," Al interrupted harshly. "Our rank is how close we are to perfection, how close we are to . . . well, to you."

Magister Lundi shook his head. "No, Al. That's just another dragon lie. Your rank is nothing more than a measure of how much Potentia you can hold. The higher your rank, the more valuable you are as a source of energy for the dragons."

"*What?*" Al felt like he'd been punched. If the Magister was telling the truth, everything he'd gone through was because of a lie. He wasn't any worse than anyone else. He wasn't any less likely to be a good worker or tenant or friend. There was no reason for his family to have kicked him out, no reason for him to be hunted.

"They don't care about people, just about how much Potentia we can gather for them. You are a zero, completely worthless to the dragons." He smiled. "But priceless to me."

Al shook his head. It was too much to take in. Both too horrible and too wonderful to believe.

Wisp put an arm around Al's shoulders. "How many other zeroes have you had try this?"

"None," Magister Lundi said. "The time was not right."

"Why is it now?" Trillia asked.

"I don't know if the dragons will be able to sense the poison. The Potentia flows from the fountain to the dragons, but I don't know if they can shut themselves off to it. We need to poison the fountain when they are too distracted to notice the contamination. Even better would be to poison it when they are actively drawing from it. For the past several years, I've been working to create just such a moment, grooming Lord Gronar to challenge Archovar for dominance. He is gathering dragons right now, preparing his challenge."

"Oh no," Wisp said, pulling his arm away from Al. His face looked pale. "That's why the Third are gathering. Castle Surflienne is Lord Gronar's stronghold."

"Yes," Magister Lundi said. "The skies will be filled with dragons, all drawing Potentia from the fountain. If we can poison it during that battle, we'll take out not just Archovar, but huge numbers of other dragons as well. And when they fall, the Third will take the castle."

"What if the poison doesn't work?" Al asked.

"Yeah," Trillia said. "If the poison doesn't work, what happens to the people?"

The excitement faded from Magister Lundi's expression. "It has to work."

"But what if it doesn't?" pressed Wisp.

"All will be lost," Magister Lundi said. "Remember Stelton, Al? This will be much worse. The land will be bathed in fire, and the magics the dragons unleash in their battle will kill everything for dozens of miles in all directions."

Trillia's eyes widened.

Wisp's fists clenched.

Al felt like he couldn't breathe. His whole family would die, everyone he'd ever known. Even Bird and Bull. Nothing would be left.

"Then Archovar will come here," Magister Lundi continued, "and kill me for my treachery, and probably all of Sadraki as well. Power will be given to the Cullers, and the Magisters will be no more."

"I can't be the only one," Al said weakly. "You must have found other zeroes over the years. Why me?"

"I do have other zeroes," the Magister said, his eyes serious, "thirteen others, all living here in Sadraki, not knowing of my plans. Tomorrow evening, before I leave for Surflienne,

I will gather them here with you and explain in more detail."

"Will it take more than one of us?" Al asked.

"I don't know. The fountain of Potentia stretches to the heavens, but no one has ever been to its root. I don't know what you will find there. And there's no way to tell exactly what will happen to anyone who goes into such an intense concentration of pure magic. Of the fourteen of you, I'm hoping that at least one will succeed in delivering the poison."

Al shook his head, uncertain. "I don't know if I can do it."

The Magister touched Al's shoulder gently. "You're stronger than you know, Al." He smiled. "Do you know how long it has been since anyone challenged the all-powerful Magister Lundi? Even the rockeaters outside Brighton fled when they saw me arrive. But not you. Even when I gave you the chance to save yourself by turning in your friend, you tried to fight."

"Yeah," Trillia said. "He's dumb like that."

Wisp looked at the floor. Al saw the muscle in his friend's jaw tense.

"Why didn't you just take him then?" Trillia asked. "Why go through all this?"

"The Third and I have been defying the Cullers for years, stealing zeroes, trying to find one with the courage to help. Now I am spied on constantly, an enemy of the Cullers, and under the suspicion of Archovar." Magister Lundi sighed. "I had hoped to meet Al in secret in Brighton, but circumstances didn't work out. When I found him, he was the center of everyone's attention. If I had taken him alive, the Cullers would have reported me, and Archovar would have killed me as easily as I would swat a fly. Besides . . ." He shrugged an apology. "He's only one zero. I hoped he'd make it here, but I couldn't risk everything to make that happen."

Al stared at the black powder. "So you want me and the other zeroes to take this powder into the Potentia fountain and spread it on whatever's there?"

"Yes. As close as possible to the time that Archovar's forces start fighting Gronar's."

"Where is this fountain?" Al asked.

"In the tower at the center of this caldera." Magister Lundi gestured toward the iron key. "That key opens its only door. Will you do it?"

Al bit his lower lip. "I don't have much choice, do I?"

Silence settled in the wooden room. "Al," Magister Lundi said at last, "the dragons have been oppressing us for so long we don't even realize it. They kill us. They brand us. They feed off our Potentia. We should be fighting them with every breath we have, but instead, we practically worship them. Since Archovar saw my breakdown on that mountaintop, you know what he's been doing? He and the other dragons have been setting me up to save people, only to kill them just before I get there. They've killed thousands, simply because they like to see my pain."

Al didn't answer.

"In Brighton, you raised your sword against five of the most powerful men in the world. I need that courage again. Except this time, you won't be alone. Thirteen other zeroes will be helping you in the tower, and outside it, I and the

Third will be fighting to buy you as much time as we can." Magister Lundi held out a key on a chain. "Here's a key to this room. Tomorrow, if you decide not to help, you can give it back."

Al looked at the key, then sighed, and put the chain over his head.

CHAPTER 26
DEFIANCE

After their meeting with Magister Lundi, Al, Wisp, and Trillia were taken to an empty house by the lake, and food and drink were left with them, platters heaped with steaming slabs of unfamiliar meat and crisp vegetables.

Al waited until they were alone before saying anything. "Do you believe it?" he asked.

Wisp shook his head. "I don't know."

Outside, the sun had dropped below the edge of the caldera, casting a long shadow across the valley. Al looked out the window at the tower on the far side of the lake. It was tall and off-white, with large round holes spaced evenly around its top, just below a pointed stone roof. Unlike the rest of the city, it looked weathered and ancient. "It doesn't look like anything special," he said. "Just a tower with holes in the top."

"Did you see his face?" Trillia asked. "I believe him." She broke off a piece of bread and crunched into it. "Anyway, you don't have a choice. You heard what he said about home. You *have* to do it."

Al fingered the key hanging at his neck. "Yeah, I guess."

"What about us?" Wisp asked. "I mean, I get that Al has a tower to visit, but there's no reason for us to be here. We should go back to Dockside, just like my dad told me to."

"Are you crazy?" Trillia asked, slicing a piece of meat from the platter. "This place is a paradise. I say we stay as long as we can." She stretched and yawned. "I'm going to get some sleep."

"See you in the morning," Al said.

Trillia waved as she disappeared into her room and closed the door.

"Al," Wisp said quietly, "I'm sorry about what happened in Dockside. I shouldn't have tackled you."

"It's okay," Al said. "That feels like a lifetime ago."

"I mean it," Wisp said. "I shouldn't have done it. I won't do it again."

"Forget it," Al said. "I'm going to get some sleep."

Al didn't sleep, though. Instead, as soon as he was in his room, he drew his sword and started practicing his parries. The whole poison thing bothered him. Poison wasn't the way people were supposed to fight. Not only that, he thought, but he wasn't sure about killing the dragons. Dragons were the creators. If not for them, humans wouldn't even exist. Al stopped practicing. That was the big problem, he realized. All his life, he'd been taught that the dragons were the creators. They kept people safe, protected them from monsters like the rockeaters.

Al stared at his sword. What if all that was wrong? What if Magister Lundi was telling the truth? That meant that the dragons were the worst monsters ever, that everything everyone knew about them was wrong. Even the ranks were a lie. Their whole society was based on a lie. At the same time, that meant that he wasn't really *uldi'iara*, that he was just as good as everyone else.

Grunting with frustration, he slid the sword back into its metal sheath inside the bag and kicked his bag under his bed. Even the sword couldn't help him think his way out of this one, he realized. He stretched out and closed his eyes.

The sound of horns woke Al the next morning. He stumbled out of bed, pulled on his clothes, and ran out of his room.

Wisp was in the common room, standing with Trillia in the open front door, looking out across the gardens. The sun was just peeking over the tip of the caldera, casting half of Sadraki in shadow, and half in golden light.

"The one day I sleep in," Al grumbled. "And they blow horns. What's happening?"

"Don't know," Wisp said.

The horns continued to blow a simple pattern of two short blasts followed by one long, repeated over and over.

"Everyone's running," Trillia said, "but I can't figure out where."

Al joined them at the door. Their house was by the lake, which was the lowest point of the caldera. From there, they could see all sides of the valley. The scene was chaos, with windwalkers, earthers, and humans all running in different directions. Some dove into houses. Others charged up the path that led out to the mountainside. The Sadraki Guard was assembling in rows on the southern slope of the caldera, just to the right of the exit.

"Oh no," Trillia whispered. She pointed to the edge of the caldera, directly over its exit.

A dragon landed on the ridge of stone, its back talons gripping the ground while it spread its wings wide and held its front legs up like arms. The size of the creature stunned Al. Even from this distance, he could clearly see its head. Its scales were the dark green of the Culler's uniform. Its claws and wings were black, as were its teeth.

Each of those claws, Al thought, had to be bigger than a man. Otherwise, he'd never be able to see them from so far away.

"Magister Lundi." The dragon's voice rumbled across the sky. "I desire an audience."

A hush spread across Sadraki. From his doorway, Al couldn't see anyone moving among the houses. The people had all managed to get wherever it was they'd been running. Only the Sadraki Guard was still visible, standing in orderly rows beneath and to the right of where the dragon stood.

"Magister Lundi," the dragon repeated.

"I am here," the Magister's gentle voice responded. "What does my lord Archovar require?"

Al stepped out of the building to watch the Magister rise up into the air. Wisp and Trillia stood beside him. "He must be using Air magic," Wisp whispered, "to make his voice louder."

"Shh," Trillia said.

"As I was traveling here to speak with you," Lord Archovar said, "I found some injured Cullers. They claimed their injuries were due to your men."

"With respect, my lord Archovar," Magister Lundi said, "my men rarely injure. Their swords are too big."

Wisp chuckled. "Got to admire his style."

"I am not here for banter," the dragon thundered. "You have obstructed the Cullers."

"Lord Archovar," Magister Lundi said. "The Cullers have always been jealous of me. Of our relationship. They would say anything to take my place as your most trusted servant. You know I would never subvert your control of the herd."

"So you have said before, but I am starting to doubt." The dragon paused before continuing. "Word has reached my ears that Gronar is gathering his forces at Castle Surflienne."

"I know nothing of —" Magister Lundi said.

"I see deception in your pattern," Archovar interrupted, "and fear."

A shiver of terror ran down Al's neck. He looked away from the dragon, and noticed the last of the Sadraki Guard disappearing into the solid rock wall of the caldera. He squinted his eyes. It was too far for him to see well, but he knew they must be maneuvering into a cave. He looked away to scan the rest of the caldera, and realized that no one was left outside — not a soul remained on the winding paths of Sadraki.

He grabbed Wisp's arm. "To the lake," he hissed. "We have to get to the lake. Hurry!"

"Why?" Trillia asked.

"Remember the Third?" Al shoved his friends toward the water. "Lundi said Archovar blasted them with fire."

Wisp's eyes widened. He grabbed Trillia's hand and pulled her off the front porch.

"I am, as ever, your loyal Magister," Lundi said from above them.

"No." Archovar's voice was hard and accusing. "You are a traitor. You plot with Gronar to overthrow me."

"My lord —" Magister Lundi started.

"I have decided I no longer need the college of Magisters," Archovar interrupted. "It is disbanded."

Fire blasted across the sky, enveloping Magister Lundi.

Wisp, Al, and Trillia ran into the lake. The water was warmer than the air and smelled sour, but they splashed deeper.

Overhead, the fire faded to reveal Magister Lundi untouched. Three other Magisters rose into the sky around him. They also wore nothing more than loose pants, revealing the skincarvings that covered their torsos. On the ground, Al saw people of all races stepping out of their houses, shedding shirts and pulling off boots, revealing skincarvings of their own. *Magisters-in-training*, Al thought.

"A couple weeks ago, I met a most interesting boy, Archovar," Magister Lundi said.

"That's *Lord* Archovar," the dragon bellowed. Fire filled the sky, boiling around the Magisters, but not touching them.

"He was the lowest of the low," Magister Lundi continued, "what the people of the stone call an *uldi'iara*. But do you know what he did?"

"You choose your last words strangely." Lord Archovar tilted his head. "But tell me, what did this zero do?"

Magister Lundi spread his arms. "He fought. When any sane person would have dropped to his knees and begged for mercy, he fought. Even with no hope of victory, he refused to yield. It is a trait I had forgotten." Magister Lundi's gentle voice turned hard. "No more."

A roar of defiance rose from the people of Sadraki. Fire and ice burst from a hundred hands toward the dragon, and the earth surged up around the giant beast's legs. Overhead, the Magisters unleashed columns of twisting fire that slammed into the dragon's chest. Clouds whipped through the sky, torn apart by the winds buffeting the dragon.

Al, Wisp, and Trillia tried to wade faster. The lake reached their shoulders now, but all of them wanted to be deeper.

Lord Archovar roared and burst out of the rock encasing him. It shattered into a thousand pieces that cascaded down the inside of the caldera. With a sound like a thunderclap, the dragon spread his wings and launched into the air. The wind from his takeoff flattened houses and knocked Magisters tumbling through the sky.

"Ants!" he roared. "You would battle me?"

"Down!" Al hissed. He, Wisp, and Trillia took a deep breath and dove. The rock at the bottom of the lake was black and sharp, but Al grabbed it and held on, keeping himself as close to it as he could. Beside him, Wisp and Trillia did the same.

Red and orange light boiled around them, a wash of vibrant color and heat. Al closed his eyes. When he opened them again, he saw his friends still clinging to the lake bottom beside him, their eyes squeezed shut. Above the water, the sky had turned dark.

Lungs burning, he tapped Trillia's shoulder and pushed off the lake floor. Wisp and Trillia followed, gasping for breath as they broke out of the surface. Thick, dark smoke hung all around them, blocking out the sky.

"I can't see anything," Wisp muttered. "What happened up here?"

"Shh!" said Al.

"Still you defy me?" Lord Archovar bellowed.

Magister Lundi's voice was no longer amplified. It sounded weak and small, muffled by the smoke. "Five thousand strong," he said. "Five thousand loyal." He coughed. "Five thousand dead."

"Your precious Third," the dragon's voice sneered. "Your beloved men of the feather. I always hated them."

"It wasn't for nothing," Magister Lundi said. "The Third will always haunt you, Archovar, just like the lives you've taken today, just like all the lives you've stolen."

"Haunt me?" Lord Archovar laughed. "The lives of mortals have no meaning."

A loud crack sounded, followed by a whooshing noise.

Lord Archovar laughed again. "Is that all you have left, *Magister*?"

"Yes," Magister Lundi said in his quiet voice.

"Then know that all your plans have failed. The Third is gone. Your city is erased. As for Gronar, my allies are already gathering. We will destroy him and his pitiful rebellion. Then we will hunt down any surviving Magisters. No trace of your meaningless life will survive."

The dragon roared, and the smoke-filled sky flashed vibrant red. Al flinched, but no flame washed over him. Instead, he heard something splash into the lake. Al, Wisp, and Trillia looked at one another, eyes wide, just their heads poking out of the still water.

"Is Magister Lundi —" Trillia started.

"Shh!" Wisp hissed.

Lord Archovar's voice sounded again. "I want nothing left alive in this caldera. Do you understand me? Nothing!"

No voice answered the dragon, or at least none that Al could hear. Only the sound of dragon wings followed, and then silence.

CHAPTER 27

PRIORITIES

"I've got to get my sword," Al said, coughing. "Come on!" He leaned forward and forced his way through the water.

Trillia splashed after him, her face streaked with tears. "I can't believe they're dead."

"Keep your voices down," Wisp said.

"Al," Trillia whispered. "Who do you think he was talking to?"

Al pulled himself out of the lake. "The Cullers," he said flatly.

Trillia covered her mouth with her sleeve. "But they couldn't have gotten here so quickly. We only arrived yesterday afternoon."

"Yes, they could have," Wisp said behind her. He had pulled the neck of his shirt up around his nose, and it muffled his voice. "According to my dad's map, they're based out of Castle T'lirian, which is less than half a day's ride from here."

Al stared at the remains of the house they'd slept in. Nothing was left of the walls or roof. The furniture was gone as well, just a part of the ash that covered everything. Around the house, the gardens were nothing more than a smoldering layer of gray.

"Archovar must have made up his mind about Lundi before he even got here," Al said bitterly. He took off his shirt and wrapped it around his hand. The fabric was soaked through from the lake. He just hoped it would be enough — and that Archovar's fire hadn't been hot enough to melt the metal.

"Al," Wisp said. "What are you doing?"

"I need that sword."

"You're crazy," Wisp said. "You can't fight the Cullers."

The burned remains of the floor felt hot through Al's boots, but not unbearable. He strode to where his bedroom had been, and spotted his sword in its metal scabbard — all that remained of his bag and its contents. Using his shirt-covered hand, he picked it up and ran to the lake to drop it in.

"Will it still work?" Trillia asked.

"The grip's burned away," Al said as he put his shirt back on. "But the hilt's metal. Even if I can't find something to wrap it with, I should still be able to use it."

"For what?" Wisp said hollowly. He threw a rock across the lake. "Sadraki is destroyed. The Magisters are dead. The Cullers are here. There's nothing left to do."

"We can poison the dragons," Al said. "We can save Surflienne and the Third."

"Our parents!" Wisp exclaimed. "We have to get that powder."

"You still have the key?" Trillia asked.

"Yeah," Al said, grabbing his scabbard from the lake. He tucked it through his belt, then pulled it up so its tip didn't drag on the ground. It looked funny up that high, but he didn't have much choice. He just wasn't tall enough to wear it normally.

"Lundi's place is down this path," Wisp said. "It's eight, no, nine intersections from here, on the left." He started running. "Come on!"

Al and Trillia followed, the gravel crunching under their feet.

The three of them ran in silence through the ash. No plants were left, and charred wooden platforms were all that remained of the buildings. Al's eyes watered from the smoke.

As they passed the fifth intersection, they heard a man's shout.

They stopped. "What was that?" Trillia whispered.

A child screamed, then another.

Al drew his sword.

"No," Wisp hissed. "You can't. We have to get the powder."

"Those are *children*," Trillia said.

Wisp glared at her. "There are children at Surflienne too!"

Instead of answering, Trillia ran toward the commotion, with Al close behind.

"Orders are to leave nothing alive," a man's voice said.

"Then let's get to it," another man answered. The second voice sounded familiar to Al, though he couldn't place it. Sprinting forward, he spotted two silhouettes standing on the platform of a destroyed house. The figures held swords in their hands, and had their backs to Al and Trillia.

Without breaking stride, Al leaped. He put all his weight and momentum behind smashing the pommel of his sword onto the back of the nearest Culler's head. The man fell limply to the ground.

When Al looked up, he saw the kids. They clung to one another, heads down, on ash-covered wood. There were two girls and a boy, all wearing pale breeches and blue tunics. Al didn't know anything about windwalker kids, but guessed the boy was no more than nine years old, and the girls were younger.

"*You*," the familiar voice hissed.

Al scrambled away from the motionless form, spinning to face the remaining Culler. It was the brown-eyed man, the Culler who had been chasing him since Dockside. He had a piece of green cloth tied around his face, keeping the smoke out of his nose and mouth, but his eyes were unmistakable, and his shirt was still slashed from his fight with Al outside Sadraki. Gripping his sword, Al jumped to his feet and took his center stance.

Trillia stood in the smoke several paces away, knives in both her hands. Her face looked pale and uncertain.

"Run!" Al shouted over his shoulder at the kids.

They didn't move, but held tighter to each other, crying.

"There aren't any guard captains to save you this time, boy."

Al jerked his attention back to the Culler. The metal of his sword hilt felt cold and unfamiliar in his hand, different than the leather grip he was used to. "Trillia," he said. "Your knives aren't long enough. Get the kids away. I can handle this."

"You can *handle* this?" The brown-eyed man chuckled. "I don't think so."

Trillia's eyes shifted back and forth between Al and the kids.

Al held his sword steady. The man was better than he was, and stronger, with longer reach. All he'd been able to do last time was survive, but he knew that wouldn't last. "The kids," he urged. Once they were safe, he could run away.

"I can't just leave you," Trillia said.

The man lunged. Al parried and attempted to riposte, but the Culler blocked it, and they returned to their guard positions. The man's weight shifted and his sword arm moved. Al parried, but his enemy's blade wasn't there. Instead, its tip sliced across Al's forearm. Al gasped.

"Get the kids!" he yelled.

A rock bounced off the side of the man's head, staggering him. Al tried to stab, but the Culler parried.

"Rocks?" the Culler said. "You think that will save you?"

Another rock hit him in the cheekbone, just below the eye. His skin split under the impact.

Trillia started to attack, but the Culler's sword tip swept up in front of her, and she froze.

Al waved her back. "Get the kids!"

A third rock, this one the size of Al's fist, zipped out of the smoke and impacted the man's nose, snapping his head backward. He shouted in pain.

Al winced, but held his sword steady, wishing he trusted his attack enough to try it.

Blood streamed from the Culler's nose, and his eyes looked like they weren't focusing. The man growled in frustration and stabbed at Al, but Al parried smoothly.

Another rock grazed the side of the man's head, and he jumped back, eyes wide, one hand over his nose. "This isn't over," he growled, and ran into the smoke.

"The kids," Al said to Trillia, forcing his voice to stay calm. "Please, now, can you get them out of here?"

Sheathing her knives, Trillia ignored him and knelt by the young windwalkers. "It's okay," she said gently. "We're going to find a way out of this. Hey Al, there's a basement!"

Al kept his eyes on the smoke, watching for the Culler.

"Makes sense," Wisp appeared out of the haze, a rock in each hand. "If Magister Lundi had one, there must have been others."

"Nice throwing," Al said.

Wisp nodded. "Nice sword-ing."

Al smiled shakily. "I'm not sure that's a word."

"Where are your parents?" Trillia asked.

The boy looked at his feet. The white fur on his face was wet from crying, and smudged with ash. "It-it was just a drill," he stammered. "Like always. They blow the horns, we go to the basement."

"Then Daddy took off his shirt," his little sister said.

"And Momma yelled at him not to," the other sister added.

The first sister buried her face in her brother's shirt. "And they went upstairs."

"We're supposed to stay down until a Magister comes to get us," the boy finished. "That's the drill."

Trillia caught her breath. "The drill?"

"Uh-huh. When the horns blow, everyone locks themselves in the basement until the Magisters come."

"He saved them," Trillia whispered. "Magister Lundi saved them all."

"Not quite," Wisp said. "There aren't any Magisters left to get them. Instead the Cullers will be coming." He grimaced. "They'll kill them all."

Al transferred his sword to his left hand so he could wipe his bloody arm on his shirt. The cut stung. "No," he said grimly, "they won't."

"You need to wrap that," Wisp said.

"How can we stop them?" Trillia asked. "It's just us!"

"I don't know," Al said. "Just let me think."

Wisp tore a strip of cloth from the unconscious Culler's shirt and wrapped it tightly around Al's arm, then tied it off. "No, Al. You need to get the powder."

"What are you talking about? If we don't help, they won't have a chance."

"And what about my family?" Wisp's face was tight with strain. "What about Trillia's, or yours? I saw you just now. You can't even beat *one* of these guys. What are you going to do against a whole bunch of them?"

"I have to try!" Al hissed.

"No!" Wisp shouted, grabbing his shoulders. "You have to save my parents!"

"But —"

"He's right," Trillia interrupted. "We can't stop the dragons. You can."

"But —" Al said, more weakly.

"Go," Wisp said, pushing him gently away. "We'll take care of the kids."

Al gritted his teeth. What could Wisp and Trillia do against trained swordsmen?

"Get out of here," Wisp said.

Trillia knelt in front of the children. "I need you to run to all your friends' houses, and then to their friends. Bang on their basement doors. Tell them the Magisters are gone. We'll meet, um . . ." She looked up at Wisp.

"At the tower," Wisp said. "Everyone can find that."

"But be quiet," Trillia said to the kids. "Tell everyone to stay quiet! You don't want the Cullers to hear you. And tell your friends," she added, "to watch for the boy with the sword." She gestured toward Al. "He's going to be coming to the tower. Tell everyone they need to help him." She caught Al's eyes with hers. "It's really, really important."

Al looked down at his sword. He didn't have any choice. They didn't know if any of the other zeroes were left alive. Even if they were, they didn't know about the powder.

Wisp glared at Al and motioned with his head.

Al took one last look at his friends, then sheathed his sword and ran into the smoke.

CHAPTER 28
NO CHOICE

Al carried his sheathed sword in his left hand as he ran. The gravel path crunched under his feet, and shouted voices drifted out of the smoke ahead of him. He slowed to a walk. Those voices could only belong to Cullers, he thought, and that meant he'd have to move more quietly. He stepped off the path and onto the silent layer of ash that covered the dirt.

Behind him, a foot crunched on gravel.

Al spun, pulling the metal scabbard off his sword.

The brown-eyed Culler stood on the path behind him, sword in hand. Blood dripped from his nose and cheekbone. "Stupid gravel," the man muttered.

"You've been following me?" Al asked. "Why?"

"Where is this powder, zero?" The man pointed his sword at Al. "What does it do? How's it going to save your family?"

Al held his sword in guard position, his scabbard in his free hand. "Nothing," he said. "It's nothing."

"This'd be easier if you just told me." The Culler's lips pulled back in a humorless smile. "Less painful."

As their eyes met, Al felt his heart pound in his chest. He knew what he had to do. Without hesitating, he turned and sprinted into the smoke. He ran without looking back, putting every ounce of effort into moving as fast as he could. The ash swirled around his feet, and the smoke deadened the sound of the man chasing after him. Al couldn't tell if he was gaining ground or not, but knew that running was his only chance.

Suddenly, the floor of a burned-out house was beneath his feet. Al stumbled and tripped. He flung his arms out, holding tight to his sword and scabbard, and landed hard on the charred wood. As the ash puffed around him, he rolled sideways and tried to crawl away, hoping the Culler hadn't seen him fall.

A hole appeared in the floor, with stone steps leading into blackness. Al slithered down them head first. Overhead, he heard the Culler's boots strike the wooden floor. They paused, walked a few steps, then resumed running and faded into the distance.

Sheathing his sword, Al scrabbled up into the smoke and crawled silently across the floor. He waited there, listening to the sounds around him. Distant voices drifted on the air, but he didn't hear any footsteps, no sign of the Culler that had been chasing him. He crept back to the path and picked his way along its edge.

The smoke prevented him from seeing more than two paces in any direction, but it also kept him hidden from the Cullers. He concentrated on moving silently and counted the intersections to Magister Lundi's house.

In the ash and smoke, the Magister's house looked no different than any other: just a gravel path leading to a charred wooden platform. The ash covering the floor was too thick for Al to see the trapdoor that opened into the cellar. He put his scabbarded sword through his belt and dropped to all fours.

The ash was warm against his hands as he crawled, the charred black wood beneath still radiating heat. He squeezed his eyes shut, trying not to imagine everything that was in that ash. *Get the poison*, he thought furiously. *If you don't get it, this same thing will happen to your home.*

When his hand touched the metal door, Al jerked away with a hiss. The metal was still scorching hot. Gritting his teeth, he covered his hand with his shirtsleeve and pulled open the trapdoor, then lowered it slowly to the floor so it wouldn't make a noise.

Al crawled headfirst down the stone stairway. He stood at the bottom, then felt his way through the darkness to the keyhole of the door. His key fit smoothly, and he went through, locking the door behind him.

The darkness in the room was complete, with no light seeping around the edges of the door. The air, however, tasted clean and fresh. Al took a few breaths to steady himself, then felt his way along the wall until he found the lantern. He lifted it and turned the knob that caused it to spark to life. Warm firelight filled the small wooden room.

In the center of the room, the wooden box looked old and unremarkable. Al opened the lid and balanced his lantern on the box's corner. The key and the silver bowl glinted back at him, the black powder a pool of grainy darkness.

Al put the key on the chain around his neck and lifted the bowl. The poison looked harmless enough. There was no distinctive smell, nothing overtly magical about it. But then, he thought, he wouldn't know if it was magic anyway. That's what being a zero meant. He sighed and looked around the room, trying to figure out some way to transport the powder. The idea of carrying the silver bowl all the way back to the tower without spilling it seemed impossible.

Boots sounded on the wooden floor over Al's head. His breath caught. The boots stopped, then walked back and forth. Al drew his sword, wishing he'd thought to close the metal trapdoor. He reached over to the lantern and turned the knob that retracted its wick. The firelight flickered and went out.

Al slid his feet into his fighting stance and flexed his knees. If anyone got the door open, he'd probably have a chance for a single lunge. After that, he'd be trapped.

Boot nails clicked on the stone steps.

"Is anyone down here?" a man's voice called.

Al held his breath.

A hand knocked on the door, then tried the latch. "It's okay," the voice said. "It's safe now. You can come out."

Al gritted his teeth, wondering how many unknowing windwalkers had done just that.

After a moment of silence, something hard thudded against the door. It didn't yield. "Forget it," a second voice called from above. "We've got new orders."

"What?"

"Everyone is to go back to the pass until this smoke clears. That's the only way out of the caldera, anyway. No reason to stumble around in this stuff."

"Suits me," the voice outside Al's door said. "I could use some fresh air."

Al stayed motionless as the boot steps receded. Even then, he didn't move, thinking about what he'd heard. If it was a trick to get him to come out, it seemed needlessly complex, especially when they could have just kicked the door down.

Finally, he let out his breath and reached over to spark the lantern to life. The firelight filled the room again, and his knees felt weak with relief. He sank to the floor, still holding his sword. If the Cullers were withdrawing, Wisp and Trillia would be okay, at least until the smoke cleared. He started to slide his sword into his scabbard and then stopped as an idea hit him.

Putting his sword on the floor, he examined the scabbard for any holes. It didn't have any; it was a solid tube of metal, perfect for carrying a certain black powder. He lifted the bowl and poured its contents inside, then slid the scabbard of powder into his belt and checked to make sure it was secure.

He picked up his sword and listened intently. No sounds drifted down through the roof, no muffled voices or creaking floorboards. Al fitted his key in the door and unlocked it, then paused to listen again. Still, there was silence. He extinguished the lantern and cracked open the door to peek out.

The stairway was empty. Al crept up as quietly as he could, then headed north, toward the tower. An eerie quiet had settled over everything. Al squinted his eyes against the ash and started to run.

When he reached the lake, he stopped to splash water on his face. The smoke was thinner over the lake, the base of the tower just visible in the distance. Al panted and held his side. The tower didn't look impressive, certainly not impressive enough to be the key to the dragons' power. He shook his head and forced himself to straighten. *No choice,* he thought. Whatever that tower held, it was up to him to deal with it. He picked up his sword and set off running again.

Up close, the stone tower looked even more weathered and ancient than it did from a distance. It was bigger than Al had realized, more than a hundred feet across at its base, with a single stone door set in its wall. Over the top of the door, two words had been carved deeply into the rock: *Peace Eternal.*

Al's heart thudded in his chest as he approached the door, both from the run and from fear. If Magister Lundi's theories had been wrong, he was about to die. On the other hand, if he didn't go inside, the dragons would destroy his home. He was the only person who might be able to save them.

He took the iron key from his neck, put it in the lock, and turned it until he heard a click, but didn't push it open. Instead, he thought of his mom rocking in her chair on the front porch, the rich smell of stew bubbling in the pot, Wisp and Trillia laughing as they tried to sneak seconds. He pulled the key out and put it back around his neck, then took three quick breaths and pushed open the door.

Brilliant white light poured out of the tower. Al shielded his eyes. Was that the Potentia the Magister had talked about? If he could see it, did that mean it would kill him after all?

"No choice," Al whispered to himself. "One." He took a deep breath. "Two." He ground his teeth together and clenched his sword tightly in his right hand. He couldn't believe he was about to do this. "Three!"

Before he could think another thought, Al stepped forward into the light.

CHAPTER 29

PEACE ETERNAL

A wave of cold washed over Al as he stepped through the door. He shivered uncontrollably. His teeth chattered, and his wounded right arm went numb with cold. The rest of his body felt as if ice ran through its veins. Tears streamed down his face, and he fell to his knees, gasping for breath.

Slowly, the sensation faded.

The shivers subsided. Feeling came back into his right arm. The icy tingling diminished to a level he could almost ignore.

Al pushed himself to his feet. He was on a ledge on the inside of a hollow tower, at the top of a narrow stone stairway that spiraled down the inside edge of the tower's walls. Above, clear sunlight beamed in through holes at the tower's top and reflected off its gleaming white walls.

It's tall enough to rise above the smoke outside, Al thought. Otherwise, there wouldn't be any sunlight. He closed the door to the tower and leaned over the edge of the platform.

Below him, the tower walls slanted outward, and the tower grew dramatically wider as it descended below the ground. Several hundred feet down, bathed in brilliant white light, lay a pale blue dragon. Thick black metal shackles bound its wings to its body and bolted its four feet, neck, and tail to the floor. As Al stared at it, transfixed, the dragon's eyes opened, and it tilted its head to look up at him. The eyes shone white, with blue irises shaped like a snake's.

Al backed away from the edge. *It's a dragon*, he thought frantically. *The fountain is a dragon.*

"Come back, little one," a deep voice rumbled.

Al panted. His legs and arms continued to tingle with cold, but less so, as though the shock of seeing the dragon had driven away the sensation.

"Come back," the sad voice said again. "It has been ages since I have seen anyone, even one as small as you. Tell me, how is it that you are not burned?"

"Potentia doesn't affect me," Al said.

"I doubt that," the dragon hissed. "It is the source of everything."

Al gritted his teeth and forced himself to look back over the edge. The top of the dragon's head and neck were covered with an intricate skincarving.

"Why do you have a skincarving?" Al asked. "I didn't think dragons needed them."

The dragon let out a long slow hiss and put its head back on the floor. "Peace Eternal," it said. "I am the key."

"I don't understand," Al said.

"Dragons used to fight all the time, little one," the dragon said. "Vicious, nasty battles over the herds and the Potentia they absorbed."

"Herds," Al said. "You mean, like me. Your herds are mortals."

"Yes, and each of us had our own herd. But that meant our power waxed and waned as the populations under our control thrived or faltered, and that made us vulnerable to one another — attack the herd and you incapacitate the dragon, you see? Finally, we thought of an answer. Instead of keying each mortal to an individual dragon, they would all be keyed to one, and that one would be carved to provide Potentia to the rest." The dragon sighed. "All dragons would get power equally from all mortals. There would be no more need for war."

"And you agreed to this?"

The dragon laughed, deep and rumbling and bitter. "No, little one, but once the mark was on me, I no longer had the use of my own Potentia, and without Potentia, a dragon is powerless. I can't even fly. They bound me here for all time, sustained by the Potentia flowing through me, but unable to touch it."

"That's horrible."

"After they bolted me to the rock, they sealed it up over me, with only the tower to let in light. For a while, they sent mortals with gifts, tasty little tidbits for me to enjoy, but as the Potentia flow increased, it became too strong for any mortal to survive. I've been alone ever since. The only creatures that could endure this Potentia are dragons, and they do not come."

"How long?"

"Centuries," the dragon said. "Millennia? I don't know. I've lost track. I used to wail and rant. Now, I mostly just sleep."

Al double-checked the scabbard in his belt. The metal felt cold against his hand, and he wondered how he would bring himself to poison this creature. Or would killing it be a mercy? He didn't know. He started walking down the stairs. "I'm coming down," he said.

The dragon paused before responding. "Why?"

Al stopped the easy lie that jumped to his lips. Whatever its crimes, this creature had suffered enough. It deserved the truth. "I have poison," he said.

The dragon didn't answer.

"There's going to be a big fight," Al said. "Dragons fighting dragons. Gronar wants to take down Archovar, and they're all picking sides."

Still there was no sound from the dragon. Al continued to descend the stairs.

"The fight is going to be over my home, today, before the sun goes down," Al said. "Thousands of people will die. My family will die. Everything I know will be destroyed."

"Poisoning me won't stop that."

"The Magister says that this powder will poison the Potentia. That all of the dragons who draw from it will die."

The dragon hissed. "The black dust," it said. "I thought we'd destroyed it all."

Al had come a long way down the stairs by now, but he had even farther to travel. The ceiling tilted over his head, forcing him to walk bent over. He checked again to make sure the scabbard wasn't spilling any of the powder. "Rockeaters found it," he said. "And the Magister took it from them."

"And you took it from him. Did you kill him?"

"What?" Al said. "No. He was a friend, well, of sorts."

The dragon laughed. "But he's dead now, just the same."

"Yes."

The dragon didn't answer. Al continued circling down the tower. He had no idea what to do with the poison once he reached the dragon. Spreading it over the creature's skincarving seemed impossible, even if the dragon *was* bolted to the floor. As he drew nearer, he saw that the dragon had lowered its head back to the floor and closed its eyes.

The bulk of the creature astounded him. It was bigger than most buildings he'd seen, and radiated a soft heat that warmed the whole tower. The heat drove away the last of the chill in his veins, and Al started to sweat.

"What are you?" the dragon asked.

Al paused. "I'm human. Is that what you're asking?"

"No," the dragon said. "Where did you grow up? How does your family survive?"

"Oh," Al said. He was almost at the floor level now, and the dragon towered above him, even lying down. The creature was not nearly as big as Archovar, but its head was still several times as big as Al. "We're farmers. I grew up in the fields outside Castle Surflienne."

"Go on."

"Let's see. I have an older sister who was going to get married, but was —"

"No," the dragon interrupted, its voice gentle. "Tell me about you. It has been centuries since I've spoken with anyone. Tell me who you are."

"Who I am? I'm just Al, that's all. Up until Testing Day, I thought I was going to be a farmer. But then I was a zero, and now I'm not anything." His voice caught in his throat. "Even if I save my family, I'll probably never be able to see them again. The Cullers chase me constantly. I changed my rank mark, but they know what I look like. It's just a matter of time before they catch me."

Al took a breath. He hadn't meant to say all that, but once he'd started, it just sort of all came out, and now he'd reached the floor. The nose of the dragon wasn't more than three paces from him.

The dragon sighed, its eyes fixed on Al. "Thank you."

"I'm really sorry about this," Al said. "Maybe if I just spread it across your skincarving, you'll be okay?"

The dragon's tongue flicked out of its mouth, a snake's tongue, but not forked. Wider than Al at its base, it tapered to a narrow point. "You could do that," it said without inflection.

"I could?" Al said, uncertain. "That would be okay?"

"That is where the Potentia leaves my body. Over time, it would poison all the dragons. I would remain down here, dreaming, until the last one was dead, and then the skincarving wouldn't work anymore, and I would rise, filled with more power than any single dragon has ever felt."

Al didn't say anything. The dragon's voice sounded sad instead of victorious.

"I don't want that," the dragon whispered. "I've had enough of power." It stuck out its tongue and held its tip in front of Al. "Feed me, mortal. It will take weeks for me to die, more than enough time for the rest of my kind to feel the poison's sting."

Al recoiled. "What?"

"Feed me, and I will sleep one last time." The dragon sighed. "Feed me, and rid the world forever of my kind. Feed me, and set me free from this life."

Al felt warm tears roll down his cheeks. He couldn't believe what had been done to this dragon, and now, after so much, the creature just wanted to die.

"Ahh." The dragon's nostrils flared as it inhaled deeply, then let out a long, slow breath. "That's the stuff."

"What?" Al said.

The tip of the dragon's tongue sliced across Al's cheek, cutting him to the bone. Al gasped and stumbled back to the wall, dropping his sword in his surprise. Cold filled his face, like someone was pressing ice on it. He shook his head, confused.

"Such pathos," the dragon said. Its tongue flicked out again, slashing through Al's clothes and leaving a deep gash across his chest. Before Al could react, the tongue flicked again, carving a second line across his torso.

The pain was intense. With each strike, the dragon's tongue left a line of searing cold. Al struggled just to stay standing.

"Can you smell it, little one?" the dragon asked. "The desperation? The fear? All your sad little life has been for nothing. Now your family will die, your friends will die, and in the end, you will die."

The tongue flicked out again, but Al jumped out of its way. The cold was fading. He couldn't even feel it in his face anymore.

"And you dropped your sword," the dragon said. "Did it fall out, little one? Poor little one."

Al pulled his scabbard out of his belt. Gripping it as if it were his sword, he took his center stance. He couldn't truly parry with the scabbard, though, not without spilling the powder inside it.

"How sad. The brave little zero lost his sword."

The tongue flicked out, lightning fast, but Al side-stepped. It moved him farther away from his sword, but he didn't have any choice.

"What are you going to do," the dragon asked, "beat me to death with your scabbard?"

Al felt stronger and lighter than he ever remembered. His wounds had stopped hurting, and he was starting to get a sense of how the tongue worked. It shot straight out, and then its tip sliced.

"You can feel it now, can't you, little one? The Potentia is changing you, becoming a *part* of you."

The tongue danced next to Al, driving him farther from the stairs and his sword, and any chance of escape. "But I'm a z-z-zero," he stammered.

"The Life Potentia is healing you, sustaining you, just as it does me."

Al risked a glance down at his chest. That, at least, the dragon wasn't lying about. His wounds had vanished.

The dragon laughed. "That's what makes this game so fun! I can play with you for years, and in the end, you'll beg to put the black dust on my mark. Then I will rise again." The dragon's neck snaked forward through its ring, allowing its head to move more freely. It lifted off the ground above Al, jaws open.

The tongue struck again, a jab straight through his left shoulder. Al cried out in pain.

"Come now," the dragon said. "Where's the begging? What about pleading for mercy? You never know." The dragon's voice softened, and its inner eyelids blinked. "I might let you go."

As the pain and cold faded, Al realized that the dragon's open mouth wasn't more than six feet from him. He shifted his weight. He could do it, he thought. It had never worked before, but this one time it had to. He pictured the tree he'd practiced against on the way to Sadraki. *Fast*, he thought. *Faster than the blink of an eye.*

"So serious," the dragon said. "What happened to all the despair?" Its voice sounded petulant and pouty. "And I worked so hard for it. Can't you do it again?"

Al lunged with the scabbard, straight over the dragon's tongue and into its mouth. At the end of the attack, he let go of the scabbard. It arced cleanly over the dragon's tongue and down its throat.

"Ack," the dragon gagged.

Its tongue slashed sideways, cutting into Al's side so deeply that it knocked him over. He curled into a ball, holding his knees. The piercing cold filled his whole body, so deep into his stomach and lungs that he had trouble breathing.

"Why did you do that?" The dragon made a sound deep in the back of its throat, halfway between a cough and a hiccup. "Did you think it would choke me?" It shook its head again.

Al shivered uncontrollably, unable to speak.

The dragon purred. "Ah, you are forgiven. That is a pain I can appreciate. Can you smell it?" The dragon's nostrils flared. "So delectable."

As the shivers subsided, Al uncurled. His clothes were slashed and soaked in blood, but his side was once again intact. He laughed as he realized that he'd done it. The dragon had swallowed the powder.

"Mm," the dragon said. "Something new. What is that? Happiness?" Its inner eyelids blinked again. "Hope? Pride? What is going on with you, little one?"

"Just thinking about everything that's happened," Al lied. He didn't know how long the poison would take to have an effect. He needed to buy time. "Nothing you'd understand."

"Tell me," the dragon hissed.

"No," Al said. "It's not important."

The dragon's tongue flicked out. Al jumped away from it.

"Tell me," the dragon repeated.

"After my testing," Al said. "I had to go on the run. I was terrified." He closed his eyes and tried to remember how it had felt in the catacombs, running with the bead in his hand. The beast liked emotion, he thought, so he'd try to give it emotion. When he opened his eyes again, the dragon's nostrils were flaring. "Master Schion put a bead in my arm to follow me," Al continued. "But I put it in a chicken." He laughed.

The dragon's nostrils were wide, its tongue flicking in and out of its teeth. "Yes," it hissed. "Tell me more. It's been so long since I've tasted these emotions."

Al leaned against the wall and told his story as slowly as he could, focusing as much as he could on the memories that brought back emotions. When he got to the part where Wisp tackled him for Master Schion, the dragon sighed with delight and rested its head on the ground.

As Al talked, he noticed that the creature's translucent inner eyelids had closed, and its tongue wasn't flicking in and out anymore. Its body rose and fell with each deep breath that it took. Al stepped toward the stairway as he continued the story. The dragon's pupils didn't follow the movement. Careful to keep the story going, Al took another step.

By the time Al's story reached Sadraki, he had retrieved his sword and was on the bottom stair. He continued talking as he started climbing, trying not to let his excitement color the story.

"And then," he said with a deep breath, "I lunged, and the black dust in my scabbard flew into the dragon's mouth."

The dragon's eyelids flew open and it roared. Its wings struggled against its restraints but were unable to break free. Al huddled against the wall and covered his ears against the noise. He was too far up the stairs for the dragon to reach him.

"Never," the dragon screamed. The word came out slow and slurred, the syllables disconnected. "You will never escape!"

A long hissing sigh followed, then silence.

Al looked over the edge and saw the dragon's malevolent eyes glaring at him. Without another word, he turned and ran up the stairs.

CHAPTER 30
SADRAKI'S LAST STAND

At the top of the stairs, Al paused to look back down at how far he'd run. His legs didn't hurt at all, didn't even feel tired. *It must be because of the Potentia,* he thought. He bounced on the balls of his feet. Whatever it was, he'd take it, especially with the Cullers still outside, waiting to kill him. He pulled the door open and stepped outside.

After the brilliant, clear air of the tower, the smoke felt almost nauseating. It stung his eyes and caught in his nose. He closed his mouth tightly. That smoke was all that remained of Sadraki. The last thing he wanted to do was let it into his mouth.

"You went into the Tower of Peace," a child's voice said.

Al jumped, raising his sword. "What?"

"That's forbidden," another voice said.

"No one's allowed in the Tower of Peace," a third chimed in.

Al squinted in the smoke and stepped away from the tower door. Children crowded around him. Windwalker, earther, and human, they were all covered with ash. He lowered his sword. "Who are you? Where are the Cullers?"

"What was that roaring?" a little human boy asked.

"Why did you go in the tower?" asked a windwalker girl.

"Wait," Al said, holding up his free hand. "Me first. Where'd you come from? Where are the Cullers?"

They all started speaking at once.

Al watched them, not sure what to do.

"Enough," a girl said sharply as she stepped into view. The kids quieted as she walked through them. A windwalker, she wore work clothes and had no fur, except for three white lines that striped the center of her blue-black head. More than a foot taller than Al, she carried a furry windwalker baby on her hip. "Having trouble?" she asked.

Al swallowed. He'd never seen a shaved windwalker up close before. The girl had fine features, with dainty little ears and a perky nose. She didn't look anywhere near as massive and bulky as the other windwalkers Al had seen, but slender and graceful. Pretty, even. "Yeah," he said, clearing his throat. "I'm Al."

"Yeah," she echoed drily. "I know. Everyone knows to watch for the boy with the sword. My name is Lena."

A windwalker shout sounded from the south, and she spun to face it. Al looked too, but the gray smoke was impenetrable. Another shout sounded, this one human, then metal clanged on metal, more shouting, and finally, silence.

The kids crowded closer to Lena, quiet.

"What's going on?" Al whispered.

Lena hitched the baby higher on her hip. Emotions ran across her face, but she managed to keep her voice even. "The Cullers are trying to kill us."

Al's hand gripped his sword tighter. "Aren't there any Magisters left to help?"

"Magister Lundi's plan failed. Only his top four were supposed to face Archovar. Everyone else should have stayed underground until Archovar left. Instead, the other Magisters tried to fight. Now they're all gone, all but a couple of students who are using the smoke to help us hide."

"But the Sadraki Guard . . . ," Al started.

"Hasn't been seen since Archovar arrived," Lena said. "No one knows what happened to them. I think they were buried." Al saw how worried she was, how tightly she was keeping her emotions under control. "Thanks to your friends, word spread across Sadraki to gather at the Tower of Peace. The children came here to be protected. The adults to defend them." She paused. "Which are you?"

Al's eyes narrowed. "Where are the Cullers?"

"In the exit to the caldera. They send out raiding parties to do the killing, three or four men at a time."

Al nodded. Without Magisters or soldiers, even three or four armed men represented a serious threat. "You need the Sadraki Guard."

"We need Magister Lundi," Lena answered. "But neither are here."

"Yeah," Al said. He stepped away from the tower door. "Stay out of the tower. It's not safe."

She pressed her lips together and nodded. "Good luck."

Al lifted his sword over his head and walked through the children. A few, like Lena, looked to be as old as he was, but not many, and all of those were carrying babies or tending to the very young. As Al reached the edge of the crowd, he found adults holding shovels and makeshift clubs, a ring of defenders around the kids.

The windwalkers stood shoulder to shoulder in the smoke, men and women, old and young, their normally white fur covered with ash. Al pushed his way gently through their ranks. The windwalkers were huge, but against trained soldiers with swords and shields, they didn't stand a chance. Looking at them as he passed by, he could see that they knew that too.

Al chewed his lip as he left the last line of Sadraki's defenders. This battle seemed hopeless: an army in the pass, a crowd of frightened people hiding in the smoke. How could they hope to beat the Cullers? He broke into a jog, heading south. Their only hope was the Sadraki Guard.

With all the buildings and plants incinerated, the landscape around Al was flat and featureless, with only the burned foundations of ruined houses to break the monotony. The smoke hung gray and bitter in the air, smelling of charcoal. It thickened as he ran, until it was so dense he could barely see his hands. He stopped and turned in a slow circle. It seemed to be smokier to the south, impossibly so. Al had never seen smoke that dense, not even after dumping water on a fire. He gripped his sword and strode forward. Whatever it was, he thought, it couldn't be good.

The smoke swirled around him, then was suddenly gone, and Al stood in the destroyed caldera of Sadraki on a brilliant blue afternoon. The valley lay empty before him, without a single house or plant still standing. A wind blew hard and steady against his face. He wiped his watering eyes and squinted into it, toward the ruined edge where Archovar had landed, where the earth had tried to seize the giant dragon. The stone cliffs there had crumbled when the dragon broke free, leaving a jagged rock-strewn cleft where the exit hole used to be.

Rows of men stood in that cleft.

"Al," Trillia's voice hissed. "What are you doing?"

"What?" Al spun. Behind him, the wall of smoke cut the valley in two. On one side, the air was clear. On the other side, the smoke hung so thick he couldn't even see the ground. Distracted, he held out his hand. The wind that was blowing from the south turned sharply upward in front of the smoke, holding it in place.

"Al!" Trillia hissed again.

"Sorry," Al said, pulling his hand back. "Where are you?"

"Over here!" Trillia shouted. She stepped out of the smoke wall and gestured to him. "Don't let them see you, you idiot!"

Al's eyes widened, and he jumped back into the smoke, then made his way to Trillia as fast as he could. The smoke was thickest at its edge. He found that if he stayed just ten paces in, it was no worse than it had been in the morning.

Wisp appeared in front of him, a rock in either hand. His face was streaked with gray ash, and his eyes had deep shadows under them. "Did you do it? We found the Magister's house, but the bowl was empty."

"I did it," Al said.

The tension left Wisp's body. "I knew you would."

"You did it?" Trillia shrieked, limping behind Wisp. She grabbed Al in a bear hug and squeezed, almost knocking them both over. "You did it!"

"Thanks," he said, hugging her back.

She let him go. Like Wisp, she was covered with soot and looked tired. Her left ankle was wrapped in torn strips of cloth, and a stick had been tied to her leg to support it.

"What happened to you?" Al asked.

"I stepped on a basement door." She grimaced. "Turns out they're not all metal. This one broke. Messed up my leg bad." She started limping away. "Come on."

"Wait," Al said. "What's going on out there? Lena said the Sadraki Guard is gone?"

"We don't know," Wisp said. "We think they were buried."

Trillia nodded. "We found some Magisters-in-training, though. They're keeping the smoke over us."

"It lets us see when the raiding parties come across the valley," Wisp said. "The windwalkers attack them as soon as they're in the smoke. So far, none of the Cullers have made it back to tell the main force what's going on."

"That can't last," Al said.

"I know," Wisp said, "but it's all we've got." A coughing fit seized him and he doubled over, putting his hands on his knees. "I hate this smoke."

Al remembered the Sadraki Guard disappearing into the side of the caldera before Archovar attacked. Magister Lundi must have built a safe place for them to go to, just like he had made sure that all the residents had basements.

"Come on," Trillia said. "We'll take you to the Magisters."

"Magisters-in-training," Wisp corrected.

"No," Al said. "That won't do any good. We need to get the Sadraki Guard."

"They're gone," Trillia said. "Buried when Archovar destroyed that side of the caldera."

Al shook his head. "That doesn't mean they're dead. Magister Lundi worked everything else out. He wouldn't have left their hiding place vulnerable to a cave-in."

"Then why aren't they here?" Wisp asked.

"I don't know," Al said. "But we have to find out. Can the Magisters-in-training work with Earth Potentia?"

"No," Wisp said. "I tried to get them to carve an escape tunnel for everyone, but they said they've only learned Air. And even then, all they're good for is moving smoke. They can't even fly."

"Then we have to go find the Sadraki Guard ourselves."

"That's crazy," Trillia said. "If they're alive, their hiding spot is right next to the Cullers' main army."

"It's not *that* close, a couple hundred yards, at least," Al said. "Besides, it's our only chance. Can you ask the Magisters-in-training to move some smoke to that side of the caldera? Give us some cover?"

"Better cover both sides," Wisp said. "That way they won't know which side we're coming from."

Al smiled. "We?"

"This is a bad idea," Trillia said.

"No worse than staying here," Wisp said. "We can sneak past 'em."

"I know *you* can," Trillia said. "You could sneak past anything. It's him I'm worried about."

"Thanks," Al said. "Love the confidence. It's just what I need."

"This isn't sneaking into a farmhouse to steal a pie," Trillia snapped. "The Cullers have real sentries, and they'll be looking for people trying to escape."

"Come on, Trillia," Al said. "You know we can do it."

"The guard probably aren't even alive," Trillia huffed.

Al let his breath out. He knew that tone. Trillia had given up the argument. "Then we'll push some rocks down on the Cullers' heads," he said, "maybe even start an avalanche."

CHAPTER 31

AVALANCHE

Al and Wisp waited on the edge of the valley until they felt a slight breeze blowing on the backs of their necks. In front of them, the thick smoke wall thinned and moved forward.

"Come on," Al hissed. "If we stay at its front edge, we'll get there before the Cullers can react."

Wisp had been resting on the ground. He scrambled to his feet and brushed the ash from his legs. "I'm right behind you."

At first, the smoke moved little faster than a walk, but it quickly sped to the pace of a hard run. Al stretched his legs to keep up. The smoke continued to gain momentum, and he leaned into the sprint.

"Wait," Wisp gasped a short distance later. "Slow down."

Al looked back and stopped. His friend was several paces away, holding his side. "What's wrong?"

"It's this smoke." Wisp coughed. His eyes were watering, and his sides heaved from the run. "I can't get a decent breath."

"Come on, Wisp," Al said. "Since when can *I* outrun *you*?"

Wisp grimaced. "Since never." He straightened and ran, his long legs carrying him past Al in the ground-eating lope that Al had never been able to match.

Al put his head down and powered after his friend, quickly catching and then passing him. He laughed in surprise. He had never caught Wisp in a race before, not even once.

They followed the edge of the valley south until they reached the rock slide caused by Lord Archovar. A small stream trickled along its edge, partly covered by tumbled boulders and jagged rocks. Al scooped up a handful of water, then took a careful sip. It tasted cool and clear, not nearly as gritty as he'd feared. "Where do you think it's coming from?" he asked.

Wisp shrugged and squatted by the water. "Maybe they had a cistern up there. It could have broken, and now the water's leaking out." He splashed the water over his face and rubbed at the ash.

Al looked at the giant rocks looming out of the smoky air, and fought back a rush of despair. He couldn't see more than three paces in any direction. "This is going to be harder than I thought."

"Yeah," Wisp said, wiping his hands on his legs. "Smoke might not have been such a good idea." He climbed onto a boulder and stood. "Come on. We can climb over the slide. Maybe we'll find something."

Al followed him up. Once on top of the rocks, the footing was manageable. They climbed slowly, searching for any sign of the missing Sadraki Guard. In the smoke, with no way to see the sun, time seemed to stand still. They climbed from boulder to boulder, searching between them for any indication of a cave. Neither spoke, both too intent on the search. Once they started hearing sounds of the Cullers' army, they clambered higher up the slope and worked their way back north. It was hard going, with treacherous footing and loose rocks.

"This isn't working," Wisp said, sitting on a boulder on the north edge of the rock slide. "It feels like we've been out here forever, and we still have no idea where to even start looking."

"Just a little bit longer," Al said. "We've got to find them. If we don't . . ." He didn't finish the sentence. It was just a matter of time before the Magisters-in-training collapsed from exhaustion. When that happened, the Cullers would kill them all.

"Yeah," Wisp said, standing. "Might as well be out here as back at the tower."

Halfway back across the rock slide, they heard a man's voice float through the air. "I hate this smoke."

Al and Wisp balanced on the rocks, motionless. "There's nothing out here," another man's voice said. "They must be coming up the other side of the valley."

Al crouched low. He couldn't see anyone, but the voices sounded near.

"Keep looking," a third voice said. "This smoke is some kind of Magister trick. They're planning something."

"This is stupid." The voice sounded farther away now. "There isn't anyone out here."

"Shut up and keep looking."

Al and Wisp waited until long after the voices had vanished, their eyes wide, their ears straining for any sound of the men.

A faint pounding sounded, so faint Al wasn't even sure he'd heard it.

"Shh," Wisp hissed.

"It's not me," Al whispered.

The pounding sounded again, three heavy booms followed by a louder one. Wisp turned his head sideways. "I think it's underneath us."

Al put his head closer to the rocks. The pounding sounded slightly louder, but the rocks they were standing on were huge. There was no way they could move them. "Let's go downhill. Maybe we'll find a building or something."

They climbed down the rock slide, stopping every few boulders to listen.

"I think it's this way," Al whispered.

"Wait," Wisp said, pointing between two boulders that were up slope from him. "Look at this. It's like the slope wasn't smooth. The rocks fell down and stacked. There's a space behind them."

Al crawled over and peered between the boulders. "I can't see anything in there." He pushed his arm through. "Hold on." He shifted position and carefully put his sword into the crack, then extended his arm until the tip of his sword hit something.

"What is it?" Wisp asked.

Al tapped the obstruction with his sword and listened to the sound. "Metal. It's a metal door, like a cellar door, but bigger."

The pounding sounded again, easily heard from between the rocks. "That's definitely it," said Wisp.

"It's got to be the Sadraki Guard." Al pulled his sword back. "How do we get them out?"

They examined the rock pile. Two boulders stood directly in front of the door, and other smaller rocks had gathered around and on top of them.

"We don't want to bring more rocks down," Wisp said.

"It can't get any worse," Al said. "No one's going to be able to dig them out while the Cullers are here, and without them, we can't beat the Cullers."

"Yeah," Wisp said. "I guess."

"Let's try this one first," Al said, pointing to the boulder directly in front of the space Wisp had found. He put his sword down next to it. "It's probably too heavy, but if we can move it, we'll be able to get in."

Wisp laughed. "You're crazy. That's bigger than you are."

"Won't hurt to try." Al put his hands into the crack and grabbed the edge of the rock, then braced his legs for maximum leverage. "You going to help?"

Wisp climbed up and sat down on the slope above, putting his heels on the boulder's top. "You pull, I'll push. On three." He took a deep breath. "One, two, three!"

Al pulled with his whole body. At first the rock didn't move, then a tingling raced through his arms and back. He closed his eyes and pulled harder. An icy coldness filled his shoulders and ran down through his fingers. Suddenly, the rock rolled free. It tumbled down the hill, knocking others with it.

"Watch out!" hissed Wisp. He grabbed frantically for the rocks around him, but they just slid with him in a shower onto Al.

"Sorry," Wisp said.

The pounding sound stopped.

Al straightened carefully. "Oof." It wasn't so much the rocks that had hit him that hurt, but the rocks that he'd landed on. He looked at the rock slide. With the first boulder gone, the metal door could clearly be seen in the side of the slope. Rocks were piled up against it, but none were as big as the two boulders, one of which they'd already taken care of. "Now we just have to do the other one," he said. "We'd better hurry, though. The Cullers must have heard that."

"How?" Wisp asked, rubbing his back. "I'm not pushing from the top again."

"Let me see." Al wedged himself between the boulder and the door. "I've got better leverage here. I can push with both my arms and legs. Then you can stand on the side and sort of pull."

"You're crazy."

Al shoved. Once again, the tingling filled his body. He closed his eyes with effort and strained with his whole body. After a few moments, the rock toppled away, and he fell to the ground.

"Huh," Al said. "They're lighter than they look." He brushed himself off, noticing with surprise that he wasn't hurting anymore from his earlier fall. It must not have been as bad as he'd thought it was.

Wisp didn't move. His face looked pale and his eyes were wide.

Al turned away from him to examine the door. It was hinged on the top and opened outward. "No wonder they were trapped," he said. "Even just a few of these big rocks at its base would stop it from opening." He grabbed some rocks and tossed them away. "I guess they didn't plan for an avalanche." He stopped talking and looked at Wisp. "Hey, are you just going to stand there or what?"

Wisp shook himself. "Sorry."

With both of them working, it didn't take long to clear the door of stones, as well as enough space to open it.

"I sure hope this is the Sadraki Guard," Al said, picking up his sword.

"I hope they don't try to kill us," Wisp muttered.

They each grabbed a side of the door's bottom edge and lifted. The door creaked as it moved and the hot smell of sweat wafted out. Then it lifted out of their hands, pushed open by the massive armored hand of a windwalker. He wore a metal helmet and a boiled leather breastplate with the silhouette of a bird in flight emblazoned on it.

Al and Wisp stumbled backward.

The windwalker's eyes swept over them, then he braced a metal pole between the side of the door and the ground, holding it open. The chamber behind him stretched into the darkness, with metal walls and supports. It looked like a giant metal box filled with windwalkers, all dressed for battle.

"Hello," Al said awkwardly.

The windwalker's voice was hard. "Where are the Magisters?"

"Dead," Wisp answered. "Archovar burned the whole valley and ordered the Cullers to kill any survivors."

A deep growling spread through the windwalkers.

"A lot of people are still okay," Al said. "They're hiding in the smoke by the Tower of Peace."

The warrior facing Al raised his right hand, and the growling stopped abruptly. "Where are the Cullers now?"

"At the entrance to the caldera. The wall collapsed, and they've put an army in the breach."

"Not a whole army," Wisp said. "Maybe three hundred men, at most."

"It looked like an army to me," Al said.

"Boys!" the windwalker's voice snapped.

"Sorry," Al said.

"We came here looking for you," Wisp said. "Everyone thinks you're dead."

"But for you, we would have been." The windwalker stepped out of the cave, his eyes scanning the smoke. "We have many who can work Potentia, but none powerful enough to break through the wards the Magisters wove into those walls. The same magic that was meant to conceal us kept us trapped." He turned his eyes to them. "I am Commander Shora."

"I'm Al. This is Wisp."

Commander Shora knelt and wiped a hand across the ground where the boulders had been, clearing it of pebbles. "Okay, Al and Wisp, I need to know the battleground: where the Cullers are, how wide this rock slide is, how far the smoke extends, everything you can — Shh!" He held up a hand with two fingers raised, then pointed down the slope.

Two windwalkers strode out of the cave and bounded down the hill, leaping easily from boulder to boulder. There was a surprised human shout, and then quiet.

The silence seem to Al to stretch forever. He crouched on the rock, peering into the smoke toward where the windwalkers had run. At last they appeared out of the smoke, weapons bared. They nodded to Commander Shora and then turned their backs to him, eyes scanning the smoke downhill.

"How far does this smoke reach?" Commander Shora asked Al.

"The Magisters are keeping the smoke here to cover us," Al answered softly. "It doesn't reach the main Culler force."

Wisp picked up a small rock. "I've spent enough time standing watch at the smoke wall," he said, kneeling by the space Shora had cleared. "I should be able draw the whole thing for you."

"Good." The windwalker looked over his shoulder and spoke rapidly in a language that Al didn't know.

Windwalker soldiers streamed out of the opening, all wearing the silhouette of a bird in flight. Eight formed a square around them while Wisp drew in the dirt. Others moved into the smoke.

Al watched, his breath caught in his throat. Individually, the giant soldiers were impressive, but as a group they were absolutely terrifying. They all carried swords and wore armor, but he spotted several with skincarvings instead of gauntlets. When the Sadraki Guard fought, he realized, it wouldn't be with weapons alone. They'd be using magic as well.

"That's good enough," Commander Shora said. "I have the idea of it now." He stood. "I want you to go back —"

A human shout interrupted him, and he turned his head toward the sound. Two more shouts followed, both cut off abruptly.

"It won't be long before the scouts are missed," Commander Shora said. "Or more come. Go back to your Magisters. Tell them to release the smoke. My men will take it from here. Move quickly. Once the fighting begins, it will be difficult to tell human from human."

Windwalkers were still coming out of the cave. Grim-faced and huge, they disappeared into the smoke.

"Thanks for the warning," Al said. "We'll go as quick as we can."

CHAPTER 32

BATTLE

Neither Al nor Wisp spoke as they clambered northward across the rock slide. Hulking windwalker shapes loomed around them, silent and frightening in the swirling gray smoke. As they traveled, the windwalkers grew less and less common until none could be seen. At last, they reached the edge of the rock slide and the stream they'd found on the way over.

With a sigh of relief, Al knelt to get a drink. "We've done it," he said. "Now it's just an easy run."

"For you, maybe," Wisp said, walking heavily. "I'm exhausted."

"Dockside made you soft," Al teased. He still felt full of energy. "At home, I remember you running clear from the Sopfias' to the swamp, just to get away from Mrs. Sopfia."

Wisp stretched and smiled. "She was really mad, but it was worth it. She makes the best redberry pie."

"Hmph. Not as good as my mom's jam."

"How touching," the brown-eyed Culler said as he stepped out of the smoke. His face was scarred and swollen, his nose no longer straight.

Wisp froze.

Al brought his sword up.

"I knew when I saw the smoke moving that you'd try to use it to escape," the Culler said, drawing his sword. "What happened? Couldn't climb out?"

"What is it with you?" Al said. "Why can't you leave me alone?"

"I am *so* sick of you." The man shifted into his fighting stance. "It hasn't even been a month, and already I hate you more than any other zero I've ever seen."

Fear raced through Al's body. "Wisp," he said. "Run."

"I don't think I will," Wisp said. He stretched his arms and walked casually into the stream behind Al. "You can take him."

"*What?*"

The Culler laughed. "Such confidence!" He stepped forward and lunged in one smooth motion.

Al parried hard, knocking the man's blade out of line, and returned to his center stance. His heart pounded in his chest. What was Wisp thinking? The Culler was a trained soldier. He was stronger and faster and had a longer reach. Al didn't have a chance.

The Culler's eyes narrowed. He feinted a slash and followed it with a quick stab to Al's leg. Al's blade moved to block the slash, then flew back into position to parry the stab, turning the point away from his thigh. He felt a thrill of icy excitement run through his arms and shoulders as he realized that he'd turned the attack aside, despite having been duped by the feint.

"You're slower," Al said, gripping the metal hilt of his sword. He missed the wrapping on the hilt, but had been carrying it long enough that it no longer felt awkward.

"I don't think so." The Culler lunged high and leaned sideways, circling his blade tightly toward Al's chest.

Al caught the attack with his blade and shoved it away. A smile stretched across his face. He wasn't afraid anymore. He flicked the tip of his blade toward the man and brought it back in line. It wasn't a real attack, no more than a gesture, but the man parried. Al's smile widened.

"I'm going to kill you," the Culler grated, "and then I'm going to make your friend tell me who your family is. Then I'm going to hunt them down too."

Al's smile faded.

"And even if I don't," the man continued, "others will. You'll never be safe. As long as you live, you'll be hunted. Nothing can save you. That's what being a zero means."

Al felt the fear come back. His shoulders tightened, and the sword felt awkward in his hand. The man was right. It didn't matter what happened in this valley; the Cullers would always be after him.

"Don't listen, Al," Wisp urged from behind him. "He's trying to scare you."

"What are you?" the Culler said to Al. The tip of his sword gestured minutely. "You're a zero, a nothing. No one cares about you, not your family, not your friends, none of them."

"That's not true!" Wisp blurted.

"No?" the Culler sneered at Wisp. "We both know what you'd do if you thought there was any way to escape. Or have you forgotten Dockside already?"

"That was different," Wisp said.

The Culler barked a laugh. "I heard the story. You turned him in to keep your apprenticeship."

"I —" Wisp started.

"Don't feel bad," the Culler said. "It happens all the time. Once you realize someone's a zero, what's the point? It's not like they're *worth* anything, certainly not an apprenticeship."

"It wasn't like that," Wisp insisted weakly.

Al glanced over his shoulder at his friend.

In that instant of distraction, the Culler moved, thrusting his steel blade so deeply through Al's belly that its tip stuck out his back.

Al dropped his sword and fell to his knees.

"No!" Wisp screamed. He grabbed Al around the shoulders, preventing him from falling all the way to the ground.

"Stupid zero." The Culler pulled his sword from Al's body and pointed its bloody tip at Wisp. "Say your good-byes, and then convince me why I shouldn't kill you." He paused. "I'll give you a hint: start by telling me the zero's last name."

Al closed his eyes, overwhelmed by the pain. An icy coldness filled his body, and he shivered uncontrollably.

"No!" Wisp said. "Oh no. I'm sorry, Al. I'm so sorry."

The cold filling Al felt worse than the pain. He gritted his teeth and forced himself to keep breathing. Wisp's words kept coming so fast they jumbled together. "I thought you could beat him. I thought with as strong as you are now, as fast, that you could . . . I'm sorry. Please don't die. Please. I didn't mean to tackle you. I didn't know what would happen. I was just so scared. Please don't die. Please!" His arms wrapped around Al, hugging him.

Al felt the coldness fading, and with it all his fear and insecurities.

"That's enough," the Culler said, gesturing with the sword. "Time to give me a name."

"No!" Wisp shouted, still hugging Al. "I won't do it."

"Don't be stupid."

"No," Al said. He opened his eyes and shrugged Wisp off, then reached out to pick up his sword.

Wisp gasped and fell into the stream.

The Culler stepped back as Al stood, his sword coming up to a guard position. The man's eyes darted up and down Al's body. "How? How are you alive?"

"Your killing days are over," Al said.

The Culler lunged. Al parried hard, knocking the attack aside, and slashed his blade across the man's upper arm. The slash lacked style or balance, but moved so fast that Al was back in his guard position before the Culler could respond.

"You little brat!" The Culler stabbed again, circling his blade around Al's.

Al circled his own blade to catch his opponent's, then continued the motion sideways, forcing the man's blade out from between them. He stepped in and slammed the heel of his left hand into the man's already broken nose.

The blow knocked the man off his feet. He sprawled backward onto the rocks, blood streaming from his nose and mouth. He stood up slowly, shaking his head, and raised his sword in front of him.

Al returned to his center stance. He felt lighter on his feet than ever before, filled with energy. Shivers ran along his shoulders and legs.

The Culler shook his head as if to clear it, and spat blood. "No one hits that hard," he muttered. "Not even a wind-walker. What *are* you?"

Al backed away a step and lowered his blade slightly. The Culler's eyes narrowed, then he clenched his jaw and took the bait, stepping forward to lunge. As he started to extend, Al stepped in to slide his blade under his attacker's, and then shoved hard straight up, driving the man's hilt against his thumb. It was the same disarm maneuver that he'd used against the Magister. The Culler's blade clattered to the rocks.

"Don't," Al said sharply as the Culler started to chase it.

The Culler froze, staring at the tip of Al's blade. The man's eyes were wide with fear.

"This ends now," Al said. "No more chasing me. Go back and tell your people that I'm dead, and don't ever come looking for me again."

The Culler started to speak.

"You can't kill him," Wisp interrupted softly, stepping around Al. "You know that, right? He'll kill anyone who comes after him." He pointed at the Culler. "And then he'll come after you."

The man swallowed visibly and nodded.

Al gestured with his sword, and the Culler ran away.

Wisp and Al watched the smoke for several seconds before looking at each other.

"I told you you could take him," Wisp said, straight-faced.

Al stared at him for a heartbeat, and then started to laugh uncontrollably. Wisp joined in.

When they had recovered, Al sat by the stream for a drink. He examined his middle where the sword had pierced him, but there wasn't even a scar. It was just like the wounds he'd gotten in the Tower of Peace. He looked at Wisp. "How did you know?"

"I didn't know about the healing," Wisp said as he sat down. "But when you moved that second boulder, I knew something was up. I don't think even a windwalker could have moved that thing. And outrunning me on the way here? No way. There had to be something magical going on."

"Does that mean I'm not a zero?"

"No. You're still a zero. If the Potentia were inside you, you'd need a porta to access it." Wisp shook his head. "I don't know what happened to you, but whatever it is, I hope it lasts."

Al wiped his sword on his pant leg, remembering the feeling of the sword passing through him. He hoped the magic lasted too. He doubted the brown-eyed Culler would stop hunting him.

"Come on," he said, standing up. "Let's run."

CHAPTER 33

SMOKE AND FIRE

Running through the smoke, Al thought about what Wisp had said. He definitely did feel stronger and faster, and there was no denying the healing that had happened. Beside him, Wisp labored to keep up, but Al barely felt the exertion at all. By the time they reached the smoke wall, Wisp was drenched in sweat and panting hard. Al stopped. "Which way to the Magisters-in-training?"

"Follow me." Wisp jogged through the smoke, leading Al to a dome made out of smoke too dense to see through. It was about ten feet tall, and twice as wide.

Al reached a finger out to touch the side of the dome. The smoke was even thicker here than at the smoke wall.

"That's it," Wisp said. "Just step through. I'll be there in a moment."

Shrugging, Al covered his mouth with his hand and stepped forward. Inside the dome, the air was crystal clear. Four windwalkers sat cross-legged in a circle, facing one another. They had shaved arms, chests, and heads, and every inch of exposed skin was carved. Their pants were the same bright blue that the Sadraki roofs had been, with the image of a flying bird stitched in black on the outside of the left leg.

The men's faces looked sad and tired, but determined as well, with creased foreheads and clenched jaws. Three of them held their heads tilted back to the sky, their eyes unfocused. The fourth had his chin on his chest, and his eyes closed.

Trillia sat on the ground next to the circle, her splinted leg stretched out before her. "Al!" she exclaimed.

Al helped her stand. "Hey, Trillia."

"Where's Wisp?" she asked.

"Just behind me. He'll be here."

The dozing windwalker opened his eyes and focused them on Al. "Who is this?"

"Al," Trillia said. "He's a friend."

"We found the Sadraki Guard," Al said. "Commander Shora wants you to release the smoke."

The man stood in one fluid motion. "Shora?" he demanded. "The Sadraki Guard is alive?"

Al nodded. "Their bunker had been blocked by the avalanche. We pushed some rocks out of the way and opened the door for them. They want you to release the smoke. They said they'd take it from here."

A smile spread across the man's face, and the tension left his shoulders. He tilted back his head and let loose a deep-throated howl.

"Wow," Wisp said, stepping into the dome. "Guess you told them."

Al hid a smile. His friend looked completely relaxed and composed, as though he hadn't even broken a sweat on their run.

Trillia moved to hug him, but tripped on her hurt leg and ended up falling into his arms.

"Hi," Wisp said, standing her back up. "Told you we'd find them. Wasn't too hard, either."

"Yeah," Al said, placing a hand on his stomach where he'd been run through with a sword. "Not for him, at least."

"All together," the windwalkers said in unison. They were standing facing one another, and holding hands. A sharp wind blew through the bubble, tearing its walls apart. Smoke flew in ribbons through the air.

"They must be sending it to the guard," Wisp said, shielding his face.

The wind sped faster, until it flowed past them like a river of grit. Al, Wisp, and Trillia huddled together with their backs to it. Overhead, glimpses of deep blue sky appeared.

The wind continued to build, until it roared in Al's ears. He, Wisp, and Trillia sank to the ground, holding tight to one another. Trillia had her eyes closed, but Wisp's eyes met Al's and they shared a smile.

At last the wind slowed and stopped. The air was clear all around, revealing a sun that was about to drop below the edge of the caldera. To the south, a heavy cloud of smoke hung above the Cullers. They were arranged in perfectly formed squares that filled the exit to the valley. A short distance to their west, the Sadraki Guard stood in uneven lines across the rock slide.

A tendril of smoke reached down from the cloud to the Sadraki Guard, thin and tenuous, but easily visible in the clear sky. Al looked over his shoulder. The Magisters-in-training sagged against one another, exhausted. Beyond them, the tower stood tall on the edge of the lake, with the remaining population of Sadraki crowded beneath it, all staring southward.

"The guard must have the smoke now," Wisp said. "Look!"

The tendril of smoke thickened and grew, making the shape of a giant feather.

A cheer burst out of the people by the Tower of Peace.

The feather started to rotate, slowly at first, and then gathering speed until it was a spinning black funnel cloud that moved toward the Cullers. Flames shot from the Sadraki Guard and took root in the winds, lining the sides of the funnel with brilliant red fire.

Trillia's eyes were open and staring at the two armies. "Who do you think will win?"

"The Cullers don't have anyone that can work Potentia," a Magister-in-training said behind Al. "Magister Lundi forbade it."

Trillia smiled vindictively. "Then this should be quick."

Al shook his head as he peered across the caldera. As much as he hated the Cullers, it didn't feel right to wipe them out with magic. It was too close to what the Archovar had done to Sadraki. He watched the Cullers break formation before the tornado, scrambling out of its path. The twister moved straight through them, then stopped in the pass.

"They're not using it," Wisp said. "It's just to prevent the Cullers from getting away."

A howl of windwalker rage rolled over the valley, and the Sadraki Guard charged.

"Wish we were closer," Trillia muttered.

Now that the armies were out of formation, it was impossible to see how the battle was going. Shouts and screams echoed in the air, mixed with clanging metal, but the distance was too great to see details, especially with the sun sinking below the western wall of the caldera.

"Come," the windwalker next to Al said. "We should join the rest of Sadraki at the Tower of Peace."

Wisp and Trillia were greeted warmly as they approached the crowd, with slaps on the back and people calling out their thanks. Trillia beamed under the attention, smiling and laughing, and explaining that it was the least they could do. Wisp didn't say anything, but stayed at Trillia's side, holding her up.

Al left his friends to their admirers and found a spot away from the crowds where he could sit down. Of course they were the heroes, he thought, laying his sword across his knees. They were the ones who had warned everyone to get out of their basements, who had organized the resistance to the Cullers. Without them, all of Sadraki would have been lost. He brushed the ash off his legs and watched the twister burning on the southern edge of the valley. Below it, the battle was hidden by shadows. Above it, the stars were out, shining bright in the night sky.

"Your friends are quite the heroes," Lena said, sitting down next to him.

"Yeah," Al said. "I guess they are."

Lena leaned back, resting her weight on her hands. "Everyone wants to know why you were in the Tower of Peace." She paused. "And how you got in."

"How I got in?" Al asked.

"It has been locked for longer than anyone remembers, protected by magic too strong for the Magisters to over-come. And suddenly there you are, stepping out of its door."

Al laughed. "It must have been quite a shock."

"Well?" Lena prompted.

Al didn't know what to tell her. Any doubts he'd had about killing dragons had vanished after his meeting with the dragon in the tower. He knew now how truly evil they were, but he wasn't sure that Lena would agree. The dragons were supposed to be their creators. How would she react to him killing them? How would anyone react?

"So? You're not going to tell me?" Lena asked.

"I was there to kill the dragons," Al said evenly. He heard Lena suck in a surprised breath, but he didn't look at her. "Magister Lundi gave me the key and the weapon," he continued, "but he needed me to do the killing."

"You mean Archovar?" Lena said.

"No," Al said. "All the dragons. The Tower of Peace was . . ." He hesitated, not sure how to explain. "Well, it was important."

Lena stood. "Fine," she snapped. "If you don't want to tell me, don't tell me. But if you're going to lie, at least make up something believable." She stalked away.

Al sighed. So much for honesty.

Across the caldera, the burning twister collapsed into the night. He stood, sword in hand, ears straining to hear any sign of battle. Around him, the sound of talking died as people noticed the change. A tense quiet spread through the darkness.

Trillia limped over, supported by Wisp. "We won, right?"

Al shook his head. "We'll find out soon."

To the south, a line of fire raced into the night sky. As it flew, it thickened and spread until it formed the shape of a bird in flight. The image hung in the sky for a moment and then disappeared.

The people of Sadraki exploded into cheers and clapping. Wisp and Trillia hugged each other.

"Yep," Al said to no one in particular. "We won."

CHAPTER 34
THE DRAGON WAR

When the Sadraki Guard appeared out of the darkness, marching in formation across the caldera, all of Sadraki cheered and ran to meet them. The orderly rows of soldiers quickly dissolved before the crowd.

Al and Wisp supported Trillia between them while they watched the family reunions.

"How are we going to get back home?" Wisp asked after a while.

Trillia snorted. "I'm sure they'll lend us some horses."

Al groaned. "Not again. Can't we just walk?"

"We'll probably have to," Wisp said. "With Trillia's leg like that —"

"I can still ride sidesaddle," she interrupted. "Only one foot in the stirrup."

"Sounds painful," Al said.

"Excuse me," a familiar voice said. Al turned to see Captain Stani. The giant windwalker was covered with ash, and his breastplate so battered and bent that the insignia of the flying bird was barely discernible. He had two soldiers with him, one on either side, each looking as battle worn as he.

"Captain Stani," Al exclaimed. "You're alive!"

"Commander Shora would like to see you, Al."

"Um," Al hesitated. His eyes flicked to the two soldiers flanking Captain Stani, then back at his friends. "Me? Why?"

"Go on," Trillia urged him. "He probably wants to give you a medal or something."

"I don't think so."

"Stop being paranoid," Wisp said. "Come on. We'll go with you."

The soldiers escorted them through the crowd to where Commander Shora stood talking to a group of soldiers. As they approached, the windwalkers withdrew. Captain Stani and his men saluted and stepped back, leaving Al, Wisp, and Trillia alone in front of the commander. He glared down at Al, his arms crossed.

Al looked down, his heart sinking. He knew what was coming. Even after all that had happened, he was still a zero, and with Magister Lundi gone, there was no one left to protect him.

"Captain Stani tells me that you're the zero," Shora said. "The one that Magister Lundi brought in to kill the dragons?"

Al nodded without looking up.

"Well," the commander said sharply. "Did you? Did you kill the dragons?"

Al raised his head. Commander Shora was staring down at him, his eyes bright and intense. "Yeah," Al said. "I did."

The commander closed his eyes and inhaled a long slow breath. When he opened them again, his face had relaxed. "Thank you." He dropped to one knee so his head was only slightly higher than Al's and gripped him by both shoulders. "Because of you, all this wasn't for nothing.

Our people, our city . . ." He swallowed. "It wasn't for nothing."

"We thought Magister Lundi's plan was a secret," Trillia said.

"Lundi didn't tell many people," Commander Shora said, releasing Al, "and none of those he did tell knew the details, only that he'd found a way to kill the dragons, and he needed a zero to do it."

"A zero," Al repeated. "Yeah."

Commander Shora stood. "At last the dragons are gone. Now we can rebuild in peace. Are you certain they're all gone?"

"I think so," Al said, suddenly uncertain. "I mean, they should be."

"What do you mean, you think so?" Wisp demanded, his face suddenly pale. "What about our families?"

"I did what I could," Al said. "I destroyed the fountain. If Magister Lundi's plan —"

"Enough," Commander Shora's voice cracked over them. "Captain Stani, secure mounts and supplies for these children. See that the girl's leg is splinted properly and take them and a dozen men to Castle Surflienne. If all is well, ask for supplies. If not, return with all speed. If Archovar still lives, we need to evacuate."

As quickly as that, Al was at the center of a whirlwind of activity. One windwalker brought him a horse, with a bedroll and blanket on it. Another handed him a scabbard for his sword. Trillia's leg was splinted, and soldiers mounted up around them. As they left Sadraki, Lena rode up alongside them.

"Commander Shora rides to the Culler stronghold in the morning," Lena said. "He will end them for what they did here."

"Good." Captain Stani nodded. "Stay close to me on this ride. When we get to Surflienne, you are to ride back here with news of what we find."

"Yes, Father."

As they left the caldera of Sadraki behind, the cold mountain air hit Al like a slap in the face, taking his breath away. He shivered and leaned closer to his horse, envying the windwalkers their fur.

Once they were all on the mountainside, Captain Stani clicked his teeth and sped up. Al clutched his reins as his horse followed. Riding downhill, he discovered, was much different than riding up, and Trillia's shouts to lean back instead of forward didn't help much. It also didn't help that everyone was watching him, or that Lena shook her head in amusement every time he almost bounced out of his saddle.

By the time the sun rose, Al was stiff and sore, and feeling miserable. Whatever it was that had healed him before apparently didn't heal bruises.

"Look," Wisp shouted, pointing west. "Dragons!"

All eyes followed his finger. The dragon silhouettes were unmistakable despite the distance. There were four of them soaring through the sky, heading south.

"It didn't work," Trillia said hollowly. She was riding sidesaddle, favoring her hurt leg. "The dragons aren't dead. That means . . ." She didn't finish her sentence, but bit her lip and looked down at her horse.

Al slumped in the saddle. If the dragons still lived, then everything he'd done was for nothing. His home was gone, and Sadraki would soon follow.

"No," Captain Stani said, squinting his eyes and turning his head to follow their path. "This could be good. Those dragons are headed toward Surflienne. It might be that the battle hasn't happened yet, that the forces are still mustering. If dragons make war like mortals do, they won't attack until they are at full strength. We still have time." He reined in his horse. "We'll stop here for a rest, then press on."

When they started to move again, Al noticed that most of the windwalker soldiers didn't remount. Instead, they left their armor and weapons on their horses and jogged beside them. As tall as they were, their long strides easily kept pace. Al slid off his own horse to run beside it. He knew he wouldn't be able to last very long, but the exercise felt good and took his mind off of what they might find when they reached his home.

To his surprise, he didn't exhaust himself. To the contrary, he felt rejuvenated. His muscles tingled as he ran, and his breath came strong and easy for the whole day. They saw dragons four more times before nightfall, each time in groups of three to five, all headed south. Al started to think that maybe Captain Stani was right, that the dragons were still gathering.

Captain Stani pressed the horses hard, never stopping for more than a few hours at a time, traveling both day and night. Hollow-eyed and tired, they reached the horse pastures north of Castle Surflienne two days later, just before noon, with the sun burning cold and lonely in the blue autumn sky. Captain Stani called a halt while they were still under the cover of the trees.

Al and Wisp walked forward to look out over the fields. Castle Surflienne still stood, alone on its hill, with Dockside a short distance away.

"We made it," Al said.

Wisp let out a long sigh. "Yeah," he said. "We did." He turned to help Trillia maneuver through the trees with her hurt leg.

"Where are the dragons?" she asked.

"I don't know," Al said. His eyes fixed on a short stocky figure walking up the road from Surflienne. The man's head was down, his eyes on the road in front of him. Al's breath caught in his throat. "Bird?"

Bird stopped and looked up, eying the windwalker soldiers suspiciously. "Al?" he said. "What are you doing here? I thought you were in Sadraki."

"Me? What about you? What happened to heading east into the mountains and across the Thumb?"

Bird heaved the vegetable sack that Al recognized from Bull's kitchen off his shoulder. "I tried, but when I reached the ridge, I found dragons on the other side. They were everywhere, laying low and using the mountains for cover. I hiked back to Castle Surflienne as quickly as I could, but everyone was being evacuated."

"Why didn't you go with them?" Captain Stani asked.

"Overseer Pilgrommor was leading the evacuation, but there was a Magister helping him." Bird shrugged. "I don't get along with Magisters."

"Pilgrommor?" Al echoed. What was his dad doing leading the Third? Was that the job that his dad couldn't risk?

The reason he'd abandoned Al? Had he been working with the Third all this time?

"So everyone is belowground?" Captain Stani asked.

"I didn't stay to check," Bird said. "Just walked as far and as fast as I could."

Al gazed at Castle Surflienne. The fields and sky were empty. There were no people or dragons, or even horses.

Wisp shielded his eyes against the sun. "There are archers walking the walls."

Al shielded his own eyes. At this distance, the walls of Surflienne were tiny, but he thought he could see movement on them. "That must be the Third," he said. *And my dad is with them*, he thought.

"Why have guards on the castle if everyone's in the catacombs?" Trillia asked.

"Because that's what you do," Captain Stani said from behind them. Around him, windwalker soldiers were mounting their horses. Helmets were put on, armor adjusted, battle-axes brought to hand. "When the enemy comes, you stand and fight."

"Not against dragons," Bird said.

"*Especially* against dragons," Stani growled.

"Are you insane?" Lena shouted. She strode between the soldiers, her eyes narrowed and angry. "Why are you mounting up? What are you going to do out there?"

"Warn them." Captain Stani's voice was flat and hard. "They've never seen dragon's fire. They don't know that it'll flatten that castle. Anyone not already in the catacombs needs to get there."

Lena glared at him. "It doesn't take all of you for that. One person on a fast horse is all that's needed."

"And who would that be?" Captain Stani asked quietly. "Who would you send out there, while my men and I hide in the trees?"

"Anyone," Lena shouted. She looked around wildly, then pointed at Al. "Him! They're his people. Send him. He doesn't even need a horse!"

There was a chuckle at that. "She's got you there, Captain," a soldier said. "We've all seen how the boy can run."

"That's enough," Stani said.

"No, it's okay." Al said. "I'll go. She's right. There's no reason —"

"Too late," Wisp interrupted. "Look."

In the distance, the horizon to the southeast had filled with dragons rising out of the mountains. They flew so thick and close together that the countryside below them was covered in shadow.

"And over there!" Trillia shouted, pointing to her right, where another cloud of dragons was launching itself into the sky.

"They're so big," Lena said. "Taller than the trees. Where could they have been hiding?"

"Mount up," Captain Stani commanded. He pointed at a soldier who was already on his horse. "You, ride to Surflienne. Tell them what happened at Sadraki, and get underground."

"Sir!" The windwalker kicked his horse into a frantic gallop down the road.

Stani's eyes surveyed his men. "You three are with me. The rest of you ride back to Sadraki. Warn them that the dragons still live. Go as fast as you can."

"You too," Captain Stani said to Al and his friends. "You

saw what happened at Sadraki. This will be a hundred times worse."

"And you," Lena said to her dad. "You're coming too."

"No." Captain Stani's eyes tracked his soldier galloping toward the castle. "I won't run again. I won't hide while another city is destroyed. Someone needs to be here. Someone needs to bear witness to what these beasts do."

"But you can't *do* anything," Lena hissed. "This is suicide!"

"Enough!" Captain Stani's voice cracked as he glared at her. "Get on your horse and get back to Sadraki."

Lena stared at him for a moment, then spun and stalked to her horse.

"This is going to be bad," Bird said softly.

Al nodded. He'd seen the earther run. There was no way he could get away in time. "Take my horse."

Bird snorted.

"No," Al said. "I mean it." The dragon armies were flying incredibly fast, and it looked like they would be meeting directly over Castle Surflienne, directly over his father.

Trillia turned on Al. "What are you doing?"

"Captain Stani's right," Al said. "I can't explain it, but I can't go. If they're all going to —" His throat closed, and he felt his eyes welling with tears. "I just can't. That's my family down there." He thought of Stelton, the city that had been burned away without anyone ever knowing. "If I can't help them, I at least have to . . . to bear witness."

"No, you don't!"

Wisp stepped closer to her. "He's right, Trill."

The windwalkers were turning their horses, tossing

away gear and supplies to lighten their load. Only Captain Stani remained apart, with three of his men.

"But the dragon fire!" Trillia shouted at Wisp. "Magister Lundi said it would burn for miles!"

Wisp took her arm. "You should go," he said. "I'll help you mount."

Trillia's mouth dropped open, her eyes wide. "For luck's sake, Wisp!"

Wisp gave her a grim smile. "Who knows? Maybe the fire won't travel uphill."

Al looked back at the dragons. The edge of the western army was directly overhead, covering the trees around them in darkness. He felt Captain Stani's hand rest on his shoulder.

Bird settled next to him and handed him a dried apple. "You are absolutely the dumbest, most pigheaded *uldi'iara* ever to walk the earth."

Al nodded.

"Ride a horse," Bird grumbled. "As if *I* could ride a horse."

A dragon far above trumpeted. It was a sound unlike any Al had ever heard, like a hundred men blowing trumpets all at the same time. The call was answered by the other army. Behind Al, hooves pounded the earth as the wind-walker horses charged away.

Wisp stepped to the tree line, one arm supporting Trillia. She chuckled. "Well, we always wanted to see the dragons."

Bird snorted. "You're all insane."

Suddenly, one of the dragons faltered. Its wings drooped awkwardly, then it fell out of the sky and crashed into the ground. The impact shook the trees.

Bird jumped to his feet. "What happened?"

Two other dragons trumpeted and blasted fire across the sky, but the flames faded as soon as they appeared, and the dragons that had launched it plummeted to the ground.

"It's the Potentia," Al whispered. He felt Stani's hand tighten on his shoulder. "As they use it, it's killing them."

"It's working," Trillia shrieked. "It's actually working!"

Another dragon twisted and fell, and then another. Dragons from both armies slammed into the ground, their bodies limp and lifeless before they landed. Others turned and flapped heavily away, disappearing into the horizon. Most, however, stayed in the sky, clawing and biting at one another.

Fire flared. Tornadoes swirled. Each time, the attacks vanished as quickly as they appeared, and more dragons dropped to the ground.

"They're using magic just by flying," Al said, his eyes fixed on the giant creatures. They fought savagely, even without their magic.

"Not as much," Wisp said. "And some are bigger than others." He winced as a black and green creature almost as big as Archovar crashed into the castle, knocking out its northern wall.

"Think they'll figure it out?" Trillia asked.

"No," Captain Stani said. "Dragons use magic as naturally as breathing. It wouldn't occur to them it could be dangerous. More likely each side will think it's an attack from the other."

The battle raged overhead, the sky flickering red and gold with flames. More and more dragons fell, filling the fields around the castle with corpses, until only a few still circled overhead. Above those, the two largest could be seen. Gronar and Archovar, Al guessed, though they were too far for him to be sure.

The two creatures circled each other as the last of their followers weakened and fell. Finally, Gronar arrowed toward Archovar, red wings folded against his dull red body, mouth open. A roar of fire burst forth. Archovar beat his wings, and wind slammed the fire backward over Gronar.

Al expected Gronar to pull out of his dive, but the dragon zoomed past Archovar and kept going, until he hit the ground with a force so great it shook leaves from the trees.

Archovar raised his head and roared.

"He's not flying right," Captain Stani said softly. "Look at his wings. You can see it."

Archovar spread his wings and glided down in an ever-tightening spiral to land clumsily in the horse fields. He turned his head back and forth, then fixed his gaze on the trees.

"He can't," Wisp said as the massive dragon stared at them. "He can't possibly see us."

"Al," Bird said urgently. "We've got to get out of here."

Archovar crawled across the fields, his wings dragging on the ground to either side of him. His movements had none of their earlier grace, but it did not make him look any less dangerous. The ground shook beneath the weight of each massive step he took. "I know you're there," he rumbled. "I know you're behind this. I don't know who you are, or what you are, but I know you're there. I can feel it." His voice dropped lower. "I can feel *you*. Come out, my little feather." He paused. "Or are you all out of poison?"

Al sucked in a breath. "He's figured it out."

"Yes," Archovar hissed. "That's right."

Captain Stani's hand left Al's shoulder and he shoved past, his massive two-handed sword held before him. His men stepped up as well, forming a line in front of the trees.

"No," Lena screamed, appearing out of the trees. She ran for her father, but Wisp grabbed her. "Come back!"

Al's fists clenched. His heart raced so fast he could hear the blood pounding through his ears. Archovar's eyes seemed to pierce right through him.

The dragon raised his head. "Mortals," Archovar sneered. "Do you think I need magic to defeat you? You are like ants before a thunderstorm."

"No," Al whispered to himself. "No, no, no. We can't fight him, not like that." He could see how weak Archovar was. His eyes looked glazed and tired, exactly the same way the dragon in the tower had looked at the end, and his wings didn't seem to be working anymore. Even so, Archovar was huge, more than powerful enough to squash them all, and with his long legs, he was far too fast to run from.

They had to use the poison, Al realized. They had to make Archovar so angry that he forgot himself and used magic, then hope the poison would kill him in time.

Al drew his sword and ran out of the trees.

CHAPTER 35

BEING ZERO

"Al!" Captain Stani bellowed. "Get back!"

Al shook his head and ran as fast as he could along the line of the trees. He needed to get the dragon's attention away from them, away from his friends. He put his head down and sprinted.

Archovar roared, a sound so loud that it left Al's ears ringing. He stumbled to a stop.

"So it was you." Archovar's eyes focused on Al as the great dragon stepped closer, his body blocking out the sun. "You are the one who plays with poison."

The dragon's voice was tight with rage. Al shifted his feet into his neutral stance, his sword pointed at Archovar. It was useless, he knew, but it made him feel better. "One?" he said. "Oh no, Archovar. I'm not *one*." He flexed his knees, preparing to dive out of the way. "I'm five thousand."

Archovar's head jerked back as if stung.

"Five thousand strong," Al said clearly. "Five thousand loyal." He took a breath. "Five thousand *avenged*."

The dragon's drooping eyelids opened wide. "Not yet," he whispered. "There are still things I can do, ways to purge this toxin."

"The men you've killed will always haunt you," Al said, remembering Magister Lundi's last words to Archovar. "No matter how high you fly, you cannot escape us."

"No!" Archovar hissed. "I am Archovar! A dragon! You are nothing."

"You're no dragon, Archovar. You're a worm, a powerless old worm. Rank zero. What is it the earthers call it? An *uldi'iara*?"

With a wordless roar of rage, Archovar opened his jaws wide and blasted fire.

Al dove to the side, dropping his sword and scrambling across the ground as fast as he could.

Behind him, the burst of fire dissipated harmlessly into the air, and Archovar collapsed to the ground.

For a moment, all was silent. Archovar lay motionless, his wings splayed awkwardly to either side. Al stood shakily, hardly able to believe what had happened.

Captain Stani whooped and ran over to him. "You did it!" He lifted Al off the ground and into a crushing hug. "You did it!"

Al felt light-headed. When he'd seen Archovar open his mouth, he had been sure he was going to die.

Captain Stani laughed and put Al down as his friends approached. Wisp supported Trillia with one hand and held Al's sword with his other.

Trillia pushed away from Wisp, placed her fists on her hips, and looked Al up and down. "That was crazy."

Al blushed and tried to shrug, but his knees felt weak.

Wisp handed him his sword. "Crazy brave," he said. "Next time, let me know ahead of time." He met Al's eyes. "I'll come with you."

"You know what this means?" Bird said. "No more Cullers."

Al stopped in mid-motion, his sword half in its sheath. "Really?"

Bird nodded. "With the dragons gone, the Cullers'll be kicked out of every town and castle that shelters them. No one likes them." He paused. "Believe me. I know."

Al felt a tension leave his shoulders. All the fear and worry he'd felt since Testing Day flowed out of him. He sheathed his sword.

"No more Cullers," he breathed. At last it was over.

"No more dragons," Trillia murmured. "It's hard to believe."

"Well," Al said, "some may survive. But you're right. The fountain fed our Potentia to the dragons. Without it, the few dragons left won't be nearly as powerful."

Wisp nodded. "They'll have to draw their Potentia directly from the elements, just like we mortals do."

"Hmph," Trillia grunted. "I think it's time we stopped thinking of them as immortal."

"That's the truth." Al stared at the dead dragons filling the fields around Castle Surflienne. Two had hit the castle, crumbling the north wall. Al hoped his dad was okay, and the thought brought his family to mind. He'd been mad at them ever since Mr. Evanson had told him they didn't want to see him, but now he didn't know how to feel.

How many people would have died if the Cullers had discovered his dad? Did that make it okay for him to send his own son away? He shook his head. He could almost understand what his dad had done.

Almost.

"So you *were* telling the truth," Lena said.

"Yeah," Al answered with a smile. Behind her, he saw Captain Stani and his men readying their horses. "I was."

"You're the *uldi'iara*, aren't you? The one Magister Lundi told Archovar about, the one who fought when he should have run."

"That's him," Trillia said. "He's dumb like that."

"Thanks," Al said drily. "Really appreciate that."

"Yeah." Wisp put an arm around Al's shoulders. "He's really not that bright. It works for him, though. I never would have been able to rescue your dad without him."

"That was you?" Lena said, turning to Wisp. "Commander Shora said it was two boys, but I didn't know . . ."

"He helped." Wisp smiled. "You might say I let him tag along."

"Oh brother," Trillia groaned.

"Lena," Captain Stani's voice rumbled, "there's time for talking later. Right now, we have to catch those men I sent north."

Lena looked over her shoulder, then back at Al.

"Lena," Stani's voice grew sharper. "Now."

Lena let out a frustrated huff. "I've got to go."

"Okay," Al said. "Maybe I'll see you when you get back."

"Maybe." She turned and ran to her horse.

Captain Stani saluted Al from his horse. "Wait here. When we come back, I'll escort you to the castle."

After they'd ridden away, Wisp raised an eyebrow at Al. "Maybe?" he mimicked Lena's voice.

Al elbowed him in the ribs. Wisp chuckled.

"I wonder what it's like to kiss a windwalker," Trillia mused. "Would the fur tickle?"

Al blushed. "She doesn't have any fur on her face."

"And what about how tall she is?" Wisp asked. "He'd have to stand on tiptoe."

"That's right," Trillia said, looking at Al. "It might be like kissing your mom."

Wisp grinned. "But furrier."

"Okay, okay!" Al said, throwing up his hands. "I met her outside the tower. She was taking care of the children. That's all. There's nothing more."

"Maybe not *then*," Trillia said. "But now you've killed a dragon."

"*A* dragon?" Al smiled crookedly. "Better count again."

Wisp rolled his eyes at Trillia. "He's never going to let us forget this."

Trillia harrumphed. "It's just not fair," she said. "He got to kill dragons, and all I got to do was run around in the smoke."

Al laughed. "I know," he said. "Zeroes get all the breaks."

ACKNOWLEDGEMENTS

Thanks go to my parents and to all the fantastic writers who have helped me (Julie, Dawn, Jamie, Libby, Karen, and many others), and in particular to my amazing wife, June, and to my first son, Jonathon, without whom none of this would exist.